RAPTURE

Ⲃ

The Russian Library at Columbia University Press publishes an expansive selection of Russian literature in English translation, concentrating on works previously unavailable in English and those ripe for new translations. Works of premodern, modern, and contemporary literature are featured, including recent writing. The series seeks to demonstrate the breadth, surprising variety, and global importance of the Russian literary tradition and includes not only novels but also short stories, plays, poetry, memoirs, creative nonfiction, and works of mixed or fluid genre.

■ □ ■

Between Dog and Wolf by Sasha Sokolov, translated by Alexander Boguslawski

Strolls with Pushkin by Andrei Sinyavsky, translated by Catharine Theimer Nepomnyashchy and Slava I. Yastremski

Fourteen Little Red Huts and Other Plays by Andrei Platonov, translated by Robert Chandler, Jesse Irwin, and Susan Larsen

ILIAZD

RAPTURE

A NOVEL

Translated by
Thomas J. Kitson

Columbia
University
Press
New York

Columbia University Press
Publishers Since 1893
New York   Chichester, West Sussex
cup.columbia.edu

Published with the support of Read Russia, Inc.,
    and the Institute of Literary Translation, Russia

Cataloging-in-Publication Data available from the Library of Congress

ISBN 978-0-231-18082-5 (cloth)
ISBN 978-0-231-18083-2 (paper)
ISBN 978-0-231-54329-3 (electronic)

∞

Columbia University Press books are printed on permanent
    and durable acid-free paper.
Printed in the United States of America

Cover design: Roberto de Vicq de Cumptich
Book design: Lisa Hamm

CONTENTS

INTRODUCTION

The Golden Excrement of the Avant-Garde

PRELUDE

In the years before Iliazd's death in 1975, he could be seen strolling through Paris's Latin Quarter, wearing a Caucasian sheepskin coat and holding a shepherd's staff. An unusual flock surrounded him—the thirty or so cats that lived in his two-room studio. By then, he had become France's most revered publisher of the *livre d'artiste* (artist's book), working regularly with Pablo Picasso, Alberto Giacometti, Max Ernst, and Joan Miró. His mysterious ability to herd cats probably reflected the strength of an artistic vision that could integrate such original talents into books that were always, ultimately, "by Iliazd." But one suspects that he also identified so closely with his cats for their nine lives, their mythical ability to survive catastrophe and land on their feet, as he had more than once.

Rapture emerged from an earlier exile's life in Paris, virtually unknown to the collectors who treasure Iliazd's artistic editions. It is a testament to the survivor's ability to reckon up and move on, the reformulation of an artistic credo adopted during an even earlier life lived under another name among Russian avant-garde poets and painters. Iliazd shared with his friend Picasso a deep faith in the artist's restlessness and the need to undergo transformation, but he also trusted the power of time to transform artistic objects. "A poet's best fate is to be forgotten" in the expectation of rediscovery by new enthusiasts and interpreters. *Rapture* is such a neglected treasure.

The great works of avant-garde modernism usually arrived with a bang. Their scandals—whether in the theater, like Alfred Jarry's *Ubu Rex*, or the courtroom, like Joyce's *Ulysses*—have become integral to the way we think about them. Iliazd was no stranger to scandal. In fact, for a time, his reputation in Russia was based on nothing more than his outrageous lectures and manifestos. Russians even today think first of his "extreme" experimental dramas written and published during the Russian Civil War. When Iliazd (then still known as Ilia Zdanevich) left the former Russian Empire, he fell effortlessly into the scandalous last Paris Dada soirées, where the tactic of shocking the bourgeois had become routine and the Surrealist movement announced itself in violent attacks on the stage.

Rapture did not arrive this way in March 1930. Nor did it meet the eager, protracted anticipation Joyce was able to muster for his *work in progress* before its final advent as *Finnegans Wake*. It was ignored. The unassuming yellow-green book, published at Iliazd's own expense, went on sale in only one Paris bookstore with a long history of supporting the new art. Within several days, Iliazd had inserted strips of paper into unsold copies with the challenge: "Russian booksellers refuse to sell this book. If you're that inhibited, don't read it!" Obviously, this was not exactly the usual bang, but it was hardly Eliot's "whimper."

A world, nevertheless, had ended with the displacements brought on by the 1917 Russian Revolutions. Iliazd had passed, like so many refugees in the aftermath of the First World War, through the chaos of postwar Istanbul and now found himself not just in exile, but even on the margin of the Russian emigré community in Paris. He was cut off from his former associates and not yet fully engaged with the French artists who would become so important to him later. He envisioned *Rapture*, his first published work of prose fiction, as a final statement on his former life, already delivered with confident hope from inside a new life that was still taking shape.

By coincidence, within weeks of *Rapture*'s unremarked release, news of an all-too-final bang reached Iliazd: Vladimir Mayakovsky, the star of the Russian avant-garde, had shot himself through the heart on April 14, 1930, sending a spectacular signal that the old life had indeed come to an end.[1] Mayakovsky's lament that "the love boat broke up on daily routine" expressed his inability to imagine himself outside the heroic public role of the revolutionary artist. Art should be for life's sake, but his heroism had failed to transform the conditions of everyday life. Iliazd still believed in "life for art's sake," and his belief allowed him to continue his work unnoticed, to enter a period that looked like dormancy, and to emerge quietly, catlike, in a new guise.[2]

1.

On the surface, *Rapture* takes the form of an adventure novel about Laurence, a treasure-mad young bandit. It tells the story of his doomed love for the mysterious beauty Ivlita and recounts how Laurence establishes a reign of terror over several mountain villages. He then departs with his gang on a series of forays down to the flatlands and the provincial capital, drawn into schemes promising ever larger prizes that turn out to be ever more elusive and evanescent. Laurence leaves a trail of victims and eventually finds himself pursued by government authorities, abandoned by his comrades, and hiding with a pregnant Ivlita in a cave. Finally, Ivlita, too, betrays him. Shortly after being imprisoned, he breaks out with the help of some nameless admirers and sets off to avenge himself on Ivlita. He arrives just in time to see Ivlita die giving birth to their stillborn child, and he succumbs to death beside them.

The story is energetic and fast-paced, as the Russian critic D. S. Mirsky noted in a short French-language review not long after *Rapture*'s publication. It bears a quality perceived at the time as "cinematic."[3] But while the story may be engaging for its own sake, Iliazd is playing a game of concealment and revelation with treasure-seeking readers. What should we make of the murdered onanist monk who sees satyrs gnawing rifle barrels, as though they were imitating the poet in Rimbaud's *A Season in Hell*? Why do we find among Ivlita's neighbors a goitrous (or wenny) family with fourteen children ranging in age from four to sixty divided into "toiling" and "spoiled" classes and a second family of cretins who live in a stable and emerge in the evening to sing unpronounceable, incomprehensible songs? And why has Ivlita's father, a grieving retired forestry official who philosophizes and collects books in languages he can't read, built such a fancifully carved mahogany house? Why, further, does he fail to distinguish his daughter from his dead wife? *Rapture* represents, as I noted above, Iliazd's reckoning with the Russian avant-garde. He is settling accounts with personalities (including himself), evaluating themes and techniques by mixing allegory and roman à clef, but passing them through the Freudian dream work of condensation and displacement. In order to begin to see how, we need a somewhat longer history of the furiously creative movement known as Russian Futurism and Ilia Zdanevich's place in it.[4]

Ilia Mikhailovich Zdanevich was born in Tiflis (modern Tbilisi), the capital of the Georgian province of the Russian Empire, on April 21, 1894.[5] His father, a teacher of French, came from a Polish family that had been exiled to the area after the Polish uprising of 1830. His mother was a cultured Georgian woman, a former student of Tchaikovsky, and kept her home open to Tiflis's artistic and intellectual elite. She also greatly desired a daughter, and in the mythology he later constructed for himself, Zdanevich made much of being treated as a girl well into his childhood.

Zdanevich's father kept track of news from France, and since the family was curious about artistic trends in particular, Zdanevich learned of F. T. Marinetti's 1909 "Manifesto of Futurism" not long after it appeared in *Le Figaro*. Zdanevich was already writing poetry in imitation of Russian Symbolists like the sun-worshipping Konstantin Balmont, and quickly became fascinated with Marinetti's antisentimental shift in values. Solar worship quickly yielded to vehement attacks on the sun in the spirit of Marinetti's "Let's Murder the Moonlight." Zdanevich asked his father to translate Marinetti's manifestos so he could study them more closely.

Although Zdanevich was far from the capital, St. Petersburg, as he learned about Marinetti's Futurism, he would have read in the leading artistic journals about what soon became known as "the crisis of Symbolism," the reigning school of poetry in Russia during the first decade of the twentieth century. Symbolism was roughly aligned in the visual arts with the post-Impressionist aestheticism of the World of Art movement, perhaps best known in Western Europe and America for its impresario, Serge Diaghilev, and his Ballets Russes. Zdanevich's erstwhile favorite, Balmont, belonged, along with Valery Briusov, to an older generation of Decadents who had imbibed the themes and techniques of French poetry from Baudelaire on. More recently, a younger generation of Symbolist poets (Viacheslav Ivanov, Alexander Blok, and Andrei Bely) had immersed themselves in the experience of a mystical world soul associated with the Goethean *Ewig-weibliche* and the philosopher Vladimir Solovyov's writings on Sophia, the Wisdom of God. Their explorations, building on the "musical" invention of the Decadent generation of Symbolists, inspired an unprecedented wave of linguistic experimentation—always in the service of some other goal. Ivanov, for instance, a Nietzschean specialist on the interplay of Dionysius and Apollo in the Greek sources, characterized poetry as a vehicle *a realibus ad realiora*. As a result, younger poets began to sense that, for all his technical brilliance, Ivanov was not interested in "the word as such." Poets within Ivanov's circle had already turned to primitivism as an antidote to the cold sheen of civilization. They were also experimenting with folk arts to extract a new mythology and devise accompanying theatrical rites that would reestablish solidarity in modern society. Futurism, not just for Zdanevich, provided an opportunity to focus on the tools of poetry while mocking all of these "higher" goals.

Several factions of younger poets and artists rose up to challenge their elders, who were also in many cases their teachers. Primitivism flourished, but its practitioners largely discounted the mystical search for the essence of the people in favor of examining formal technique. Where such mysticism survived (in the work of the poet Velimir Khlebnikov, for instance), it tended to be grounded in minute studies of dialect and etymology, in the specific nuances of word roots and variants. Poets began to talk about the "thingness" of words and of poetry as a craft. Among them, the Acmeists (Nikolai Gumilev, Anna Akhmatova, and Osip Mandelshtam) formed the Poets' Guild as an alternative to Ivanov's more exalted Academy of Poetry. Khlebnikov, who insisted on using only Slavic words, devised the term "budetliane" (people of the future) in 1910 to describe a group of poets and artists that would eventually include Mayakovsky and take on other names (Hylaea, Cubo-Futurists).[6] He deepened his idiosyncratic research into the roots of Slavic languages and, together with Aleksei Kruchenykh, arrived at some of the most radical treatments of the word as material for analysis and resynthesis. Another group of poets called themselves Ego-Futurists, after Igor Severianin's 1911 manifesto. Their belief that poetry should express unbridled subjectivity rather than mythologizing and moralizing justified yet more experiments in neologism.

Futurism, it should be said, came to Russia not just through verbal art, but also through the painting and sculpture of Marinetti's compatriots, Umberto Boccioni, Gino Severini, Carlo Carrà, and Luigi Russolo, as well as through Picasso's application of Futurist techniques to some of his Cubist work. Because Futurism was subsequently adopted and adapted through so many channels by Russian artists and writers, it never became a unified movement with an acknowledged leader. Consequently, squabbles over priority arose almost at once among those who first appropriated the name in Russia.

When Zdanevich arrived in St. Petersburg in 1911 to study law at the university, his brother, Kirill, acquainted him with a group of young painters calling themselves the Ass's Tail, gathered around Mikhail Larionov and Natalia Goncharova. These artists were feverishly assimilating and transforming styles and techniques drawn both from their Western European counterparts and from Russian folk artifacts, religious icons, and popular printed sheets (*lubki*). Larionov apparently found the eloquent Zdanevich useful as a spokesperson for his particular brand of Futurism. The still-teenaged Zdanevich spent the first year of his public life as a Futurist primarily cowriting manifestos with Larionov, presenting polemical lectures, and participating in open disputes.

According to Zdanevich, he was the first to proclaim the name Futurist in Russia when he took the stage during a debate over painting styles hosted by the Union of Youth in St. Petersburg on January 12, 1912. In contrast to Khlebnikov's impulse to "slavicize" the movement, Zdanevich tended, at first, to faithfully reproduce all the characteristics of Marinetti's stance, down to his own vocabulary and rhetoric, often quoting directly from Marinetti's manifestos. Nevertheless, as he became more accustomed to the theatricality of public speaking, Zdanevich rapidly developed his own way of mixing Marinetti into homegrown Russian debates on aesthetics. In his lecture "On Futurism," delivered in Moscow on March 23, 1913, to coincide with Larionov and Goncharova's Target exhibition, he combined the hoary Russian materialist claim that a pair of boots is worth more than Pushkin with Marinetti's pronouncement that "a roaring car . . . is more beautiful than the Victory of Samothrace."[7] He goaded his audience by waving an American Vera brand shoe, claiming that it was more beautiful than the Venus de Milo because of its ability to separate human beings from the earth and raise them out of the muck. His lecture ended, as he fully intended, in a scandal, with the audience attacking Zdanevich, who defended himself with tea glasses and a large platter. He ended up forfeiting his speaking fees to cover damage to the theater—but in compensation he had suddenly become famous in his own right.

Audiences witnessed the corollary to Zdanevich's act a year later when he held forth on "Shoe Worship" at the Stray Dog Cabaret, the center of Petersburg bohemia, on April 17, 1914. In this parody of Symbolist mythmaking, delivered while Zdanevich pretended to sleep on stage, he wove a complicated panegyric to shoeshine men, the priests of the shoe cult. Their "holy hands, black and grimy from polish, turn your shoes into mirrors that amusingly reflect the sky."[8] In transforming the instruments that raise human bodies from the earth so that they also reveal the sky to human minds, the shoeshine men selflessly bring about the end of their own usefulness by preparing human beings for their next advance: joining the French aviation pioneer Louis Blériot to live in the air, where shoes need no longer be worn. Zdanevich displaced Marinetti's overly luxurious machine fetish with a mass-produced object like those worn by every member of his audience (and an object, besides, of Freudian fetish). Iliazd's parodic treatments in *Rapture* of Symbolist themes and their Marinettian Futurist negations ("scorn for woman," "murdering the moonlight," "wireless imagination," "rootless humans") follow the same pattern by making images and metaphors concrete while widening as far as possible their circles of connotation, multiplying the levels of meaningful resonance they generate.

Most of Zdanevich's writing up to this point, as it happens, addressed problems of visual art rather than poetry, but he was beginning to assess what the various Futurist poets had accomplished. When his mother begged him early on not to subject himself to the shame of public scandal, he assured her that he was biding his time, hoping to trade on his notoriety in order to advance his own ideas about poetry in the future.[9] He had begun experimenting with verbal forms analogous to the Rayonist abstraction Larionov was promoting at the time. Only now did he feel he was ready to move beyond the derivative poetry of his early notebooks.

Hylaea's "A Slap in the Face of Public Taste" appeared in December 1912, signed by Mayakovsky, Khlebnikov, Kruchenykh, and David Burliuk. Each of them would subsequently have ample justification for laying claim to recognition as chief Futurist, and Zdanevich moved to position himself in this competition for first place by criticizing their poetry in his lectures and pseudonymous articles.[10] Burliuk, always more impresario and instigator than poet and painter, was easiest to dismiss. Zdanevich believed that Mayakovsky, though talented, simply extended the Decadent trend in Russian poetry into cruder, less cultivated forms. He always thought of Khlebnikov as a genuine poet, new and exciting, although he, too, in Zdanevich's opinion, owed most of his technique to Russian Symbolist tradition and demonstrated little essential connection to Futurism as Marinetti had defined it. Kruchenykh was the real wild card, dangerously exploring genuine abstraction in poetry and reducing text to texture. Zdanevich felt threatened enough to tactically accuse Kruchenykh of plagiarizing one of Larionov's manifestos when Kruchenykh and Khlebnikov published their programmatic "The Word as Such" in September 1913. Still, Zdanevich characterized Kruchenykh's experiments in *Pomade*, which featured the poem "dyr bul shchyl," the debut of Russian Futurist "beyonsense" (*zaum*), as somehow overly sentimental.[11]

Zdanevich was at last preparing to publicize the new ideas he'd been working up together with Larionov and his friend, the painter Mikhail LeDantu, when he encountered Kruchenykh's abstract poems. Futurism had done its work, but in rejecting the past, it encouraged a new academicism. Each artistic movement claimed to promote an exclusively correct style justified by a superior realism grounded in turn on a scientific or mystical fact. That fact might be Symbolist access to unseen metaphysical realities, traditional realist representation of the world and life "as it is," Impressionist truth in an artist's immediate perception, or Futurist reference to the physiology of optic nerves. They began to promote "everythingism" to interrupt this endless succession of novelties without shutting down fruitful experimentation in the arts. Everythingism was founded on recognizing the sheer conventionality of works of art, their ultimate divorce from any claim to a basis outside of artistic activity. For Zdanevich, everythingism truly allowed artists to overcome the constraints of time and space by encouraging them to draw on all possible means of communication, no matter where or when they were first discovered and developed. "Everythingks" would not reject tradition, but neither would they respect the proprieties of style. To the charge of eclecticism, Zdanevich asserted a fundamental distinction: Eclectics borrowed and mixed superficial forms indiscriminately for equally superficial effect without understanding their artistic function and reason for being; an everythingk finds an integral place, fully motivated by the artistic problem or task addressed in the work, for every borrowed element and technique so that it contributes to the work's unique overall structure and texture (the main considerations for judging an abstract work). By drawing on disparate sources and techniques, the everythingk artist weighs and offsets their peculiar distorting effects to achieve "equilibrium" in each work.

Although this notion of equilibrium might suggest that every-thingism is a retrograde reassertion of the artist's genius for creating organic works, an important new note in Zdanevich's drafts for an everythingist manifesto invokes concerns that would also arise among the Zurich Dadaists, especially Tristan Tzara and Hugo Ball. Zdanevich urges artists to strive for "fullness" in a work without any concern for achieving coherence by excluding contradictions. At one level, this meant integrating chance into strictly composed structures. Zdanevich expected equilibrium to emerge from forms that exploit both simultaneity and sequence (or perhaps, as in Saussure's lectures on language, "synchrony" and "diachrony") and exist at once in a state of authentic originality and utter dependence on other works ("the work as such *and* as a part of art"), relying on open theft as a strategy.[12] Zdanevich and Larionov even released a "Da Manifesto" in the form of an imagined interview during which they answer "yes" to all questions posed, no matter how contradictory the result.[13]

Zdanevich felt strongly the need to move beyond his role as propagandist and aspiring theorist toward practical application of everythingism—toward the moment when he could be called a poet. In October 1913, he attacked Nikolai Kul'bin, an older proponent of Futurism, in another talk from the stage of the Stray Dog, as though he were chiding himself: "But revolution only turns out to be revolution if you get things done."[14] He had, in a way seemingly uncharacteristic for the hotheaded avant-garde, put off publicizing everythingism for several months until he could connect it at least to Goncharova's work, if not his own. He delivered two lectures on "Natalia Goncharova and Everythingism" to accompany exhibitions of her work in Moscow in November 1913 and in St. Petersburg in March 1914. For our purposes, the lectures are notable not only because Zdanevich first publicly presents everythingk positions, but also because he makes two creative departures in the texture of his writing from the still-prominent rhetoric he inherited from Marinetti. We can see fragments of *Rapture* emerging like studies for a larger painting out of Zdanevich's simultaneously playful and aggressive provocations.

The November lecture includes an imaginary biography of Goncharova that provides her with a fairy-tale childhood and a career that takes her to several historical civilizations and places her in contact with their artistic masters. The biography is meant to demonstrate the primacy of art over life, so that the "artistic facts" of Goncharova's career are projected onto her life to create a true biography.[15] The theory is certainly of interest, and Zdanevich applies it to himself later in his "Iliazda" lecture, but the biography contains, more concretely, stylistic parodies and narrative material that reappear especially in *Rapture*'s depictions of Ivlita. In his March 1914 talk, Zdanevich offers "an engaging film scenario for movie directors" called "The Fallen Man." Its hero, "son of an expansive Italian rich man," joins a cell of genuine revolutionaries, "Natalia Goncharova included in their number." He abandons them at the height of a planned uprising and runs away with "a gang of shady characters"—Mayakovsky and his henchmen, especially the Burliuk brothers. He falls still further, associating with figures representing the even more suspect Ego-Futurists and the Mezzanine of Poetry, and dies "a disgusting, inglorious death" in a hospital.[16] The passage is nothing more than an amusing weapon in Zdanevich's ongoing polemic with other Futurist groups, but, like an accidental mutation that turns out to be beneficial later on, this melodramatic—and silent, we should recall—allegory of Futurism in Russia looks now, as Régis Gayraud has pointed out, like the genesis of *Rapture*'s main plot.[17]

Once Larionov and Goncharova had moved to Paris in May 1914, Zdanevich's attention turned from theories of painting and invective directed against his rivals toward attempts to write "manifold poetry," an alternative to "the poetry of a single mouth."[18] Zdanevich intended manifold poetry to be performed in an "orchestral" fashion like a score, not read in silence on the page. It would convey "the sounds of a marketplace, not the line at the cash register."[19] The need to free words from time, specifically the time needed to pronounce phonemes in sequence, required new techniques of simultaneous pronunciation. Among the many metaphors Zdanevich tries out in the notebooks to his unpublished manifesto on manifold poetry (metallurgy, bartending), he develops a long passage about "everythingk-woodsmen" cutting the "grove of trees [that is, words—T. K.] sententiously nodding their heads." The everythingk-woodsmen aim to "extract their heat and saw them up into parquetry blocks for the palace of poetry" and "logs for the factory of everythingism."[20] Zdanevich's metaphor in this unused sketch from his notebooks illustrates a fundamental procedure he applies later not just to words, but to "stolen" characters, plots, myths, and entire symbolic systems, cutting them up to make them burn more brightly or to reassemble them into structures entirely his own. Furthermore, it's no surprise that before becoming a bandit, Laurence, the hero of *Rapture*, works at a sawmill, where, as it turns out, he is already a murderer of transformed humans "nodding their heads," and that Ivlita's father, the former forester, lives in a magnificent house made of fancifully carved mahogany—just such a "palace of poetry."[21]

Manifold poetry represented Zdanevich's first contribution to beyonsense, and he believed he had found a method less arbitrary than Kruchenykh's "poems in [his] own language." Its first fruits were onomatopoeic poems inspired by early World War I flying aces like Roland Garros ($_{GA}$RO^{LAND}). Zdanevich worked out a more complex approach to beyonsense after joining Olga Leshkova's and LeDantu's Bloodless Murder group in Petrograd at the end of November 1916.[22] The group performed the first of his plays (he called it a "dra"), "yAnko olbAnian kIng," on December 3.[23] The play was inspired by their colleague Janko Lavrin's war coverage from Albania and was composed in a combination of phonetic Russian and beyonsense words masquerading as Albanian.[24] The tsarist censorship prevented its publication in 1916, but when it finally appeared in Tiflis in 1918, it was Zdanevich's first book under his own name.[25] Such long gestations remained characteristic of Zdanevich's work throughout his life.

In the meantime, Zdanevich had finally met Kruchenykh. Zdanevich had been engaged during 1916 as a war correspondent for the liberal Petrograd newspaper *Rech'*, covering the Russo-Ottoman front in Eastern Anatolia. He was based in his family's home in Tiflis, where Kruchenykh was doing his wartime service as a draftsman for the railroad in Georgia, and the two became acquainted in March 1916.[26] Some of Zdanevich's polemic energy had been blunted by his experiences near the front, and despite Zdanevich's formerly keen sense of competition, it turned out that he and Kruchenykh shared interests and inspirations. Both engaged critically with Khlebnikov's theories about word formation. Khlebnikov had derived some of his ideas from etymological and morphological studies, but many were less convincingly the result of purely speculative association between sounds or shapes of letters and particular concepts and emotions. Both had primitivist interests. Kruchenykh found a source for beyonsense in folk charms and curses, as well as in ecstatic religious glossolalia.[27] He also liked to collect writing by children and the insane. Zdanevich had long been impressed by painted shop and tavern signs in Georgia, especially by the work of Niko Pirosmanashvili (or Pirosmani), whose paintings he, his brother Kirill, and LeDantu collected for Larionov's 1913 Target exhibition. He had been thinking more and more about the nonstandard orthography he found on these signs. And both had become interested in Freud, especially *The Interpretation of Dreams* and *The Psychopathology of Everyday Life*.[28] Their rivalry gradually heated up and eventually boiled over into three years of feverish collaboration and almost graphomaniac productivity.

But first, Zdanevich had to return to Petrograd to finish the exams for his law degree. He received it just before the February Revolution and then was caught up, along with other Futurists, in organizing a Union of Cultural Workers (Soiuz deiatelei iskusstv) to press for artistic freedom from government interference of any kind. Despite his dedication to the cause of leftist art and his impassioned speeches in the name of the Free Art faction, he failed to be selected for the Union's steering committee in spring 1917.[29] Mayakovsky was among those selected, and Zdanevich felt a lasting bitterness over the episode. When Professor Ekvtime Takaishvili invited Zdanevich to participate in an archeological expedition to investigate medieval Georgian architecture on Ottoman territory then under control of the Russian army, he readily accepted and left Petrograd at the beginning of May. As a result, he missed the subsequent revolutionary upheavals, from the July Days through the Bolshevik takeover in October and the first stirrings of the Civil War in January 1918. Zdanevich and Kruchenykh had the good fortune of spending the next years in an independent Georgia largely spared the devastation of the Civil War.

Kruchenykh and Zdanevich formed the Futurists' Syndicate in late 1917.[30] As Tat'iana Nikol'skaia has pointed out, the Futurists in Tiflis were freed from the game of scandal and riot, the need for continual self-advertisement, and the endless polemics that took up so much of their energy in Moscow and St. Petersburg before the war.[31] The public in Tiflis showed genuine interest in new artistic trends, and even when the writers presented lectures, plays, and poems that were undeniably much more scandalous than ever before, audiences took them seriously. Futurists from different camps performed and published together, sharing the stage and page with local Georgian Symbolists from the Blue Horns group and with Sergei Gorodetsky's section of the Acmeist Poets' Guild.

The following spring, Zdanevich, Kruchenykh, and the newcomer Igor Terent'ev joined to form "41°," a self-styled "duet for three idiots."[32] Zdanevich gave frequent lectures at the Fantastic Cabaret for the newly founded Futurist University. (Kruchenykh pointedly employed Khlebnikov's Slavic neologism, *vseuchbishche* [all-study institute], rather than the standard foreign borrowing *universitet*.) He covered numerous topics, including "Dodi Burliuk's Lorgnette," "Theater at an Impasse," "Orthography and Straining," "On the Magnetism of Letters," and "Tyutchev, Singer of Shit."[33] Now, however, he was known as a poet rather than merely a propagandist, the author of a series of dras under the collective title *drUnkeyness*: "yAnko olbAnian kIng," "dUnkee for rEnt," "EEster AIland," and "asthO zgA." Even Gorodetsky the Acmeist found them "amusing."[34]

While Zdanevich fleshed out his orchestral poetry and learned the printer's trade in order to represent it on the page, Terent'ev took up the study of how chance contributes to artistic creativity. He produced a book on the topic, *17 Nonsense Tools*, as well as an article, "The Highway to Roundabout Discovery." One of the techniques Terent'ev advocated for producing meaningful nonsense was called "shooting at random." In *Rapture*, Iliazd treats Terent'ev's term in the same way he tends to treat idioms and metaphors—by making it into a concrete image. The inept former forester in the novel illustrates one aspect of this idea when he reacts to his daughter's abduction by grabbing his gun, firing without taking aim, and scaring himself nearly to death. But the image also describes the wenny old man's hunting habits. In his madness, he never misses his prey—thanks not to reasoned skill, but to some implied intuitive sense. It's also worth noting, as far as gun play goes, Zdanevich's continual reference to a Russian juridical term that describes an act that fails because of the agent's inadequacy or incompetence: "a criminal attempt using unsuitable means."[35] The phrase has come to designate any failure due to inadequacy. Zdanevich adopts this phrase to describe the entire practice of poetry.

And, while we're on the topic of failure due to inadequacy or impotence—Zdanevich's writing in Tiflis incorporates an intensified use of sexual and scatological double entendre, again under Kruchenykh's immediate influence. Kruchenykh was studying not just Freud, but Havelock Ellis, especially his volume on autoeroticism. Before coming to Georgia, Kruchenykh had initiated a new method of literary study, "shiftology," by inspecting the classics of Russian literature for secret sexual and scatological obsessions. The most reliable method for bringing these secrets to light was listening for puns across word boundaries when the poems were read aloud.[36] Terent'ev also contributed to this line of research with his *Tract on Outright Obscenity*. According to the Georgian poet G. Robakidze, Zdanevich began prefacing his readings with the claim that "Futurism is erotic solipsism."[37] The scatological aspects of Zdanevich's *dras* probably also find a source in Alfred Jarry's *Ubu* plays. Inevitably, despite the generally amiable atmosphere among Tiflis artists, Kruchenykh, Terent'ev, and Zdanevich were compared to boys writing bad words on fences. Zdanevich, however, manages to organize this play of beyonsense in his *dras* into something that for English readers might be most conveniently compared to Joyce's manipulations of standard English in *Finnegans Wake*. Like Joyce, he weaves material from other languages through Russian and alters standard orthography to engage multiple simultaneous meanings that similarly tie trivial slips of the tongue to deep mythologies within an intermittently discernible plot.[38] Vladimir Markov, the first historian of Russian Futurism, called the collective output of 41° between 1917 and 1920 "the clearest crystallization of Futurism's avant-garde elements and its evolutionary, if not necessarily aesthetic, climax."[39]

As the Soviet Union gradually absorbed the independent Trans-caucasian republics, Zdanevich started saving up for a ticket to Paris by working for the American organization Near East Relief.[40] He may have been drawn to Paris by news of Dada actions, but he told his contacts when he arrived in France that he had left Georgia because it was getting to be impossible for anyone to deal with "pure art" free from politics.[41] In any case, he arrived in Istanbul in November 1920 and found himself in the midst of a sizeable Russian diaspora, most of whom were waiting, like him, for permission to move on. It took nearly a year for a wary French government to issue a visa to this "grammatical revolutionary and murderer of words," as the French journalist André Germain later called him.[42]

Within two weeks of arriving in Paris in November 1921, Zdanevich was already using Larionov's contacts to arrange a lecture in "picturesque" French on "The New Schools in Russian Poetry," where he introduced Parisian society to the history and tenets of Russian Futurism. Naturally, his lecture included propagandistic distortions that exaggerated the importance of 41° and laid claim to independence from any French influence whatsoever. He summarized the work of 41°, emphasizing "Terent'ev's First Law": Pragmatic language finds its center of gravity in meaning, poetic language in sound.[43] This "eternal dualism" maps onto a whole series: heaven and earth, day and night, body and soul, reason and intuition, thought and feeling, Dr. Faustus and John the Theologian.[44] When writers and speakers focus exclusively on pragmatic language, "shifts" (Freudian "displacement") or deformations occur in morphology, etymology, syntax, phonetics, and orthography to assert the emotional and instinctive, sexual and obscene (following Freud) aspects of language.[45] These shifts are both "a useless consequence of language decay" and "a means of poetic expression" that should be compared neither to "magic tricks" nor to "music."[46] Zdanevich announces plans to open a new 41° University and makes the Tiflis venue sound far more substantial than the cabaret reading series it was in reality. He concludes, "Reason is mendacious, poetry is immaculate, and we, too, are immaculate when we are alone with it."[47]

By December 21, Zdanevich was already being advertised as a "mezzo-soprano" in a piece arranged for "Dada Lir Kan" by Sergei Charchoune, a Russian Paris resident from before the war who had become a regular participant in Tzara's and Francis Picabia's Dada soirées. The prospect of uniting 41° with Dada excited Zdanevich's Russian compatriots who were already active in the Dada group (Valentin Parnakh and Sergei Romov, in addition to Sergei Charchoune).[48] Zdanevich participated selectively and became friendly with members of different emerging Dada factions, but he remained wary of identifying too closely with Dada, skeptical as to whether their poetic missions were really directed toward the same end.[49] Unfortunately, by the time Zdanevich arrived in Paris, Dada was reaching a crisis. Picabia had already broken with Tzara, and André Breton was giving clear signals that he felt Tzara's approach to literature and art was not quite serious enough. Zdanevich was thankful to his Dada connections for the attention he received from the French-language press. Still, he poured much of his energy into preparing a magnificent edition of the last of his dras, lidantIU as a bEEkon, engaging Paul Éluard to write a French preface.

Before he could finish, Paris Dada was over. Iliazd had used the occasion of a visit by Mayakovsky in November 1922 to announce the formation of the "Through" (Cherez) group of young émigré writers, who intended to establish close ties with both French and Soviet avant-gardes.[50] Mayakovsky's promise to organize a corresponding group in the Soviet Union led to the founding of LEF, the Left Front of the Arts, in January 1923. Zdanevich also quickly became active in the Union of Russian Artists in Paris, later filling the office of secretary and, in 1925, president.[51] Since Tzara's reputation for destructive scandal prevented him from renting halls in

Paris for Dada soirees, Iliazd and Through took responsibility in July 1923 for arranging the "Evening of the Bearded Heart," a program of music, poetry, film, and a performance of Tzara's "Gas-operated Heart." Breton, accompanied by Robert Desnos and Benjamin Péret, rushed the stage and began beating Pierre de Massot before being removed by police from the hall. After an intermission, Éluard confronted Tzara directly as the play was beginning and the evening ended in a mêlée that sealed the final separation of Breton's group from Tzara's.[52] Initially, Iliazd and most of his Russian associates took Tzara's side, but it wasn't long before the Russians were back on friendly terms with the group that became known in 1924 as the Surrealists, since, for a time at least, they shared aesthetic and ideological interests.

Once these dustups settled down, Iliazd had every reason to believe he would be able to support a Russian-language artistic grouping independent of the dominant anti-Soviet Russian émigré circles. Surrealists were eager to collaborate with Through, and the Union of Russian Artists held annual fund-raising balls that became legendary events in Parisian life, attracting high-profile collaborators like Picasso. France finally recognized the USSR and included a Soviet Pavilion in the 1925 Exposition of Decorative Arts, where work by Constructivists like Alexander Rodchenko was displayed alongside a copy of Iliazd's lidantIU as a bEEkon.[53] It looked as though publishing opportunities for leftist artists living in France would soon open up in the Soviet Union. The Union of Russian Artists went so far as to pass a resolution declaring loyalty to the Soviet Union in January 1926.[54] Iliazd was even able to find work as a translator in the new Soviet embassy.

But there were countervailing forces. Inflation in Germany brought a new wave of young Russian writers from Berlin. Writers who joined a series of newly established competing organizations, including the Poets' Guild (whose Acmeist founder, Nikolai

Gumilev, was revered as an anti-Bolshevik martyr and was executed in 1921), were gradually given privileged access to the most important émigré salons and to major Russian-language journals and newspapers. The Union of Young Poets and Writers received a blessing from Vladislav Khodasevich, a leading conservative poet and critic, to explicitly combat Futurism's prestige and Boris Pasternak's influence among young Russian émigré writers.[55] Writers like Parnakh, who had enthusiastically moved to the Soviet Union beginning in 1922, sent or brought back disturbing news about bureaucratic stonewalling, growing anti-Semitism, and worse. And no sooner had the Soviet government established direct contact with leftist artists in Paris than official policy turned against the avant-garde in Russia, including Mayakovsky.[56] Iliazd became increasingly isolated in what he called "poetic reclusion."[57] One of his last remaining disciples, the poet Boris Poplavsky, addressed the situation in a poem dedicated to Jean Cocteau and titled with Iliazd's favorite ready-made phrase, "A Criminal Attempt Using Unsuitable Means":

We're in coffins for one, fit tight
Where our breath coos without purpose
We wear straitjackets in the night
And rap back and forth our verses.[58]

By 1928, Poplavsky could not endure yet another unrealized edition of his poetry. The lure of publication in the major journals drew him, too, into the mainstream of the emigration. Iliazd's French contacts among writers diminished after he broke with Breton, the "Roman pope" of Surrealism, when Breton forbade all criticism of Soviet bureaucracy.[59] Iliazd, still quixotically claiming to speak "in the name of the young writers," made a spectacular break with all the Russian factions at a meeting of the Franco-Russian Studio on

April 29, 1930, where he requested the floor after a paper on emerging features of the Russian émigré novel and a response from a committed Communist who claimed there was no Russian literature outside the Soviet Union. A Riga newspaper account reported that this "exemplar of literary failure" who "writes endlessly under the strange pseudonym 'Iliazd' " and whom "no one publishes" or "takes seriously" asserted that the whole world should learn from Soviet literature and that émigré writers were "pretenders at best."[60] One month after he published *Rapture* and two weeks after Mayakovsky's suicide, Iliazd committed a corresponding professional suicide. Mayakovsky had set a period to the end of the Futurist era and Iliazd acted in homage to his old rival.[61]

2.

This professional suicide was merely a second, tardy, and very public death. Iliazd had already acknowledged a significant break in his creative life much earlier, in the elegiac tone of his intended foreword to the final dra, *lidantIU as a bEEkon*, published in Paris in 1923. The brash manifesto attitude is gone; Iliazd had no pronouncements or prescriptions for the future of art. The book is "a wreath on the grave of what we lived by these last ten years." After briefly reviewing the spectacles, scandals, and shocking experiments that filled those years, along with the aspirations that occasioned them, Iliazd writes, "We know that all our youth was for nothing, and I vainly swore I would prevail because I was young. . . . Farewell, youth, beyonsense, the acrobat's long way, equivocations, cold intellect, everything, everything, everything."[62] Illiazd's foreword announces the reckoning that would come in *Rapture*, and announces it as a sublimation, claiming that with *lidantIU as a bEEkon* he has reached the point of perfection for the approach he had chosen and now "throws it away," much like Wittgenstein kicking away his ladder. The loss marks a distinct gain—he dies that he might live, christened with a new name, Iliazd. In a sense, his dramatic farewell to "everything, everything, everything" functions as a greeting, an attempt to see the world, "everything," as if for the first time.[63]

The break is real, and the farewell to beyonsense as a technique is genuine. In the midst of life's way, after years of avant-garde experimentation, he had, like Dante, lost the direct path, albeit often intentionally. Iliazd avoids neologism in *Rapture* and merely describes instances of beyonsense—the unpronounceable name of the hamlet and the songs the cretins sing in the evening—without ever providing the actual words. Nevertheless, the novel is filled with "inhuman" sound, like the last stanzas of Baudelaire's "To the Reader": animals, plants, wind, water, avalanches, and machines. And the novel evinces a longing as deep as Novalis's or Khlebnikov's, if more pessimistic, for establishing lines of communication with the inhuman, from the rocks beneath our feet to the stars over our heads. In the rest of his work, he returned to beyonsense only to collect and reprint exemplary texts in a polemic 1948 anthology, *The Poetry of Unknown Words*. Iliazd wanted to demonstrate to Isidore Isou and the Lettristes that he and his colleagues, including Dada poets like Kurt Schwitters and Raoul Hausmann, had thoroughly explored decades before what Isou was naively claiming to discover anew.

If the beyonsense dras, as Regis Gayraud claims, "erect bridges between every human being's individual unconscious and various mythological and religious notions 'surfacing' from the collective unconscious," *Rapture* sublimates in a consummate form what had been dredged up in those earlier exercises.[64] Iliazd simultaneously renounces and preserves what he has lost. An excremental, absolutely useless and needless waste ("youth . . . for nothing") turns out to be a priceless sign of lavish cosmic generosity. The work's title encapsulates both aspects of sublimation: our mourning for something we believe we once possessed while we raise it to the dignity of an unattainable ideal. In Russian, as in English, it sits in the midst of a sizeable etymological web connecting raptors, ravishers, and rapt admirers—rapacious, ravenous behavior with rapturous ecstasy, utter deprivation with unhoped-for fulfillment. For our English ears, it draws in reivers and the bereft. I can't help thinking of Flannery O'Connor's title *The Violent Bear It Away*, which comes, of course, from a "hard saying" about the Kingdom of God and those who attain it. But I also wish to recall a verse from one of *Rapture*'s most important intertexts: "The thief cometh not, but for to steal, and to kill, and to destroy: I am come that they might have life, and that they might have *it* more abundantly" (John 10:10 AV). I can't quite agree with the Serbian scholar Milovoje Jovanović's assertion that Iliazd intends his title to invoke only violent loss and death.[65] Nevertheless, the novel is full of the thief's work, leaving everything ravaged.

Rapture may seem an oblique memorial for the losses of war, revolution, and civil war, but no more strange in this role than *lidantIU as a bEEkon*. Ostensibly concerned with problems of artistic representation, Iliazd dedicated the final dra to the memory of his fellow everythingk Mikhail LeDantu, killed in a train accident while returning from the front in 1917. Some readers may find an engaging meditation in Virginia Woolf's use of the word "rapture" in her death-haunted *To the Lighthouse* and *The Waves*. Bernard in *The Waves*, for instance, takes stock of how Percival's death has affected each of the other characters with these words: "All had their rapture; their common feeling with death; something that stood them in stead," where making some accommodation with human finiteness, with mortality, can be seen as the condition for really living. Lily Briscoe, in section IX of "The Window" in *To the Lighthouse*, also thinks about rapture in the course of a meditation on autonomy and secrecy, artistic representation, and the latter's use for capturing the experience of love and grappling with absence. *To the Lighthouse* happened to appear while Iliazd was waiting for news about whether a Soviet publishing house would accept his novel. These associations are mere coincidence, something in the air across Europe, but I suspect deeper ties, perhaps emerging from shared Nietzschean themes, with Thomas Mann's own mountain novel, in which Hans Castorp descends to die in the Great War.

What then, can be saved? Iliazd called *Rapture* "a commentary on the idea of poetry as an always vain endeavor." Gayraud expands on the thought: "The attempt is vain because it is aimed at infinity, at eternity. But poetry remains a precision instrument."[66] In that sense, Iliazd's work calls out to Baudelaire's "artificial paradises" of hashish and opium employed to satisfy the "taste for the infinite" by means alternative to religious devotion and mysticism.[67] In *Rapture*, Iliazd recalibrates his everythingk tools to make yet another "criminal attempt," knowing in advance that it will be a "needless echo" like the one that ends the novel, or, as he expressed the same idea elsewhere, "the beard growing on a corpse's face."[68] Iliazd applies his "woodsman" skills this time not to words and phonemes, but to mythological, religious, folk, and literary plots (and, let's not forget, to the story of Russian Futurism), cutting apart scenes and characters to reassemble them into multilayered "orchestral" symbols. But where an allegory or a roman à clef always points us toward the appropriate "higher" interpretation and derives energy from readers' desire to understand it, Iliazd's novel inspires an aptly frustrated joy in the tensions between ultimately irreconcilable source plots. The poets in *Rapture* are "pretenders," as are we when we attempt to draw one neat meaning from its weave.

Let me illustrate Iliazd's treatment of plots and myths by choosing, for the sake of argument, two sources that are as intimately related as can be, the Gospel of John and the Revelation to John, both ascribed to the same author and foundational to a single religious system. As we move in *Rapture* from an obvious parody of the Gospel of John to a riff on the Revelation to John, we tend to want characters who inhabit a role in the first plot to inhabit a corresponding role in the second. We want heroes to continue to be heroes and villains to remain villains (even if they eventually repent). But more often than not, we find that Iliazd does not place his characters in the new scene as we would expect. This treatment prevents us from identifying a master plot that would allow us to interpret the novel in a single key. Moreover, as characters shift from "positive" to "negative" positions within borrowed plots and myths, all are subjected to the trials that beset finite beings: longing, temptation, self-doubt, delusion—but also external violence and the vagaries of chance. Sometimes they triumph; sometimes they fail. None of the plots and myths brought to bear on the novel's composition expresses the whole truth, but in their aggregate, their partial truths point toward a common human condition, the desire for more than bare life, to which culture is the response, in all its bafflingly proliferating manifestations. *Rapture* simply takes its place on the heap (not necessarily on *top*). According to Hugh Kenner, Wyndham Lewis called Joyce's *Ulysses* "a time-book, a midden-heap of *temps retrouvé*, a lingering over what had long faded from the world."[69] Iliazd continues to follow his everythingist practice and revives fading and faded plots and myths by overcoming time to bring them together simultaneously. The consciousness of the artist draws on them all to accomplish a particular task, "*to create*," in Lewis's words, "*new beauty*."

Lewis's invocation of the "midden-heap" has a further aptness for our purposes. Iliazd was also a student of ethnography and archaeology, recognized as an expert when it came to comparative studies of Byzantine, Armenian, Georgian, and Spanish and French Romanesque church architecture. He was quite sensitive to shared features of widely dispersed cultures. Yet, despite his experiments with evoking a collective unconscious, it seems to me that he was far more fascinated by the diversity of cultures than by their convergence. In contrast to Khlebnikov, who saw beyonsense as the royal road to a common, nearly telepathic language, Iliazd reveled in the effect of what we would now call "dissemination." A project like James Frazer's *Golden Bough* could serve as a treasure house for material without convincing Iliazd that it all boiled down to one fundamental myth. Likewise, Iliazd's treatment of a collective unconscious is illuminated less by Carl Jung's notion of a collective unconscious filled with archetypes than by Jacques Lacan's later interpretation of Freud, where "the unconscious is structured like a language." Iliazd's affinities are, after all, with the Russian roots of structuralism in Viktor Shklovsky's OPOIAZ (later known as the Russian Formalists) and Jakobson's Moscow Linguistics Circle.

Iliazd's novel is utterly lacking in a religious key, and there is little actual mysticism as opposed to mystification, despite his Soviet evaluators' misgivings.[70] As I pointed out previously, Iliazd makes it difficult to form judgments about his characters precisely because plots do not consistently map onto one another. The difficulty only increases when Iliazd also shares out characteristics derived from recognizable fictional characters and mythological figures. Consider, for example, some of the ways an important source character like Jarry's Père Ubu enters the novel. Laurence displays Père Ubu's penchant for cruelty when he derives pleasure by scattering coins and causing a brawl at his reception banquet. But the former forester wields Ubu's pataphysical mechanism for assuring good weather, drawn from Jarry's science of imaginary solutions, or "the science of that which is induced upon metaphysics."[71] At the same time, the former forester experiences a suspicion, directed primarily toward his daughter/dead wife, that someone might take over his home, an idea borrowed this time from one of Ubu's victims in

Ubu Cuckolded, the "professor of polyhedrons," Achras. "Paternity," however, is never well established, and when the former forester expresses this same suspicion in his wary welcome of Laurence, the source is clearly Manilov's mannered reception of Chichikov in Gogol's *Dead Souls*. The effect on our ability to judge recalls the Dostoevskian responsibility "of all for all," voided of its particular Christian content—all the major characters fall short of that striving for eternity that is the glory of poetry. Ultimately, the roman à clef falls apart: While we may agree with Gayraud that Laurence can most closely be identified with Mayakovsky, the wenny old man with Khlebnikov, Jonah (who attempts to rape Ivlita after an avalanche destroys the hamlet) with Burliuk, and the former forester with Zdanevich himself, the bandit's yellow blouse doesn't always fit, nor should it.[72] Each in some way falls victim to the distorting vices Hölderlin singles out in his 1795 preface to *Hyperion*: acquisitiveness and tyranny, the excessive desire to possess and the excessive desire to dominate. Each character is a manifestation of the poet, flawed by definition. Ivlita, likewise, need not be confined to just one of her hypothetical source figures. Some of these sources can be read in her name: Eve, Lilith, St. Julitta, Juliet, Miss Julie. Some are revealed by her involvement in plots or by her attributes: Diana, Daphne, Isis, Sophia, Mary, the Woman Clothed with the Sun, the Whore of Babylon, Solveig, Sonia Marmeladova, Marya Lebyadkina, Christ, Baba Yaga—or Sleeping Beauty, for that matter.

This list of Ivlita's "masks," so to speak, suggests that Iliazd is coming to terms with Marinetti's "scorn for women," a fundamental Futurist tenet repeated in every one of Zdanevich's lectures on Futurism. Kruchenykh also frequently invoked the phrase. In Kruchenykh's "research" on beyonsense, he asserted, along with Khlebnikov, that the phonetically liquid letter л (*l*) could be characterized as "damp" and, when combined with the typically feminine ю (*iu*) in "liubov," the Russian word for "love," presented all kinds of pitfalls for the masculine Futurist artist. Marinetti associates the theme with his hatred for moonlight, and Zdanevich, in his "shoe worship" and "face painting," with hatred for the earth and everything natural. Damp, fog, moonlight, and love are all themes associated in *Rapture* with Ivlita, but also with Laurence's first victim, the monk Mocius, who paradoxically pursues and threatens him. Mocius's name invokes a further, related, set of associations: Mokosh', a Slavic fertility goddess, patron of weaving and, like the Parcae, tied to fate; Mocius, Hieromartyr of Amphipolis, who battled Dionysian cults in Macedonia before the legalization of Christianity; Moses, "drawn from the water," in Jovanović's reading; and, in a multilingual pun, "mockery."[73] Love threatens Laurence, the one crowned with "laurels," whether victor or poet, with stagnation and sleep.

As it happens, these troubling letters, *l, iu, b*, are the initials of Mayakovsky's great and tragic love, Lilia IUr'evna Brik, who had already entered the developing mythology around Mayakovsky as the source of a certain "softening" noted by Kruchenykh in his 1918 article, "Mayakovsky's Amorous Adventure."[74] She became love personified and Mayakovsky frequently inscribed her name and initials in his poetry. She was later marked as the femme fatale who dragged Mayakovsky down from the heights of revolutionary activism into the "poshlost'" of "byt," the vulgarity of day-to-day existence with its petit bourgeois aspirations, most succinctly represented in *Rapture* in Laurence's acquiescence to the novel's betrayal scene.[75] But betrayal in *Rapture* is as ambiguous an action as any other and flows both ways, just as water in the novel flows sometimes uphill and sometimes down—it could be the justified abandonment of the poet by a neglected muse.

Symbolists like Alexander Blok had recorded this changeability of the muse or the Eternal Feminine from the comforting Beautiful Lady (with all attendant religious and chivalrous connotations) to the threatening, but exciting, Stranger (usually a prostitute-like figure). For Zdanevich, the chameleon's constant change presented an imperative for Futurists, but he went on to push "changeability" (*izmenchivost'*) into praise for violent transformation and generalized faithlessness (betrayal, treachery, apostasy, and infidelity [*izmena*]). He put into Larionov's mouth a revolutionary rejection of all notions of legitimacy and fidelity in "Face Painting (A Conversation on Gaurishankar)," a talk at the Stray Dog on April 9, 1914: " . . . apostates are our ideal fathers, prostitutes our ideal mothers."[76] But changeability is also susceptibility to transfiguration, metamorphosis, and alchemy. What Apuleius's *Metamorphoses, or The Golden Ass* was to the *drUnkeyness* cycle, Ovid's *Metamorphoses* is to *Rapture* with its transmutation of people into trees, as well as numerous borrowings from individual stories. The book ends not with Penelope and Odysseus's rooted bed (emblem, in Zdanevich's lecture, of a rejected heraldic motto: *semper immota fides*), but with, contrary to Marinetti's dream of rootless humanity, human beings rooted by their metamorphoses. Petr Kazarnovskii has identified "inversion" or "perversion" as the constructive principle of Iliazd's novel, harking back to Huysmans's *Against the Grain* with its relentless emphasis on artifice.[77] For me, however, every inversion in *Rapture* is liable to reversion, or perhaps revision, spiraling into previously unimagined forms. Changeability (and exchangeability) in the novel is thoroughgoing: every image is supremely ambivalent, every assertion morphs immediately into its opposite, the philosopher's stone turns not just iron, but shit to gold—and gold to shit.

And every theme passes into another. Follow an image and you find yourself wandering through often-contradictory spheres of reference. I could pick up the tree theme, or take up the history of early modern popular culture or, as Elizabeth Beaujour has suggested, the history of social banditry.[78] When we consider any of these spheres, we see how much "life" this novel gobbles up and digests, how much detail it wrests from descriptive sources outside the world of strictly literary reference and divests of reality. Iliazd constantly reminds us of *Rapture*'s artifice. We, like Laurence, turn up all kinds of jewels, but as the wenny old man suggests, every treasure brought to light is a red herring. The real treasure is nonobjective (it has no object, whether purpose or prototype) and lies in the novel's pointed silence, with the cretins' abject timelessness, the inside-out of the "mind's mind" Ivlita craves, untouched by natural or human history or by society, neither exchangeable nor communicable. The artist's vain attempts to grasp it produce an inevitably tainted art that only whets our thirst and points to what cannot be attained. The lost Dante found a renewed faith and the return of will and desire, moved, himself, by "the love that moves the sun and the other stars." Iliazd rediscovers in *Rapture* the engine of Freudian drives, the struggle of Eros and Thanatos, propelling the artist toward ceaseless transformation in a hopeless and often hidden quest to embody an elusive poetic ideal. In that sense, the novel is, as Gayraud claims, "a return to a species of Symbolism bearing the experience of the avant-garde."[79]

It should nevertheless be said that, while Zdanevich draws on a vast fund of Russian sources, for English readers Dostoevsky will loom large over the novel. I have already mentioned Iliazd's idiosyncratic appropriation of the "responsibility of all for all." He also displays a penchant for doubling characters. He gradually loads specific terms with complex semantic content as they pass from one context to another (Dostoevsky usually does this by letting the words pass through the mouths of different speakers, but Iliazd's is not a psychological novel and his characters do much less speaking). Finally, he includes significant references to *Crime and Punishment*, *The Idiot*, and *The Demons*. Here we have a rational murder committed impulsively and the subsequent struggle of the murderer to recognize the nature of his guilt. Ivlita, like Sonia reading the account of the raising of Lazarus from her Gospel of John to Raskolnikov, attempts to instruct Laurence by interpreting the prehistoric paintings and artifacts they find in their refuge from a punitive expedition. (This cave, by the way, recalls Christ's nativity *and* his tomb, not to mention Plato's cave.) We find in *Rapture* the same fairy-tale and folk themes Dostoevsky uses to depict the relationship between Nikolai Stavrogin and his wife, the crippled Marya Lebyadkina: Ivan Tsarevich, the falcon, and the red dragon. And Laurence resembles Stavrogin in his moments of moral lassitude and in his susceptibility to being used in others' schemes. Perhaps the most tightly realized relationship of any character to prototype in *Rapture* is the revolutionary party agent Basilisk's to Dostoevsky's verbally incontinent Pyotr Verkhovensky. Dostoevsky is also an inspiration for the narrating voices, the shifts into parodies of lyrical, ethnographic, picturesque, and bureaucratic prose, not to mention Brother Mocius's carnivalesque Dionysian and Orphic funeral, suddenly erupting scandals, and moments of outright satire.

I would speculate further that Iliazd's *Rapture*, this tissue of words, looms, in turn, over Nabokov's works as one of those "Viceroy" texts for Nabokov's own "fantastically rare" *Nymphalis danaus* Nab., the species in *Ada* that mimics "not the Monarch butterfly directly, but the Monarch *through* the Viceroy."[80] Kazarnovskii has pointed to a similarity between the novel's unresolved ending and Nabokov's treatment of Cincinnatus C. at the end of *Invitation to a Beheading*.[81] Ivlita, however, triggers an immediate, perhaps too easy, question about *Lolita*, Nabokov's great meditation on art and crime (his own "Crime and Pun") and the transmutation of life into art.[82] I've already mentioned my suspicion that the veil of punning obscenity Eric Naiman lifts from *Lolita* for us in *Nabokov, Perversely* could have derived from practices perfected by 41°. But I'm also struck by a late scene in *Rapture* in which Laurence feels an overwhelming sense of regret and deep loss as he listens to the cretins' songs wafting up from the valley below, like Humbert Humbert on a mountainside above Telluride, Colorado, reflecting on the distant sounds of children at play. Both novels end with all main characters dead—focused on a stillbirth at Christmas.

Finally, I'd like to qualify one of my earlier claims. Iliazd does not entirely reject the beyonsense tricks of the *drUnkeyness* dras. Jovanović has noticed a Khlebnikovian phonetic battle in *Rapture* between *l* and *r* or life and death, respectively.[83] English happily allows a neat consonant exchange of this "minimal pair," a possible Freudian slip of the tongue, to transform "ravish" into "lavish," which generates its own yo-yo movement between themes of unstinting generosity and prodigious waste—all the shades of prodigality.[84] In this novel, that minimal shift, keyed as it is to the unconscious, can often be far more consequential than characters' psychological motivations. The scatological and sexual themes that emerged in the dras also remain, most prominently in Mocius's association with masturbation ("erotic solipsism") and in the cretins' shit-choked stable (they produce two equally useless things: excrement and sublime song)—certainly enough to foreclose any possibility of publishing the novel with a reputable house in Russian Paris.

3.

This, then, is the peculiar book Iliazd hoped to publish in 1927. He sent the manuscript to his brother Kirill, who had gone back to the Soviet Union around the same time Iliazd came to Paris. Kirill had connections to *Red Virgin Soil*, the chief publishing venue for "fellow travelers," writers who were not members of the Communist Party, but were not averse to supporting the Soviet government. In December, based on the first three chapters, Kirill expected he could get the novel published first serially, and then as a separate edition. But conditions were rapidly changing in the Soviet Union. By February, Kirill informed Iliazd that "40 publishers are being shut down right now . . . and it will be harder to get into print, although your novel is very good and I think it will move forward."[85] *Red Virgin Soil* became a particular target of a militant "proletarian" writers' faction on the ascent, and its editor was arrested as a "Trotskyist." The new editors rejected *Rapture* in May 1928 and Kirill offered the manuscript to the Federation publishing house, where the editorial board declined it nearly unanimously. According to Gayraud, the board criticized, aside from a perceived " 'mystical state of the spirit,' an aesthetico-contemplative indifference to the characters, failure to indicate place and time, and a language that was 'very strange, even clumsy at times, as though illiterate.' "[86]

Iliazd attempted to craft a satisfactory, even tendentiously tailored reply to Bolshevik objections, interpreting "rapture" as "a feeling that anticipates and accompanies revolution," placing himself at Petrograd's Finland Station in March 1917 for Lenin's fateful return to Russia from Swiss exile, where Zdanevich witnessed the "unforgettable," "enraptured gazes of the sailors." He objected that the editors would not call Gorky a religious writer because some of his characters pray. He disputed the charge of indifference by drawing attention to the author's evident attitude toward despotic power and punitive raids, among other things. He defended the novel's supposed lack of a specified time and place by claiming to be "an internationalist, not a student of Leskov." Consequently, if the writing gave the impression of being " 'a translation from a foreign language,' so much the better. But as to 'illiteracy,' this, at any rate, is an exaggeration."[87] Iliazd's letter did not change the editors' minds.

That same year, Iliazd asked Parnakh to translate the novel into French. Parnakh was making a living writing for French-language art and music journals after returning to Paris from his sojourn in the Soviet Union. He apparently agreed, but there is no surviving evidence that he ever managed to translate any of *Rapture*.[88] Iliazd published the novel at his own expense in 1930, under the old 41° imprint, emblazoned with a curious illustration that may be a variant of Jarry's *gidouille*, the spiral that graces Ubu's belly. It looks at once like a mountain, a labyrinth, a variety of fossil ammonite, and a coiled pile of shit. He sent copies to his old associates in the Soviet Union and heard that many of them liked it. But there were no reviews in the Soviet press. Olga Leshkova, his former companion in Bloodless Murder, noted that the novel was better received in Leningrad, where she shared it with Evgeny Zamyatin and Korney Chukovsky, than in official Moscow.[89] Most of the 750 copies remained unsold after Russian bookstores in Paris refused to carry the book because of the obscenities it contained. Mirsky published his French review, where he commented on Iliazd's unfortunate isolation in the Russian émigré community and urged quick translation of the novel, believing that it might even have something to teach French writers. Only Iliazd's former disciple, Poplavsky, published a full-fledged notice in the Russian émigré press about this "most original work" that "taken altogether frames . . . something approaching the 'age-old questions' the revolution and its tumult have no power whatsoever to change."[90] Charchoune mentioned Iliazd's *Rapture* in his 1932 article on "Magical Realism" among young writers of the emigration. He noted that this noteworthy example of the new prose had already been forgotten because Iliazd was one of only two writers who were "neither ours nor yours."[91] Faced with a situation in which it had become nearly impossible not to choose sides, the other, Parnakh, had gone back to the USSR for good the previous year.

And then, after one more unsuccessful proposal in 1970 to translate the novel into French, it disappeared to be unearthed here in the United States, like one of the ammonites Iliazd collected.

Elizabeth Klosty Beaujour introduced a facsimile reprint of the 1930 printing for Berkeley Slavic Specialties in 1983, a few years before Régis Gayraud's 1987 French translation. Beaujour's reprint brought the novel to the attention of a new wave of Russian émigrés from the Soviet Union, while Gayraud's translation was the long-awaited first step toward making it accessible beyond its Russian audience. For a long time, Mayakovsky, who had been "canonized" by Stalin, remained the only visible, widely available poet of the avant-garde for Soviet readers, although a group of dedicated academics and writers tended other legacies, especially Khlebnikov's. Gorbachev's glasnost made it easier to publish their works, sometimes in large editions that were sold as soon as they appeared on the shelves, but Zdanevich's novel remained out of print. The fall of the Soviet government in 1991 finally removed barriers to content. Unfortunately, it also wiped away the well-funded Soviet publishing system. When Sergei Kudriavtsev's Gileia publishing house brought out a new Russian edition of *Rapture* in 1994 with a Russian introduction by Gayraud, it was again in a small edition funded in association with a Düsseldorf specialty house. The edition largely escaped the notice of Russian readers. Perhaps the novel's most visible boost came in October 1999, when the late Russian/Israeli critic Aleksandr Gol'dshtein included *Rapture* on his list of the "best of the best" twentieth-century Russian novels for the influential newspaper *Nezavisimaia gazeta*. Gol'dshtein praised the "incomparable" novel's "magical prose, like a wizard's spell, . . . rendered deep and flowing in a language that flushes our vision clean."[92] In 2008, Kudriavtsev's Gileia published the novel again in *Filosofiia Futurista* (*A Futurist's Philosophy*), a better-funded, larger collection of Iliazd's writings with commentary. This edition attracted more attention from Russian readers, especially among younger poets like Petr Kazarnovskii, who reviewed it for *Novoe literaturnoe obozrenie*, one of the leading journals of literary scholarship and criticism in Russia today.

It also incorporated a few emendations Iliazd made after *Rapture*'s 1930 publication. I have followed this edition in my translation, with minor exceptions.

I hope that the novel has not, as Gol'dshtein conjectures, "forever passed fame by." And I think Iliazd would appreciate encountering a small circle of new readers through this translation, an American English louse on the corpse's beard of his art. I have already mentioned more than once a phrase he liked to repeat: "A poet's best fate is to be forgotten." The line comes from an obscure seventeenth-century French poet, Adrien de Monluc, some of whose works Iliazd published in luxurious editions during his later career as a printer specializing in the livre d'artiste. For Iliazd, the phrase was another twist on John the Theologian's and Dostoevsky's "corn of wheat."[93] It meant to die and be resurrected, to be lost in the earth and dug up again by chance at some unforeseeable time and place after undergoing subterranean processes of fossilization and metamorphosis—to be recognized with passionate interest, lovingly polished, and presented once again to an audience the poet never imagined or intended.

4.

Iliazd did not disappear with his novel. He landed on his cat's feet and refashioned himself. By 1930, he had enough money to publish *Rapture* because he had been working successfully as a textile designer for Coco Chanel. His interest in fashion was nothing new. After all, he had praised the supreme artifice of Paul Poiret in his 1914 face-painting lecture on changeability and infidelity.[94] Sonia Delaunay recruited him to paint shawls in 1922 and he had gone back to working with textiles after being fired from the Soviet embassy in 1926.[95] In September 1926 he married Simone-Axele Brocard, one of Chanel's models, and went to work in 1927 for a textile factory that was acquired the next year by Chanel. On Serge Diaghilev's recommendation, she appointed him as head designer. He even invented and patented a new weaving machine that was adopted in all of Chanel's factories. In 1931, he became a factory director, but resigned two years later.

Iliazd took a break from writing novels, none of which, aside from *Rapture*, was published in his lifetime. He returned to his interest in church architecture. In 1933, he supplemented the drawings he had made of Byzantine, Georgian, and Armenian churches during his 1917 expedition and his 1921 layover in Istanbul with new drawings of Romanesque round churches he visited in Spain. This accumulation of material provided the basis for a series of presentations at Byzantinist congresses over the next four decades. In the 1960s, he was able to extend his comparisons through travel and study in Yugoslavia, Greece, and on Crete, as well. When his wife left him with two children in 1935, Iliazd planned to move to Spain permanently, but the outbreak of the Spanish Civil War intervened. He was rejected when he tried to enlist in an international brigade on the Republican side and never returned to Spain again after Franco's victory. For a time, homeless and unemployed, he survived thanks primarily to help from friends—Picasso foremost, but also Tzara.

In 1938, Iliazd took a step toward printing the first of his meticulously designed books with work by leading artists. This undertaking would seal his artistic legacy in Western Europe. He returned to writing poetry—now, as for most of his subsequent work, operating within the constraints of traditional sonnet form, in five-foot iambs, and constructing entire "crowns" of sonnets. The cycle "Afet" provided the text for his first livre d'artiste under the revived 41° imprint. Iliazd worked, as he would for the rest of his life, with l'Imprimerie Union, the same Russian-founded printing house where his Dada associate Sergei Romov had worked before moving to the USSR in 1928 and where Apollinaire's *Calligrammes* had been typeset. Picasso provided etchings, the first of many for Iliazd's editions. They collaborated right up to Picasso's death in 1973. From the start, Iliazd's careful planning of every aspect of his editions set them apart. Louis Barnier, a later director of l'Imprimerie Union, remarked, "When some publisher released a livre d'artiste with work by Picasso, Rouault, Bonnard, they were books by Picasso, Rouault, Bonnard, but when Iliazd published a livre d'artiste with work by Picasso, Giacometti, Miró, Ernst, they were books by Iliazd."[96] Through the 1960s, Iliazd funded his publishing by searching out rare books for an antiquarian shop, where he was paid a small commission.

During the occupation of France, Iliazd met and married a Nigerian princess, Ibi Ronke Akinsemoyin, who was studying at the Sorbonne and who gave birth to his third child. Akinsemoyin died in May 1945, seven months after the liberation of Paris, from the tuberculosis she contracted during her internment as a British subject. I have already mentioned Iliazd's postwar anthology, *The Poetry of Unknown Words*. The collection was not only directed against the Lettristes. It also included one of Akinsemoyin's poems and served as yet another memorial in print, further confirming what was evident already in *Rapture*—beyonsense had become, for Iliazd, a language of mourning. Many of Iliazd's late poetic cycles, in fact, are explicitly conceived as memorials for Republican soldiers of the Spanish Civil War and for French Resistance fighters of the Second World War. The extravagant splendor of *The Poetry of Unknown Words*, graced by the work of twenty-two artists, far exceeded the needs of Iliazd's polemic, and it has become a classic of the livre d'artiste genre.

Iliazd spent much of his time after the war with Picasso in the South of France, experimenting with ceramics alongside the artist. There he met the ceramicist Hélène Douard-Mairé, who became his constant companion and, in 1968, his third wife. From the early 1950s, Iliazd was able to pursue his publishing work on a continual basis. Iliazd's inventive "books" were not so much bound codices as specially designed cases containing carefully arranged leaves of different kinds of printed and unprinted paper. Marcel Duchamp was sufficiently impressed by Iliazd's attention to technical as well as visual design to engage him for a new edition of his *Boîte-en-valise*. During this period, Iliazd chose to print texts not just from his own and others' modern poetry, but also from material he excavated from library archives. He published obscure travelers' accounts of his native Georgia, baroque French poetry, and, in one of his most spectacular editions, *65 Maximiliana, or the Illegal Exercise of Astronomy* (1964, with Max Ernst), Romantic treatises on astronomy. His final book, Adrien de Monluc's *Le Courtesan Grotesque*, illustrated by Miró's etchings with aquatint, appeared at the end of 1974, a year before his death. Any of Iliazd's editions incorporating his archival finds might serve to illustrate how poets benefit by being "forgotten."

Iliazd's fame has always been fragmented among the many phases of his life and the many roles he has played. Book artists and collectors have long valued his Parisian publications, and historians of modern art are aware of his collaborations with Picasso, Giacometti, Ernst, and Miró. This body of work, tied to some of the most readily recognized names in modern art, has supported Iliazd's fame in Western Europe and the United States. The Centre Georges Pompidou presented an exhibition dedicated to his artists' books in 1978, followed in 1987 by another at New York's Museum of Modern Art. A 1976 exhibit at the Paris Museum of Modern Art focused on his collaborations with Picasso. Johanna Drucker, an accomplished printer in her own right and now a pioneering professor of digital humanities and media studies, emerged from this milieu. She proposed the first (unrealized) plan for a synthetic biography of Iliazd while working closely with his widow, Hélène Zdanevich.

Other audiences have concentrated on Iliazd's Futurist phase. Slavists in Western Europe and the United States, like Russian audiences, have long been familiar with Iliazd's Futurist work, but are generally unaware of his later career publishing artists' books.[97] After the collapse of the Soviet Union, he was given a major exhibition in Georgia. And his beyonsense books have also held a prominent place in exhibitions dealing with the Russian avant-garde in general. Only now, however, are all the aspects of Iliazd's life and work being brought together. A retrospective exhibition at the Pushkin State Museum of Fine Arts opened in December 2015. Although initiated by a new generation of Russian book collectors, it was dedicated to Iliazd's entire career. For many Russians, who know nothing of his life after his departure for Paris, the exhibit was a revelation.

Until now, Iliazd's prose from the 1920s and his more "traditional" poetry written from the late 1930s until the end of his life constitute the most neglected segment of his output. Beaujour published fragments of a 1928 novel titled *Posthumous Works* in 1987 and 1988, but none of Iliazd's unpublished novels were available in full before Kudriavtsev's Gileia published *Parisites: An Inventory* in 1995.[98] *Letters to Morgan Phillips Price* followed in 2005, and *Philosophia* anchored the 2008 collection of Iliazd's writings.[99] His late poems existed only in luxurious limited editions held by libraries' special collections and private collectors, out of reach for most readers. Their texts have now been collected into a single volume published in 2014 by Gileia, unavoidably stripped of Iliazd's elaborate visual settings.[100] Gayraud, along with André Markowicz, has been translating Iliazd into French since the 1980s and has now accumulated a substantial body of work. This long-overdue debut will be the first complete literary work by Iliazd available in English. And my introduction has been a rare attempt to hang on to this Proteus long enough to begin to see him whole, to herd these many cats' lives into one.

POSTLUDE

Just as the end of Russian Futurism around 1925 had triggered a flood of memoirs and retrospective work among its participants, the 1960s initiated a cascade of golden anniversaries and important birthdays for the international avant-garde more generally. Iliazd wrote a series of French memoirs, first in response to a meeting in 1962 with the Italian Futurist, Ardengo Soffici, who asked him to tell the story of Russian Futurism.[101] He extended this memoir in 1965 with "Approaching Éluard," an account of artistic life in Paris in the 1920s intended as a preface to a book of Éluard's poems, and then again in 1968 to mark the fiftieth anniversary of 41°. Meanwhile, his brother Kirill was given permission to visit France in November 1966, their first direct contact since 1921. His last book with Picasso was likewise retrospective. In *Pirosmanashvili 1914*, Iliazd reprinted his early article on Niko Pirosmani, the Georgian artist who had meant most to him at the beginning of his career. Its frontispiece is a drypoint portrait of Pirosmani by Picasso, the artist who meant most to him at the end, etched solely on the basis of Iliazd's anecdotes and reminiscences of the earlier painter. It was released in December 1972, just months before Picasso's death, a year prior to Iliazd's own eightieth birthday celebration. Drucker has written of this project,

> Drawing to the end of his energies, Iliazd had evidently wished this book to perform a double closure: as the end of the cycle of large books, and as the close of the full cycle of his life's work. There was a mirroring effect between the beginning and the end, a deliberate, marked recognition of the self-consciousness which had dictated the construction of the oeuvre as a whole.[102]

Iliazd took an everythingist approach to his own life, pulling together elements from all of its phases. The Caucasian outfit he wore on his

Paris strolls with his cats recalled a charming 1916 caricature by LeDantu of the "Fu-tourist" Zdanevich trekking through the mountains followed by a herd of goats.[103]

Now we are another fifty years on, in the midst of centenary celebrations. I have invoked Dante's vision as a model that Iliazd "perverts" in *Rapture*. I would like to end with a longer retrospective glance toward Augustine. *Rapture*, like Augustine's *Confessions*, narrates a series of errors and misplaced longings, and demonstrates the rhetorician's reformulation of himself and his art toward a new end. Iliazd, like Augustine, contemplates eternity, the arbitrary relation of signs to meaning, and the dream of direct communication in eloquent silence. *Confessions* is also, in part, the story of Augustine's shame before the "violent," less complicated, less educated, monks who "bear away" the Kingdom while he hesitates, slave to other forms of "rapture." But whereas Augustine famously addressed God at the beginning of his book, saying, "Our hearts are restless until they rest in you," Iliazd embraced the restlessness and allowed his semiautobiographical hero in *Philosophia* to identify, with characteristic ambiguity, "a secret in motion."[104] The artist needs to keep moving and changing, but the goal of art is also elusive and unstable. Augustine looked forward to a final transfiguration in resurrection, while Iliazd welcomed ceaseless metamorphoses, the cat's nine lives, continual rebirth here on earth, even after death. The cat buries the waste product of its digestion. Shit turns to gold.

As though to bring everything full circle, Lili Brik, Mayakovsky's great love, came to Paris for the opening of an exhibit on the poet. Playing the novel's "herald of snows," she paid Iliazd a visit a month before his own death in 1975, on Christmas, like the heroes of *Rapture*. Hélène found him in the kitchen, still standing up like a tree.[105]

I would like to thank Dick Davis, translator from Persian, for allowing me to entertain this project many years ago in his class on literary translation at The Ohio State University. I am indebted to the circle of translators who meet once a month with Bobbi Harshav, and to Ross Ufberg, who introduced me to them, for giving me the impetus to complete it. Katia Mitova graciously took time to read and comment on the first chapters. I am also grateful to the editor of Columbia University Press's Russian Library series, Christine Dunbar, for her enthusiasm and support. Finally, I echo Iliazd's dedication in thanks, above all, to my wife, Valentina Izmirlieva, and daughter, Hannah.

RAPTURE

To my wife and daughter

The snowfall was rapidly rising, revoking the bluebells, then the gravel, and in no time Brother Mocius was striding over whiteness instead of moss and blossoms. It wasn't cold at first, and the refreshing snowflakes crept down, sticking to his cheeks and sinking into his beard. Through the turbulent air, the valley slopes, studded with crags, had begun to dress up in lace and soon disappeared altogether; and then their outlines trembled, shifted, whirled, and whipped Brother Mocius across the face, freezing and fretting his eyes. The path, hidden from view, slipped frequently out from under his bare feet, and the traveler now and then wound up stumbling into the chinks between drifts. Sometimes his foot got stuck, and Brother Mocius tumbled and floundered, rattling his penitential chains, then got up again with some effort after eating his fill of an icy treat

Finally, trumpets sounded. The winds broke free of the surrounding ridges and, diving into the valley, beat about fiercely, but you couldn't tell why. On the right, unclean spirits made the most of the disarray by sending up an infernal roar, and from behind, something like violins or the whine of an infant in pain barely bled through the tempest. Voices added to voices, unlike anything recognizable, more often than not. Occasionally, they tried to pass for human, but ineptly—so all this was obviously a contrivance. Someone started romping on the heights, pushing down snow

But Brother Mocius was not afraid and never thought of turning back. Crossing himself from time to time, spitting, wiping his face with his cuff, the monk followed his habitual, easy path along the valley floor. True, of all the rambles he'd had to take through this pass, and, yes, even through the neighboring, less accessible passes, today's was by far the most unpleasant. Not once had the pilgrim observed such ferocity, especially at this time of year. In August, such fuss. As though this journey were prompted by nothing in particular. No need for the mountains to get so worked up. But if fate saw him through and they didn't cast an avalanche down just now, he'd be out of danger in an hour or two

The valleys the trekker was making his way through, up to his knees in snow at every step, ended in a steep grade just before the pass to the range's southern slope. Brother Mocius reached this grade about three hours after the blizzard started. He could climb up only on all fours. His arms sank deeper than his legs. The snow yielded so readily that when his staff slipped from his hand, it was buried without a trace; at times, everything gave way under the monk, and he hid his head, trying to stop the slide. Brother Mocius could no longer see what was happening around him. But he could feel: he wasn't up to it. He became lighter, brighter; he rose, levitated. He didn't hear the ravines rumbling, paid no heed to their foolery. Thirst alone coursed through his body and became more intense the longer he gnawed on ice, until the snow first turned pink, then was covered in blood. Finally, the grade became less steep, and still less: here was a place so level you couldn't take even a step without fatal fatigue. Brother Mocius broke open his iced-up eyelashes, froze, and collapsed onto his back

Above him, the storm kept raging. Monstrous shades moved around him or trod upon him, breaking him. It was hard to look, but he had to keep an eye on gargantuan coiling death, to monitor his own extremities, horrifying, now that they'd been touched by it: the way his fingers, tying themselves in knots, swelled, turned wooden, were overgrown with lichens and pinecones, split—and life (transparent, not crimson) dripped from the cracks. But things are light and easy again, not painful, not stifling. This brushwood still somehow sweeps snowflakes from eyelids; you can cross yourself and observe the eerie magic. It's growing warmer because of the snow; and at just this moment the weary wanderer is permitted to fall asleep. After driving away all other sounds, the storm intones a prayer for his repose

Brother Mocius, dying, was on the verge of wanting to recall something, and maybe even someone, but there wasn't time, and, besides, the state of his soul allowed no thought for things past and unimportant. The blissfulness of this glacial slumber was, if you like, sinful, but still, sent from on high in the midst of this life as a reward and the forecourt of paradise. And the interred monk awaited the opening gates and the unearthly light that surely must pour forth. The wisdom inexhaustible and lavish charity of him who has sent this so ravishing death

But Brother Mocius slept and was not sleeping, and the order of events was such that his mind rose from the dead and got to work. A sequence of trivia, more and more numerous, compelled him to ascribe them meaning and then to refer them to the order of things below. The buried monk did not know why, but concluded that his soul had not yet parted ways with his body: death had not taken his soul. He remained waiting, and gradually the thought arose that waiting was tedious and he needed to hurry events along. It was already clear that death had laid hold of Brother Mocius—but it had also dropped him, either by accident or by command from on high, and now he had regained his freedom, otherwise known as earthly existence, since *there*, there is no personality, and that means no freedom, and you dissolve into absolute necessity

After checking to confirm that this was indeed the case, the traveler got back to moving. He tried using his hands, but didn't succeed at first; then his right hand found a way out and discovered the crust formed by the snow his body heat had melted. The crust turned out to be brittle, and with the help of his other hand, Brother Mocius set to breaking up the vault and digging his way through the thickness above—which was easier, since the snow was dry and airy, and, evidently, not much had piled up on top of him

Brother Mocius exerted himself, strained until he farted with a self-satisfied giggle. Suddenly the vault caved in; he could stand up without trouble, shake himself off, and look around. So it is

Brother Mocius climbed up to the head of the glacier that sat in the very saddle of the pass and flowed down both sides. A few clouds, puffs of fog, and a fringe on the cliffs recalled the morning blizzard. An unobstructed view in every direction! Admire your alpine environs! Continue on your way unhindered! But neither praise nor thanksgiving escaped from the monk—only an even filthier giggle, as though he were pleased at swindling someone. In his gaze, however, recently so resolute, radiant in the moment of death, there was a glint of fear, uncertainty, awareness of his own impurity. Had death turned squeamish when it saw whom it was dealing with? And the monk hurried along the ice to the highest point of the pass, just a little way off

To the left, not more than a few steps from the place where Brother Mocius had just been lying, the glacier calved and plummeted into a small tarn that filled the cauldron beneath the pass. Although ice and slush were floating on the preposterously lilac water, a rabble of alpine butterflies was bathing very peacefully, taking flight over the surface or plunging below. To top that, the water was so transparent, you could see the stones, and when the wings were promenading on the bottom, you could make out their teeny-tiny antennae

Summits, spiteful and disfigured, were staggered around the lake, but today they were neither shifting nor threatening. Brother Mocius felt no urge to inspect their suspicious crags, so he turned to face the valley he had just passed through, now lying on his right, surrounded by bulwarks rising up farther off on the main range, and therefore less dangerous. Particularly fine is that stake over there, hammered into heaven. They say some cutthroat clawed his way to the very top a thousand years ago, but couldn't get down. He's been crying out into the frosty air ever since, begging someone to rescue him. He must have been sitting on the opposite slope, since Brother Mocius couldn't spot the screamer this time, either

A herd of turs cut across the glacier on its way down. At first the animals loped along in a scatter, but the holy fool spooked the kids, and the hoofed beasts bolted from the steep, down from ledge to ledge, and then all at once to the very bottom, toward the barely visible herdsman's shelter where Brother Mocius had passed a storax-scented night with no presage of the morning's misadventures

As usual, there were just a few cracks in the glacier and no reason to be apprehensive: they were covered. Now the walls were narrowing, forming a passage. You couldn't relax here—quick as a wink, they'd come crashing down; and the monk stepped as soundlessly as possible, taking care not to say a word. Stones were leaping continually; this time, too, several streaked past and disappeared. A cluster of stalactites broke away, but without much noise. Here's a heap of ice with a signpost stuck in it. The pass!

How many times Brother Mocius had walked by this place during his long ascetic struggle, setting out yearly from his own monastery to visit the neighboring monks who lived south of the mountain chain. And no matter how much the years sharpened his sense for spiritual things and made him indifferent to earthly grandeur, even now the monk could not contemplate without rapture, and a touch of curiosity, the wonderful canyon, grandest of all, now opening up before him, which he must cross, trudging on about twelve more hours before reaching the first huts

Since the ice field on the southern slope was much scantier, the wayfarer put the modest ravine, filled with ice and snow, behind him in less than half an hour and emerged onto a stony meadow. Now he could laze a bit, remove his chains, bash the bishop, chew his nails, and venerate his flask. His cassock was filthy (where had the mud come from?) and tattered, his elbows bloodied, his feet hopelessly frostbitten; his eyes were burning and his mouth was full of abomination. He'd not only lost his staff, his faithful companion, but also his cap. How had the brandy been spared? Someone popped up from behind a rock, cackled, and launched a stone at the holy fool

But imps are no longer menacing in these parts and, after sprinkling earth on your wounds, you're at liberty to stretch out in peace and contemplate the wonders—not for long, it's true, since the sun has also made its way over the pass. Look at that first-class glacier, sky blue from the worms seething in it. Like to get some: the prior complains of constipation and says there's no better remedy than the heads of those worms, but he has only a few left in his jar. And here's the cave where the satyr dwells. Saw him last time from a distance, gnawing the rifle of some unfortunate hunter. Good thing the stream is already swollen: if you could clear it, might have to suffer all kinds of things

And Brother Mocius relished the spectacle of icy masses, twisted like rams' horns and rearing into the sky; and the numerous flocks of winged creatures, soaring way up high, level with the sun; and the springs spurting out with a hiss from under the cliffs and spouting upward. Clouds (concealing beasts reluctant to display their ugliness) sprawled on the overhangs to bask in the sunshine. The highest peaks, where no one ever has, or ever will, set foot—never mind those tall tales about Englishmen—were generally situated far from one another, so that, in general, you had to travel for weeks to get from the foot of one to the foot of another; here, they all huddled together, so close it wouldn't take five hours to reach the farthest and most majestic. Innumerable pieces of ice broke away from the heights and hung in the air, pretending to be diamonds and supported by an unknown power (nothing special among these lavish miracles), and inexplicable singing burst out of the crevasses. Brother Mocius stood up and began to howl

Instantly, who knows from where, angels small in stature, followed by swifts, flitted out and started tracing patterns above Brother Mocius while chiming in. Eagles, their white beards loosed to the wind, stooped, screeching. Swarms of fierce bees streaked by, obedient and humming; diverse butterflies swished, vipers crawled from their dens, whistling, and hyenas leapt out, sobbing and weeping. Howl, peep, roar, flutter. Everything was keening. Even the humble gentian and saxifrage, customarily dumb, as is meet for plants, contributed a barely audible squeak, not to mention the slender lizards, darting in with their hatchlings

The monk's voice rose. Drowning out hundreds of others, Brother Mocius howled, and at such volume that he did not, himself, know whether the howl was his own or belonged to the fountain in the canyon's lower reaches, far away, it would seem, for the moment. Accompanied by the winged creatures, the singer followed a barely discernible path, forsaking the ice for pastureland. Here, goats and chamois ambled under the watch of spirits with dense feathers and rudimentary feet; the animals fought (not maliciously, but in jest), locked horns, and took a long time separating. Sinless, they would stare at the sun for hours without squinting

The streams ran together and cut a deep channel. The path descended, hugging the edge of the ravine. The snows receded ever higher. The singers retreated behind the clouds. The grasses became more substantial, some like umbrellas as tall as a man. Dwarf pines. Now the canyon that had seemed beyond compass narrows, turns, and vanishes in the forest. Only halfway, and the sun was already cooling off, communicating a foul luster to the glaciers that had drawn back into the distance. And with a sigh, the monk gazed at the country he'd left behind

Not counting the bear family taking its postprandial ease in the neighboring clearing, Brother Mocius was once more completely alone. He noticed this suddenly and promptly turned anxious. In vain he scanned the summits, trying to catch sight of his recent companions. A wasteland. And the mountains gloomier, more silver, more mundane. Where had everything hidden away? Before, the angels small in stature would accompany Brother Mocius to the very waters, until he plunged into the forest. And what about the beasts who showed the way and cleared his path? Why had they all abandoned him and—more to the point—abandoned him covertly? He lifted up his eyes. It's unnaturally clear and pure

And just then Brother Mocius recalled how death had spurned him in the pass, and it seemed that his hands were changing again. It seemed? No. So it is: they twist, overgrown with bark, turn wooden. And suddenly stones were flying from the slope; shades appeared in the bushes, sneezing, spitting, coughing. The air filled with bats, ready to latch on. The heavenly orb had just set, but night had already fallen. Fireflies, or something worse (God knows what) winked. At first, the pilgrim decided to stand still, but when something scratched him and then pegged him with a stone, he took off running, tangled in his cassock. Further down, he was less frightened, the smell of pitch made it easier to breathe, and his hands seemed to revive. If you don't stray from the path, you might not be saved—but keep walking

The moon caught fire and dressed the forest in motley. Nothing was audible except the fountain nearby, and you couldn't have heard anything anyway. Needles gave way to leaves, pitch to the odor of humus. Brother Mocius tried chanting the evening prayer;

his voice returned. Suffering fatigue, thinking about impending sleep, tormented by hunger, the wayfarer marshaled his strength, hurried on without stopping. Another two hours and he would reach the vineyards

And again, Brother Mocius felt guileless and lighthearted, like he had when he'd awakened beneath the snow and begun to break free. The day he'd lived through receded beyond the pass. Fear of death—that is, fear in the face of new, otherworldly obligations you're not sure you'll be able to meet—disappeared, as did the sinful weariness, more deeply rooted in him than this fear. Now the monk thought how good it would be to meet some hunters and get some cornbread, how his brandy had run dry, how, in a week, he would make it to the sea, and how his return crossing would, most likely, be less troublesome. Cutting across a brightly lit glade, Brother Mocius frightened some deer, but didn't even glance in their direction when he heard them breaking through the forest. The jarring cry of some raptor, not far away, touched him just as little

As he was nearing the place where all the water that runs down from the glaciers and swells the raging river gushes into the sky to come crashing down a little way off, lamenting, and then slips away to the sea, Brother Mocius realized that the play of moonlight on the spray hanging over the area really had grown old, and he was about to begin descending along the winding path, when the brush parted and a stranger emerged, tall, but dressed like a highlander. Brother Mocius was not gladdened, only surprised, and cried out to the stranger coming toward him. But his words, evidently, did not carry beyond the fountain. Then Brother Mocius drew nearer and hiccuped in sudden fright

Instead of greeting the monk, the stranger clutched and lifted him up like a sacrifice over the abyss

T he hamlet with the incredibly long and difficult name, so difficult even its inhabitants couldn't pronounce it, was situated right next to the glaciers and forests and renowned for being populated exclusively by cretins and people with goiters—an undeserved reputation explained by its extreme inaccessibility. It really was inconceivable to climb up through the canyon along the stream. You had to go north, ascend against the current of the main river, and then, taking to the east, surmount a forested ridge accessible in good weather not just to people on foot, but to horses, and finally descend to a modest glade, where you would have counted, all told, about twenty chimneys. But since good weather was rare in this place noted for abundant precipitation, the inhabitants had to lug building materials, manufactured goods, and salt up on their own backs

In fact, there was only one entirely goitrous, or wenny, household, with a few more cases peppered among the other families: a share no greater than in neighboring villages. The cretins, also just one family, occupied a hastily constructed stable. They normally crept out in the evening, heedless of bad weather, and, seated on a log structure that had once served as a trough, broke into abstruse songs composed just like the hamlet's name. At some distance rose the house, made entirely out of mahogany and distinguished by lavish carvings, that belonged to the former forester, although no one could conclusively confirm that this man had ever been deemed competent to hold such an office

The entirely wenny family consisted of an aged wenny, his wenny old lady, and fourteen wenny children, ranging in age from four to sixty. The old man was approaching eighty and had irrevocably lost his mind, without, however, losing his ability to sleep with his wife, shoulder loads of firewood, and be the wisest shepherd in the neighborhood. He knew the mountains and their scant pastureland so well that whenever the goats consumed all the fodder underfoot, the old man was the one the shepherds turned to for advice on where to find grass, and the wenny would unfailingly locate, in the most unexpected place, a completely uncharted dale or outcropping where they could find sustenance until winter. In his contempt for the canine race, the wenny did the howling and barking himself, and at night, whenever he was scaring off a bear, even the glaciers would cringe at his piercing, plaintive howling, bitterer than a brute beast's. Several neighbors maintained that the wenny had long been dead and that a satyr was living in his hide

The wenny wife was a very ordinary old lady, well-preserved and beautiful, despite her monstrous goiter and hunchback; they sharply distinguished their children by class: toiling and spoiled. Their progeny thirty and older belonged to the first class: six sons and a daughter, likewise very ordinary. The grown sons had been deprived of all liberty and lived in accord with the will of their father, who had invented a unique occupation for each. The oldest supervised the bridges that served the hamlet and the road to the pastureland. There were four bridges, one made of planks, while of the other three, further upstream, the first was a log thrown from one bank to the other, and each of the two following bridges was a pair of towering firs felled so their tops dipped into the water. Here, in crossing, you had to crawl along one tree until you were level with the stream and then leap skillfully onto the other tree that dropped down from the opposite bank

The second son's trade was whittling quarterstaffs for the great hunt. The old wenny was chairman for life, and that's why he presented this kind of weapon to everyone who participated. The other sons' occupations followed along the same lines. As for the daughter, an exceptionally old maid, she never left the kitchen and, strumming a guitar of her own design, sang songs borrowed from the cretins, mixing them up and misquoting them every time

The spoiled class of children, thirty and younger, sons and daughters, was not even suited for the work mentioned above, since all were epileptics. They were not allowed to leave the confines of the hamlet and either shuffled all day about the squalid yard or hung around the former forester's place and carved even more novel wooden ornaments for his magical house

When the wenny was neither absent on business nor in the pastures, he invariably grabbed his rifle as the evening approached and headed off alone to the neighboring mountain. His progeny sat quietly in the yard, listening intently. In an hour, a shot would ring out, the children would cry in chorus, "Got it!" (the wenny never missed) and in another hour, the old man would return with a roe deer they roasted whole and consumed on the spot, their cheering backed by the guitar

The former forester's habits in no way resembled the wennies' way of life. Likewise wenny, but with a modest goiter that could pass for his Adam's apple, the prematurely widowed former forester had moved there from town many years back, and, after buying land, spent a large sum constructing a whimsical, spacious house that would have served to embellish even a hamlet not quite so absurd as this one. There he lived, never going out, with his only daughter

The former forester got married late in life, when he was already bald and paunchy (he'd been an Adonis in his youth), to a girl about

twenty-five years younger, if not more. He wanted to have a son—
not for reasons that direct men's minds in such cases, not out of pro-
priety, but for rather extraordinary reasons he explicated at length
to the future mother and to everyone within earshot. "I'm too much
past my prime for a daughter," he would repeat. "Just think, in about
sixteen years, when my daughter starts blooming, who will I be? A
decrepit old man who doesn't excite any rapt admiration! Will she
really grasp how handsome I had once been? And the slight age difference between her and her mother will make them rivals, since
her mother, as she fades, will envy and obstruct her daughter's success. I need a son: what will my mug and my goiter matter to him?
He'll respect me *and* find his mother still beautiful"

But events refused to comply with the forester's wish, and a daughter was born. And the next year, when his wife died before delivering
the son she was carrying and the cesarean section failed, the old man
shaved his head (another caprice), sold all his goods, decided to take
to the back of beyond, anyplace he could scare up, and made no mistake in selecting the hamlet with the unpronounceable name

The change of scenery saved him from the physical and spiritual transformations that are inevitable in such cases. So, at least,
he thought. The former forester remained just as devoted to chess
and the collection of books he purchased only when he found
them completely incomprehensible or impenetrable because they
were printed in foreign languages. And since there was no one in
the hamlet he could play chess with, and he never had occasion,
over the course of many long years, to teach any of his neighbors,
the former forester played against himself for hours or composed
problems, pretending he didn't know their solutions beforehand.
He even asked one of the spoiled wennies to carve some special
chess pieces and assigned them wild names, nothing like the usual
ones—names that corresponded to the mountain and forest powers he possessed knowledge of

The former forester was neither a believer nor an unbeliever and thought there were neither angels (evil or good) nor miracles; everything is natural and normal, but there are, so to speak, unusual immaterial objects we know nothing about since, for now, generally speaking, we don't know *anything*, but will come to know, if we diligently study nature, the way he had in his youth and still did now, as a widower. In his account, the immaterial objects contained in all things constituted their souls and could, under special conditions, influence the world. They brought a man blessing or bane and bad weather, as was appropriate; and in order to bring about one and not the other, one had to know. For his part, the former forester knew enough not to fear misfortune, although, remarkably, the chief sorrow of his life, the deaths of his wife and son, never came to mind. He imagined himself secure against the forest, against the mountains, against his neighbors, and this was more than enough to justify calmly dedicating himself to leafing through books or shifting chess pieces from square to square

Busy with his chess, his speculations, and his books, the former forester overlooked his daughter growing and maturing beside him. Until she was about ten, it seems, she was under the watch of a nurse whom the father didn't notice, as though she were invisible. He never set foot in his daughter's room, never wondered what his child was up to. Then one day, to his surprise, he discovered that the nurse no longer put in an appearance (he *had* seen her, after all), but a moment later he forgot about her for good. Then the day arrived when his daughter—who had for some time been regularly setting the table, serving each course, and withdrawing—set a place for herself instead of leaving, sat down opposite her father, and ate dinner with him. During the meal, the former forester imagined that today he was seeing his wife anew, although somewhat changed, and he wasn't sure what to ascribe this change to. Several weeks later, he concluded that this *was* his wife, only dead, and began to study her new state. Observing was easy because his daughter didn't conceal herself, but spent her days in the same room with him or on the balcony. Only when, one day, the former forester caught her reading books (she was really reading, not leafing through them), the old man's heart was roused. He grasped that right beside him, imperceptibly, someone who might be stronger than he was had settled in and, living harmoniously with him until the appointed time, would, sooner or later, challenge him. And although he couldn't treat the dead woman inhospitably when she gazed, walked, and laughed the way she did, although he couldn't escape her by locking himself up, and didn't want to anyway, she was, all the same, his enemy, and the immaterial object deep in the old man watched and waited to see what would happen. And since, from that moment on, anyplace else was more serene than home, the former forester gave up his fifteen-year confinement and, after rummaging through the storeroom for his rifle and borrowing some cartridges from his neighbors, surprised the hamlet by heading out to hunt black grouse

But the old man didn't notice the most important difference between the live woman and the dead one. Among other things, even in this land where all women were beautiful, Ivlita was an altogether exceptional phenomenon. And not just because her body was ideal—while not, like all perfect things, dead—but also because it roused such vigorous sensations and attuned the observer to such rare harmony. Her movements were intrinsic to fleshly perfection; her eyes and voice signaled that more than her body was divine. And, to be precise, the young woman hadn't grown up, hadn't suffered the ponderousness of earthly existence and the tedium of growth, but had emerged all of a sudden from the mist when she appeared once upon a time beyond her father's yard, unanticipated, her existence unsuspected by any of the hamlet's inhabitants

But while her father knew nothing of his daughter's qualities, the highlanders received the young woman into their everyday lives.

Whenever anyone had to go out into the neighboring country, each of them, ducking into a tavern or a friend's place, would blurt out, "We've had a supernatural event," but would immediately fall silent, fearful that others, once they found out, would profane this treasure, and their listeners never managed to catch what exactly the event was and decided: Likely some satyr's or water sprite's new mischief, or some such nonsense. Why did Ivlita go on living beyond reachless mountains, unbeknownst to the world and in the company of subhumans? Even the old wenny voiced this concern, with some qualification: We don't know whether she's a good or evil incarnation; later on, it goes without saying, we'll see; in the meantime, there's no use worrying about it. But no matter how much the old man tried to calm their fears, it was clear that something was evil, since why else would all the villagers do nothing but watch for Ivlita fetching water or calling the goats, and, when they were traveling, pine not so much for their native hamlet as for the young woman's presence there

So, on account of her useless qualities, because of the mountains, and thanks to the back of beyond, Ivlita's lot was becoming more complicated and confused, although thus far she herself suspected nothing. And for that reason, the girl's existence remained just as dull and even as ever, nothing more than a reflection of the seasons

The onset of snow was presaged first by a cobalt sky that exchanged its dark blue hue at night for the same dark blue, only thicker, and after a few days, by winds that blew their gray currents even into this secluded dale and brought the odor of a vile sea. In the mornings, the fog lay too long, smothering the hamlet, dispersed slowly, and the shoots it bedewed shrank back: the dew was bitter and brackish. The lavishness of falling stars constantly lighting up the heavens made sleeping difficult, and the roosters' crowing was particularly throaty. There were no green leaves, only gold, but more often rose and purple; the needles turned gray until they poured from the surrounding cliffs. Fish were jumping very frequently up out of the river; you couldn't leave the hamlet without running smack into a bears' wedding. The forest, anticipating snow, was gripped with fever, and moans and groans burst from the thickets. The population grew: after stamping out the campfires that had been burning in the pastures since spring and collecting every last one of their goats, the sleepy shepherds returned, muttering something under their breath, and locked themselves away. There was no rain. There might have been some drizzle, but it was so fine, like steam, and no one could tell where it was falling from. But one morning, when she awoke, Ivlita noticed right away how especially bright her room was and guessed that beyond her door lay nothing but snow, dry and crumbly. How many new tasks and troubles she faced: getting out the skis, the special clothing, and clearing the roof. But her animation soon drained away, replaced by a stupor, a dormancy full of visions, a daily life rich in emotional turmoil and short on events. A few passages shoveled out from the snow that had now reached the roof, leading to the outbuildings and the unfrozen spring—these were all the space for taking a walk: the skis were for others; others went into the forest, set traps; Ivlita stayed home. The rumble in the woods from the avalanches that had never rolled all the way to the forest-protected hamlet was her sole worry at the moment. And if the snow had gone on for years, she would have felt neither more joyful nor more melancholy

And then, one day, the sky turned from white to azure; no new snow came, the old was melting. First it receded from walls, making way for snowdrops. Their armies, ever increasing in number, efficiently crowded it out until, at last, only a few patches remained here and there in the shade and on the northern sides of buildings. True, the snow was about to counterattack, but it ran out of breath. New needles and buds. Apple trees blossoming. Every creek, so pitiful toward the close of the year, now a whole river, muddy, raging—waterfalls resounding everywhere. The shepherds creep out from their hovels and head off on business to their neighbors and the city. Cattle and swine take possession of the clearing. At home, water is heating up and you can clean away the accumulated grime. Women's bellies swell. Now there's singing in the woods, woodpeckers, lilac, panpipes, circle dances, the first festivals—but not for Ivlita. Rains. There's never any summer. Spring drags on overlong, longer than the winter and more restive. More super-fluous variety. And by the time spring with its incessant rains and overly fickle mists becomes tedious to the point of revulsion and women stop giving birth, the herald of snows appears, autumn is coming—for about two weeks, not more, judging by how long the heart's ease endures. And so it was now, August was ending and, for Ivlita, autumn was blushing in the yard

And yet, no matter how simple this sensitive life and how alien Ivlita was to desires, she was short on rapture. Her cultivated and complex mind's mind, endowed with inward contemplation at the expense of outward, was conscious of being its own enemy. The wenny children who made up her company saw in life's phenom-ena, in nature's minutiae, the presence of powers *she* knew did not really exist. Therefore, the annual round was empty and water could not quench her thirst. Beliefs and rituals—she fled them to keep the emptiness from expanding even more. Ivlita didn't even won-der what people did beyond the passes. And that autumn, after lan-guishing to her heart's content during the course of the year, Ivlita was thinking of snow as though it were death

03

The river carried Brother Mocius a long way. He came to rest just above its confluence with the wennies' creek, wedged among the logs that float singly up to that point, where they're caught, lashed together into rafts, and sent in that trim to the sea. The lumberjacks discovered the corpse

The general astonishment knew no bounds. No doubt, the holy fool had fallen victim to a violent crime; no one could entertain the thought of him slipping or being cast down by a reckless stone or block of ice. They knew Brother Mocius too well, were aware that every year, several times, and in the worst weather, even in winter, he crossed the ranges; they believed in his holiness and recounted many stories about his miracles. The mountains could never hurt him

But in that case, who would have dared? The area between the settlement where they found his corpse and the passes to the north was uninhabited, and you wouldn't run into anyone but woodcutters and shepherds along the river. But even they didn't hike up to the alpine zones, while the body must have fallen from a fearsome height to be so curled. Who would climb up under the clouds for the love of crime?

In the taverns (there were two) and at the sawmill, conversations on the topic went on with unflagging abandon, inciting a series of bloody brawls; knives as well as fists came into play. There was no dispute as to whether the holy fool had perished violently or naturally—not a single voice was raised to defend the latter possibility; they argued only about which community the murderer could belong to, and on this point the gathered assembly began settling accounts

The monk's body, in a mahogany coffin (the coffin was tiny, just like a child's), was carried to the church and displayed for public viewing. This church made a strange impression. Constructed in times long past, when the province had been flourishing, a remarkable example of a remarkable architecture, the church was severely dilapidated now and, left to its fate, on the point of collapse. The coping had given way and had not even been replaced by a tile roof; the frescoes had fallen; there were trees in the windows. One cupola remained intact, blackened at the top by thousands of sheltering bats, and their guano, covering the flagstones in a thick layer, filled the church with an intolerable stench. Since the settlement had no clergy, there were no regular services; once a year, the cassocks gathered for the church's feast day and vainly attempted to drown out the chiropters' raving with their prayers

In such splendor, Brother Mocius's coffin fairly shone. On the first day, only locals came to view the wizened body, undamaged by the water; on the next—their neighbors came, too, and not only to gaze on the body, but also to venerate it; on the third—to tear a small piece from his cassock or pluck a whisker from his beard. And since only about a week remained before the church feast and the fair linked to it, they left the relics lying there until the day when someone would be present to perform a funeral service over them. And as the day approached, the corpse acquired a complexion that made it easy to prove, even to a complete outsider, that Brother Mocius had died violently

Folks started gathering on the eve of the holiday. Another settlement of variously sized and colored tents grew up around the hill where the church rose. The tents were laid out in streets and alleys, with the rich accommodated right around the hill itself, and the outskirts occupied by those who had carts, but no tents, and, last of all, those who had neither one nor the other. Merrymaking included music, dancing, wrestling, and prodigious drunkenness. In the course of two days, every reveler—that is, pilgrim—would consume untold measures of apple and millet brandy. But neither measures of wine nor the profusion of flutes and wrestlers would determine the degree of merriment, but rather the kinds of office the visiting clergy would have to perform on the day of the feast. If only baptisms or a wedding followed the prescribed prayer service, the holiday might be considered a flop. Only death could provoke genuine merriment. Only its presence could compel all assembled to sing, drink, kiss, and dance tirelessly. At weddings, they drank from slop basins; at funerals, they drew drafts from buckets. The musicians would attain such raving that they couldn't calm down; the dancers, once they had entered the circle, would refuse to cede their places to others; the bonfires would turn into blazes, and the orgy would drag on well beyond any proposed limit. While the people were dispersing, it would turn out that the modest cemetery not far from the church had been treated as a dump; no one, however, cleaned it up, and only the snow would veil this disgrace

But the graveyard deserved to be treated differently. Its headstones, decorated with superb illustrations, the work of the local stonecutter Luke, did more than preserve portraits of the deceased—they even narrated their lives. You didn't need to know how to read (a difficult and altogether bad business) in order to learn the deceased's occupation: whether he was a farmer or a tradesman, and in what line; whether he had children and a house;

how he died and how old he was; what dishes he preferred and what he distilled his brandy from; how much moveable property and real estate he had left behind; if the widow or widower renewed the marriage bond before the stone was set in place, this was unfailingly mentioned, and in a way most unflattering to the living. Sometimes the sculptor who had enshrined the deceased's memory would even show up at the grave many years later to append some new pertinent fact. The plot sequence, in its basic outlines, was strictly obligatory, and Luke, faced with the task of preparing the stone for Brother Mocius's future grave, ranted and raved more than anyone for a murder investigation, since, for now, he lacked the main story line for his series of illustrations

In despair, the master craftsman proposed that his interlocutors—the village headman, the scribe, and the others seated together in one of the taverns—refuse to bury the holy fool there, since they didn't know the facts, and send him north to find repose within his monastery's walls. But Brother Mocius's funeral was too great an enticement for drunkards; second, they could expect, without a doubt, miracles at the monk's grave; third, while he was carving the stone, the murderer would certainly be found; fourth—and so on—in a word, so many objections were advanced against Luke's idiotic proposal that everyone present cold-bloodedly bashed his face in and sent him home to sleep it off

The first consideration was legitimate. The funeral of the monk, who was celebrated throughout the region, proved to be especially tasty bait, and the congregation surpassed the most lavish expectations. The attendees unfurled their camp all the way to the river, and the fine weather permitted them not to hide out under carpets and carts. There were so many trumpeters with trained bears that the fair resembled a menagerie. The bagpipes' moan and the din of drums were accompanied by howling children who could neither sleep nor keep still. At night, when everyone started leaping over fires, gunshots went off more enthusiastically than in battle. But there were always many more wineskins than people, and on the morning of the feast, all who weren't vomiting their guts out were, in any case, three sheets to the wind

Brother Mocius's funeral was performed not by parish priests, but by monks who turned up from his own monastery, as well as from the monastery he'd been traveling to. The monks didn't share lay opinion as to the ascetic's violent death, since the expression in the dead man's eyes bore witness that he had seen death, while people who die violently supposedly don't see it; but since the monks weren't convinced even of this (to Luke's distress), they decided, in order to avoid any ambiguity, to accept the locals' petition and bury the holy fool in the cemetery there. No one showed up for the funeral. But when the brothers carried the coffin from the church, they had to expend much time and extraordinary effort fighting their way through the crowd and scrambling over snorers' torsos. At the cemetery, the believers pried the corpse from its coffin, filled the coffin with brandy, and, down on all fours, slurped it straight from the coffin. No one tried to prevent this, since it might have led to a lynching, and the monk's body, completely mauled by his votaries, was tossed into the hole and covered with earth. And two days later, when Luke the stonecutter had recovered enough to head over to the cemetery and take the measurements he needed, he found the coffin on top of the grave, and in the coffin—a fellow villager stifled in wine

Those who had proclaimed there would be miracles at the holy fool's grave also turned out to be right. It all started with an unseasonable laving downpour so heavy it washed all the filth away into the river, and the timber floats, backed up because of a labor shortage, were torn from the banks and spewed out into the sea. At the grave, a black tree suddenly burgeoned and blossomed fragrantly. And at night, anyone who dared could see: the silvery moon was shining over the tree. And in a couple more days, a thorny hedge had enclosed the grave, and before the first snow, the grave was proof against glance and hoof. And since miracles, although they are indeed miracles, are rather ordinary phenomena in those parts, people would soon have forgotten all about Brother Mocius's grave, but for the fact that he had been killed

As long as the murderer had not been tracked down and disarmed, no one felt safe. But not because they were dealing with a murder. Murder itself was nonsense; who hadn't, one might ask, had occasion to murder, if not while drunk, then in combat, at any rate? Murder wasn't the problem; it was ill will, the degree of malice. And the degree must have been superlative, just to resolve on acting inimically against this fool renowned for his holiness, not to mention murdering him. And the peasants and workers could not tolerate such ill will in the neighborhood, all the more so for being hidden. And the patrons of the two taverns conducted their investigation so diligently that before long you could have considered the murderer's identity established

First of all, at the end of countless scuffles over the honor of this or that village, they determined that Brother Mocius's body had come to rest there, of all places, precisely to signal that the desecrater was present in that place. Once they'd derived this important fact, they had only to search within their own circle—making their task considerably easier. Their suspicions eventually landed on Laurence, a recent deserter, splendidly robust and daring. Laurence had just come back to the mill; he'd been hiding in the woods for a few days to mark a draft commission's arrival in the settlement, and during his absence, they'd fished out Brother Mocius's body. When he was deserting, Laurence had felt the need to justify himself before his comrades (he said he was going into hiding so as not to kill on command), which indicated, since manly flight requires no justification, that the young fellow had resolved to kill willfully, and the murder, consequently, was premeditated. To be accurate, Laurence was not the only deserter, and during the commission's visit, just as during all previous visits, no one of age for conscription could be found in the village; but it had never occurred to anyone besides Laurence to voice contempt for government-sanctioned murder, so the evidence against him was unimpeachable

When Laurence's words about murder reached Luke the stonecutter and the next meeting at the tavern agreed with Luke on every point (the engraver was rabid with joy—now nothing would delay preparing the gravestone), they didn't arrest Laurence or even inform him of the charges raised against him; rather, the investigators, after deciding to keep their discovery to themselves, started tailing Laurence in order to ascertain just how glutted with ill will this person was and to prevent further outbursts. From that time, every step, every action was under surveillance. Was Laurence working? Someone stood beside his supervisor pretending to be a casual visitor. Was he sleeping? The window opened and someone inspected the room. When the young man went into the woods or onto the glaciers to hunt, shadows kept running from trunk to trunk and from cliff to cliff behind his back. But since Laurence didn't do anything criminal over the course of a month, the stonecutter, the village elder, and the others came to believe that they'd bumped up against a villain not merely eminent, but also shrewd

The investigators now assumed that Laurence was only pretending not to notice the surveillance—and not to know about the charges that were hanging over him. Indeed, Laurence was supremely aware of everything and his blindness and deafness were feigned. And could he, sensitivity itself, fail to notice the constant, crude pursuit his fellow villagers had devoted themselves to? More than once, he had a mind to toss off some stunt, liven things up for his pursuers, or threaten them and demand that they leave him alone. But it seemed to Laurence that the best defense was dissimulation, and he maintained his normal lifestyle as though nothing were happening

They didn't like Laurence at the mill, despite his fun-loving manner, his strength and agility, the fact that everywhere and always he was inevitably the hero, whether at work, out hunting, or playing games, making judicious use of his advantages and never showing off. His passion for arguing, for answering every "yes" with two "no's," for providing proofs, his tendency not to trust anyone, not even to believe himself, all with a dash of veiled, yet piquant country snobbishness, armed even his friends against him. Everyone thought of him as powder just waiting to ignite. If he had amassed a record of sincere sins, they would readily have forgiven him; they couldn't excuse his perverse obstinacy and pride. And so, no matter how exciting he was to hunt with (no one brought game in like he did; once, he even bagged a snow leopard, an extremely rare, shy beast), Laurence couldn't find any companions; no matter how fine his soloing voice, he couldn't assemble a chorus. He hung around by himself, lived alone after leaving his parents' home, but without becoming antisocial or feral. On the contrary, in his conduct, he was worldly, attentive, played at kid-glove manners, and although they appreciated him at the sawmill as by far the most able, they didn't trust him: before you can blink, he'll drop some work you can't put on hold and take off. They were surprised he hadn't yet run down to the city and they lavished attention on him

His desertion, by riveting him to the mountains, eased the sawmill owner's fears, and new, less balmy days ought to have dawned for Laurence. Before he had managed to take stock of this fact, Luke's inference made its appearance, and life instantly became unbearable. But in the same way that Laurence pretended not to notice he was being tailed, he maintained at the sawmill the air of a man doing a favor by working. There was no more deliberation, however, about calling him to order, since the stonecutter's suspicions had ceased to be a secret held among the vigilantes

Within a month of the memorable gathering at the tavern that determined the gravestone's subject matter, not just the whole village, but also the entire district, and even the faraway city were in on the matter. And so, one evening, when several gendarmes halted their steeds on the square in front of the village hall and the taverns, no one asked them why they had deigned to pay a visit; they were expected. They were escorting an outlandish omnibus with two passengers: a forensic investigator, already of "actual" rank (in bureaucratic terms), and his secretary. This parade made the whole population come running, despite the late hour

Usually, a visiting investigator's duties were limited to formalities, for he came only in response to rumors of crime that had reached the city (he was never summoned; the local population never knew anything about any of it), and since the criminal would have vanished long before the bureaucrat turned up (in reality going off into the mountains or being hidden by someone), the investigator would interrogate the locals: the elder, the tavern owners, and a few others he felt like conversing with. The secretary would produce some inscrutable thing on paper, those interrogated would subscribe their marks—some two crosses, some three—the investigator would spend the night in the village hall, following a splendid dinner with those he had questioned, and would go back where he came from in the morning, and that would end the matter for all eternity. After his departure, it even happened that they would discuss in the tavern, with much laughter, the wanted criminal's presence in the village hall, and how the investigator had been particularly attentive to the criminal's sighing over the decline in morals, how the secretary had spent an especially long time recording his effusions, and how, at the dinner, the criminal had been appointed toastmaster and had brought all those present to the brink of ecstasy with his eloquence and stamina

And this time, too, the bureaucrat arrived planning to spend his time just as amiably, never suspecting that matters stood differently. Luke the stonecutter's allegation—that, although Brother Mocius's murder had been committed far away, the perpetrator was, so to speak, very well known to everyone, and that he was, indisputably, the deserter Laurence—was so incredible that the investigator nearly fainted. When, moreover, Luke added that the perpetrator had not gone into hiding, but was sitting right nearby, and that if he would just cross the square, he could arrest him, the investigator jumped up and shouted that it was too late to take up this matter, that he would look into it in the morning, and how dare Luke dictate how he ought to proceed, that—as it were, and so on and so forth—then threw everybody out of the room and went to bed on an empty stomach

Luke wasn't lying. Laurence, acting as though he hadn't noticed the crowd and with no thought of running away, although he was also certain that, against all precedent, they would betray him, was sitting in a tavern, calmly conversing, lazily stretching from time to time, looking like he was tired and wanted to sleep, but preferred, nevertheless, to keep up his pleasant conversation. The entrance of the stonecutter, the elder, and the others, accompanied by gendarmes, didn't even make the young man flinch. His accusers' sour faces showed how much the forensic investigator had fouled things up. Waiting until tomorrow and putting up with Laurence's bravado was inconceivable. But they also couldn't arrest him on their own, without delay: Luke had already overstepped his bounds and might provoke the outright displeasure of the majority, who didn't share the stonecutter's artistic fervor. And so they all sat down, the accusers were silent, and the gendarmes had no idea who was sitting right in front of them

But, while the elder was resigned to the situation, the artist couldn't stand it. Seated opposite Laurence, Luke fidgeted for a while and then suddenly kicked aside his stool and popped up right beside the young man. All present craned their necks and froze. It was painfully quiet. Shaking, flushed, and spluttering, the stonecutter cried out:

"Come on, own up, you're the one . . ."

The gendarmes pounced on Laurence. But he pulled a pistol from his shirt, fired several times at the stonecutter and the rest of them, and skipped from the tavern, hounded by their curses and volleys

04

Even though the wennies' hamlet was four hours' walk at most from the sawmill, none of its inhabitants knew a thing about the events that had shaken the village with the sawmill, not just because of their isolation, but also because the wennies, once they'd crossed the range, became deaf and blind to everything happening round about

None of them attended Luke's funeral, dull minus a requiem, adapted for those deceased careless enough to die outside the festal week. The snow hanging over the earth was bringing the year to a close and declaring an end to the overly drawn-out tale that had arisen because of the dubious monk and the immoderate artist; and the peasants really did hasten to fill the grave, the murder provoked no commentary, and by evening, safely locked away and deprived of their taverns until spring, they had forgotten everything, as though there never had been a Mocius or a Laurence and their victims

Accordingly, when Laurence entered the unpronounceable hamlet after noon, his presence didn't alarm or even surprise anyone. It's true, the young man had never shown his face there before, but all the hunters knew him for a tireless marksman and master trapper, and his advent seemed accidental: He's cutting through the hamlet, they say, on his way to do some hunting, seeing it might snow, the young sport. Needless to say, the rules of hospitality don't permit letting anyone pass with impunity, so Laurence was obliged to sit a moment and have a drink in the first house, then sit and drink in the next, and so on. The highlanders stood on their thresholds and waited for the stranger to emerge from their neighbor's place so they could drag him into their own. So Laurence eventually reached the wenny's house and stayed an especially long time, asking the old man about winter trails into the mountains, about the possibility of surviving there during this season, unspooling, in a word, all the intelligence he, Laurence, lacked, but when bedtime came, he refused a berth and left for the cretins. The latter were already asleep on the ground in their stable, but the wenny children were greatly astonished (since no one ever called on the cretins, out of squeamishness) when Laurence announced he would spend the night in that very place

Laurence was wary of being rousted out during the night, since he couldn't be certain the highlanders weren't concealing beneath their courtesy a resolution to assault him. But he needed sleep inordinately after blundering two whole days in the woods and drinking so much now; he was also taking account of the acute possibility that gendarmes would be searching the vicinity for him (while, as it happens, the townsmen had swiftly headed home after the murder). The cretins' stable, then, was an impregnable fortress

But when Laurence awoke in the morning, roused by his aggrieved hosts' wailing at the sight of this outlander, he regretted that his exaggerated caution had driven him to enter the place. The filth in the stable was such that probably no animal, including pigs, was capable of surviving under those conditions. The floor was carpeted with rotting, urine-soaked hay, since cretins generally pee right where they are; a corner of the stable was set aside as a latrine, but no one ever cleaned up and it was gradually encroaching, year by year, on the open space. It was difficult to say whether the cretins were wearing threadbare woolen clothes, a kind of bag with holes for head and mitts, or were themselves overgrown with wool that brought to mind sheep's wool. Their father, mother, and another full-grown dwarf stood and cried, their legs with huge feet set wide apart and their monstrous heads with meaty ears and eyelids hanging down, all three with a uniform growth of hair, and nothing more than her breasts flopping out in the open identified the mother's sex. Their offspring, distinguished only by their smaller size, latched onto their parents' legs and squealed. Fleas, despite the cold and altitude, were visibly leaping back and forth in swarms, and the hay teemed with vermin

Laurence tumbled out into the snow and nearly choked on the pure air. What abomination! That meant he'd been soundly drunk the previous evening, not to take things in. So that's what the fabled untouchables were like. He'd gladly have exterminated them all, never mind some sort of customary rights and the legend that they protected the hamlet from avalanches, but he wasn't likely to escape lynching twice. Laurence had heard a lot about these terribly sick people, about their limited minds and meager means of expression, but what he saw stunned him

Once the wenny found out that Laurence had arranged to spend the night with the cretins, he couldn't get to sleep and had been standing in the snowy yard since the crack of dawn, waiting for this enterprise to end. He refused to let the flustered Laurence into his home, but tossed him some new clothes and demanded that he bathe in the icy stream and change. Since he couldn't risk being left without shelter or friendship, Laurence acquiesced and only afterward received an invitation to enter and have a drink

The wenny's sermonizing knew no bounds

"In all my years," the old man wheezed, "no one's ever thought of seeking refuge with the cretins. No one's ever committed such a great sin. And what did Laurence go and do?

"We, the highlanders, are not bound by flatlanders' laws, since our truth is not theirs. Flatlanders are blind and live by the belly's mind; we live by the mind's mind. They die, we metamorphose into trees; they see *things*, we see *souls* as well. The plain only exists so there can be mountains, and mountains to protect the pure from the unwashed. We're hospitable, but Laurence must remember that he's one of the unwashed

"Can you tell from the sound whether a shot has hit its mark? Predict what ravine the goats will follow down to water at dawn? See tracks on the bottom when an animal runs along a riverbed? Can you say which tree will fall first from old age, and when? Where the first avalanche will come crashing down? Where lightning will strike?

"Your knowledge is negligible, your senses dulled. How do you know your misdeeds are glorious?"

The old man stood, flushed and resplendent, exalted by a presentiment of misfortunes whose advent he was trying to ward off, acknowledging, perhaps for the first time, that he was powerless, that the years counted for something after all. But Laurence made no attempt to mount up in the wenny's wake. And so he stuck to his ill-starred vaudeville

A really stupid story, you could say. Brother Mocius, a holy fool from the north, famous for hiking over the mountains in all seasons and boasting that he had seen and knew about wonders and treasures such as no one knows, had been grating on Laurence's nerves for years. Recently, while hiding in the woods from the draft commission, Laurence met the monk near a large fountain and killed him in revenge. And damned right to do it, too, since the pretender turned out to have nothing on him but some pitiful copper coins and a wooden cross. But the corpse came ashore in the village, and Laurence narrated the events that followed

"Alas, wenny. Treasures, the whole thing's so alluring. Living in the mountains might be all right, but there's nothing worse than living on the skirts of the mountains. Wonders, rumors, hearsay poison the imagination. For instance, they say you've got mercury lakes. What wealth! But can you really find your way to a lake? I walk around like a highlander, but I'm not a highlander, and no matter how much I've searched, I can't find one. People talk about money squirreled away in caves and guarded by satyrs. About veins of gold in the rocks and nuggets on the riverbanks . . .

"I didn't find any mercury lakes and I made no mistake in killing the monk. When you look into it, there isn't anything at all. You hear: Treasures, treasures! But the highlanders are paupers, even though they're supposed to know everything. For instance, you've lived more than eighty years, and what do you have besides a disgustingly hard existence and an eternal battle with nature? I'm coming to the conclusion, at long last, that you shouldn't seek riches here, but on the plain

"No one here wears silk or rides a bicycle. I'll readily agree that the flatlanders' eyes are weak and their ears are bad. It's not in my power to answer your questions. But what good is knowledge, this mind's mind you talk about, if it can't feed you better, dress you up, or hedge against goiters and labor?"

The old man listened and was transformed. His strength abandoned him, along with his grandiloquence. He kept on philosophizing. Laurence was, you might say, young, and so he was seeking out treasures. Treasures really did exist, but only as long as they went unclaimed. Find them, and they'd crumble to dust. Laurence measured out life in wealth, like a flatlander, while highlanders thought only how to put off dying as long as possible. Life existed only for attaining old age. Only then did the eyes actually begin to see, the ears to hear, and the mind to soar above the mind

But the ferocity and tension had disappeared from his face, and his pupils clouded over. It was evident that his spirit, roused at the price of a sleepless night, had grown once more decrepit and fallen asleep. Besides, they had drunk too much wine. And Laurence, done with fooling around, proceeded to swagger. He was grateful to the old man for the pointers. But he couldn't, unfortunately, jump out of his flatlander's skin. The mountains only corrupted him, Laurence, they'd never be able to catechize him. Old age isn't at all enticing. It's good to die young

"Enough talk," Laurence suddenly shouted, quaffing his horn and hurling it onto the table, "We're not in church. Worldviews are all well and good, but here's something more amusing than the mind's mind. I'm staying here. Give me some land or one of your outbuildings. Besides, they say your kids obey you like dogs. Magnificent. Let me put them to work. I'll make them useful and rich"

The wenny agreed, no questions asked. He was prepared to assign Laurence an allotment, but only when spring came, and he could live right here in the meantime. The incident with the monk really was silly, since monks were pretenders and didn't have a clue when it came to the mountains. As for his children, although they were nonentities corrupted by traveling on the plains and sometimes sighed after the life there, they'd been gloriously schooled

"They wouldn't challenge me," Laurence interjected

"Be at ease, they won't betray you. Once I've given them into your power, there won't be any faintheartedness"

Only then did he call his toiling children, whom he tyrannized, and announce that he was handing them over to Laurence for instruction and that their earnings would be excellent; that although Laurence was much younger than they were, he was smart; and so on. The unfortunates didn't dare object; they weren't even curious about what they, with their beards, would learn from this young man. But after witnessing the previous evening's expedition to the cretins, they had already determined they should expect a shake-up

Others in the hamlet likewise needed no informants at all to understand: Laurence's presence had nothing to do with hunting. Everyone knew about Laurence spending the night with the cretins and had seen him washing off in the stream, and that was enough to conclude, when the wenny met with Laurence behind closed doors, that the hamlet was on the verge of great events in its history. And when it came to light that Laurence hadn't quit the hamlet, but was even staying on to live with the wenny, their opinion was confirmed, and they figured only that events were postponed until the snows melted

Laurence's advent had even been remarked from the former forester's balcony, and it coincided with the first snow. A joyful Ivlita peeked out in the morning and saw that the white scene was violated this time by a commotion near the creek, where a long-awaited man was being baptized in the frenzied waters. That a bridegroom might appear to her in the mountains—this was something Ivlita had never before entertained. But now she perceived him, and an unhoped-for possibility drew the young woman thenceforth along new days past finding out

The wenny children who frequently came to see her no longer seemed alien and she no longer teased them. Only then, while they were conversing about Laurence and she was interrogating them about his life (although they couldn't impart any sensible reasons why he had come), did Ivlita notice that the world was being transfigured from day to day, that her sight and hearing and sense of smell were changing; she was beginning to detect and fathom phenomena the wennies had long been expounding to her, phenomena whose existence she had denied because of her coarseness

It started when Ivlita began to discern in the forest at night not only leaves whispering, trees creaking, and eagle owls groaning, but also voices—vague, garbled, seemingly not at all human—that were nevertheless completely comprehensible, and you could say with no mistake what the source of one or another of them was experiencing. Then she started hearing how the snow fell, the snowflakes' barely perceptible sough became clear, and all at once she realized that it wasn't just a sough, but a peculiar form of speech. So that proverbial voice of nature Ivlita had heard of so many times was gradually made intelligible. Evidently, all things had a language, and this language didn't exist, like human language, for exchanging opinions and thoughts, but emanated, mirroring the mind of things, the way a song bereft of words streams out. Ivlita would throw open the window and look at the snow that had ceased oppressing her, listen closely, and begin warbling. At the other end of the hamlet, the cretins would creep out and sing. And Ivlita understood surpassingly now why the wenny's daughter imitated them. In their senseless speech was as much weighty content, far removed from life's trivial worries, as in the forest idiom . . .

Once Ivlita began to hear, her eyes were opened, too. She already saw that trees were not trees, but souls who had passed their earthly way in human form and were passing it now in the guise of trees. It turns out that trees advance, cliffs migrate, the snowy veil undulates. Ivlita also saw: the souls of snow leopards, wolves, and fallow deer coming out of the woods, strolling peacefully together and dropping in on the cretins, and angels flying down from the snow-covered summits; and, paying no heed to people, they all go on living, not their own life, but their death, their freedom from the empty human way of life that had possessed Ivlita up to that time. And Ivlita felt like living, once she was dead, her own death, too . . .

Laurence stayed on for a long time in the hamlet not knowing a thing about Ivlita. The snow and the fact that the wennies continued treating Laurence like an outsider and didn't breathe a word about her even once while enumerating their native land's noteworthy features caused some fairly ordinary events to be postponed. True, the former forester's house attracted attention because of its fanciful construction, and the young woman's voice enveloped the dale in the evenings. But Laurence was too preoccupied to get carried away with lacy woodwork or feminine song. He had to head off first into the mountain deeps and then, on the contrary, delve secretly into the valleys, visiting villages, scouting things out, and getting to know the place. Sometimes he had to be absent for weeks, and Ivlita, never leaving her window, languished with boredom and anticipation. Some strangers usually came back with Laurence: his gang swelled. In the villages, adherents, disciples, and vassals appeared. Laurence's influence grew strong. To recover his citizen's rights and acquire still more new, exclusive prerogatives that would render to Laurence's authority soul and body not just the wennies, but also the entire country, he lacked just one thing—a word. He need only proclaim himself sovereign, that was all, and then he would be able to show up at the lumber mill—and at the taverns—where no one would dare tail, betray, or oppose him

This is the marvelous word: *bandit.* And when Laurence donned the yellow woolen shirt worn under a felt cape proper to his new vocation and, festooned with arms both of cold steel and fire, showed up one fine Sunday at the village hall where the stonecutter Luke had made his complaint to the investigator, he was met—although, it seemed, no one was expecting Laurence and the winter didn't promote transportation—by a multitude bearing gifts of broadcloth remnants, cartridges, and refreshments for the archon and his wenny retinue. The populace stood in the large hall. Each held a purse in plain sight. Laurence entered, accompanied by the headman and the village elders. The headman presented each of those gathered (although Laurence knew them all thoroughly), announcing how much money he'd brought and the extent of his property and plowland, so it would be clear how fair the amount of tribute was. Several times, due to fudged accounts, Laurence had to interrupt the headman and point out the actual state of affairs. But Laurence was in a fit of magnanimity, and when the tribute didn't seem sufficient, instead of taking the perpetrator hostage, as one might expect, he ordered the balance to be ready by this or that deadline. The justice of his resolutions provoked, every time, an ecstatic clamor. The new bandit's father and brothers also brought tribute, taking advantage of a substantial discount based on family ties

The reception ended with a superb dinner. The village hall was crowded, so they opened up the idle sawmill and had soon rigged up a table that ran its entire length. Since bandits avoid getting drunk, everyone drank in moderation. The anxious mood gave way first to levity, and then to sincere pleasure. Many sang, even more danced, right on the table. Standing, likewise, on the table after demonstrating his marvelous adroitness, tirelessly bowing in response to the accolades, Laurence engaged the gathering with a speech for the better part of an hour, during which he summed up the accord with his native village, swore fidelity to the obligation he'd assumed not to kill or rob its inhabitants from that time forth, announced, beating his breast and sobbing (everyone copying his behavior), that he would donate the means necessary to adorn the graves of the stonecutter Luke and Brother Mocius in an unprecedented fashion, and finally began scattering fistfuls of the money that had just been brought to him, admiring the free-for-all and fisticuffs raised on account of the silver

A few days later, the post was robbed on the highway, its convoy shot dead

05

As long as the populace beat and slashed its own, the administration couldn't care less. If one of its function- aries fell victim, a certain annoyance would arise, but the annoyance would quickly pass and the functionary would be for- gotten. But whenever the plebs dared to rob the treasury, violating the administration's own inalienable right to pick the treasury clean, intervention aimed at capturing those responsible and stifling such boldness became unavoidable

An incalculable number of sundry military and civilian folk, most repulsive in mien and base in soul, would converge on the villages lying in the vicinity of the crime scene. Since the populace never knew anything, they would arrest all the elected officials and lead them away God knows where, impose a tithe on the populace and, finally, conduct a wholesale search, since the tithe always seemed insufficient and they would be forced to resort to confiscation and payments in kind. But while rending and throttling, they would hardly have imagined even for a moment that they would get at the bandits using these methods. They believed in one measure only— purchase, and that's why they would post a reward for capturing the bandit chief equal to the tithe taken from the populace. The bandits, however, if danger threatened for any reason, had only to renounce the tribute due them, and equilibrium would be restored. The actual outcome of the comedy was this: The populace, aggrieved by the deportation of its best people, would beg the bandits to carry out their exploits elsewhere in future, so that everyone would suffer equally, and the gang, with utmost courtesy, would honor the request. It's true that some bandits would, nevertheless, end up in jail whenever the gendarmes managed to wound anyone at a crime scene or overtake them. All this happened extremely rarely, and the administration's saving grace was the fact that bandits themselves were rare; they were born, not made. This moderation in nature even allowed the lowly who captured anyone to boast before the lofty of the measures they'd taken and to receive rewards and distinctions for what they'd done. And so, if you don't count several functionaries and rich men who paid with their heads, everyone was, at bottom, satisfied with this state of affairs; it nourished them, and the gang became a source of economic flourishing in a country that had, until that time, dragged along in a pitiful condition

That's why the news that the village with the sawmill had sworn fealty to Laurence, and also about the robbery of the post, broadcast around the region, provoked extraordinary excitement. Never had life seethed so in the dumb days of January. Just as though spring were already approaching now, not months later, and as if there were neither impassable snow nor loathsome frosts

Laurence, accompanied by the wennies, returned to the hamlet. He knew that as long as the authorities were fooling around beyond the mountains (as though it were not already generally known that the word "authorities" was a synonym for "fools," and some further proof was required), he could calmly feed on the remnant of winter and the majesty of the backwoods. The title *bandit* freed him of all misgivings regarding the highlanders, and there was no need to seek refuge with the cretins

The loot was ample; Laurence gave generously not only to his comrades in arms, but to the whole hamlet. Each of them now had enough money to make needed spring purchases, and since the flat-landers were obliged to provide services equal in value to the tithe, what was bought would also be delivered. One of the wennies even proposed blazing a real trail to the hamlet, if not a cart lane, in order to crown the beneficent turn of events, but Laurence, who saw in this suggestion the basest lack of gratitude, flew into such a rage that the wenny son had to retract his own words and add that if the opinion he'd expressed was incorrect, it would, perhaps, be better to make the hamlet completely inaccessible, immuring it once and for all. But when Laurence rejected *this* idea and proclaimed that his work was just beginning and that he would maintain an open chan-nel to the outside world, although in a new spirit, the shared radiant mood gave way to evil premonitions

The former forester was first to inform his daughter about Lau-rence's activities. He subjoined no evaluation whatsoever, whether because he was wary of speaking ill or simply because it didn't con-cern him in the slightest, and that was reason enough; and Ivlita, forced once again to make up her own mind, unexpectedly found herself facing difficulties. It didn't matter that Laurence was a ban-dit, but killing, what about that? Was it good? Of course, it was good, when . . . But when, precisely? So, from superhuman spheres she had to sink to judging humans, good or bad—a distinction she didn't recognize; and she found the need for evaluating deeds bur-densome. After her eyes had been opened this winter and she had seen to the bottom of nature, Ivlita supposed she had crossed the final frontier, and there was nothing left beyond penetrating mortal secrets. Once she recognized the objective reality of spirits, she had herself become one of them, and impoverished human life had very nearly turned into an insignificant detail. And now this life was tak-ing unforeseen revenge, mocking Ivlita, revealing to her a world of evaluations and excuses, a human world she, as it happened, did not know, and its presence embarrassed her

Ivlita tried to avoid complications, replying neither "yes" nor "no," that there was, she said, no evaluating, any murder at all was permitted, one must defend oneself and attack, that the world of people was no more exalted than the animal world and wolf law no worse than human. But her peace was shattered, and even if Ivlita had never again bumped up against human affairs, she could not now but know they existed. The young woman had never before been curious to find out what was going on beyond the mountains. Now she thought with alarm about the hostile world that surrounded her and perceived that she could not break through her surroundings

Laurence. He had bestowed sight on her, he had dissolved her in nature, had elevated Ivlita, and he had likewise debased her, snatching from her the rapture she had nearly attained, casting her down, robbing *her*, too, killing *her*, too. In place of magnanimous snow, pines, mountains, and a river—a blizzard, danger, not a wink of sleep. The wind tears through so that the house shakes, ready to topple over, and there's no shelter from the cold. Avalanches break the woods all around, the dale moans at night, and when it's day's turn, it's not much brighter than night. If you cower under hides so you can't hear a thing, can't see, thoughts assail your mind even more insistently. Ivlita grew timid, indecisive. She lay ill, complaining of a headache; she was feverish, but not dying. She listened in horror: the hurricane blew incessantly beyond her window, she hoped her malady's duration depended on the foul weather

Finally, Ivlita felt better, and everything really had quieted down in the yard. Again, the same trembling whiteness and the snowflakes falling imperceptibly, as though they did not even exist. The hamlet was bustling, cleaning up, people were clearing paths, fixing damage. But what a change to this familiar scene! As though its soul had flown, its colors faded. As though everything had turned away from Ivlita. Not that nature stood before her once more inanimate. But it had backed away, withdrawn far off, and it occurred to Ivlita: there was no recovering this loss. She no longer felt like singing or laughing. She sat for hours, unmoving, distractedly gazing all around, failing to notice her weeping father, leaving her food untouched

Then Ivlita started going out into the yard to stroll between the walls of snow that led down to the stream. The wennies, when they learned that Ivlita was ill, came particularly often, bringing her gifts in the form of dolls molded from bread or clay or made from empty spools impaled on sticks. This was a new world, miserable, no substitute for unloved nature. At home, lying on the floor in front of the stove, Ivlita arranged the dolls, named them, played with them; in short, it was just like her childhood. But the dolls acted differently, they did nothing but beat one another in spite, kill one another, and Ivlita saw that this way, too, had been choked off. One day, she hurled them into the stove

The wennies stubbornly avoided revealing to Laurence the reason for their frequent trips to the former forester's. Uneasy, the young man decided to go with them and see for himself. Along the way, one of the sons blurted out that the forester's daughter was, you might say, sick. What's the big fuss? Aren't women always getting sick? Why would a stranger get involved, it's just not done

While they were cutting across the hamlet, Laurence was curiously scrutinizing the only two-story house, which rose up from a hummock, surrounded by hawthorn, preposterous with its curves, and as though perforated throughout by carvings on its shutters, balconies, and doors. What weird woman lay ill in that castle?

The forester, when he caught sight of his guest, ran out, inviting him to come into the dining room. He bustled around, bowing, taking pains to settle his new arrival there in the carved armchair, his favorite piece of furniture. The purpose of the visit wasn't clear to the old man, so after several minutes' silence, he inquired, made anxious mostly by the usual ploys of bandit politeness. Laurence, with a refined courtesy that compelled the forester to reminisce about the city, replied that he simply thought it necessary to call on him, since he saw no obstacle to their acquaintance. "Not a single obstacle, you understand." To conclude, the master of the house, in polite fashion, offered his guest some brandy: "Rye, apple, or grape?" "Apple, please"

Ivlita, festive, emerged in a cherry-red dress to bring the guest his parting drink. So tall, Laurence had never seen women like her in the mountains. Her thick braids, thrown over her shoulders, were the color of straw and reached her knees. Her eyes, there aren't eyes like that here. Laced up in a corset, her superb bosom, her long legs. Ivlita was holding a curved drinking horn, not the usual ram's horn it was customary to drink from in such cases, but a prodigious one, made of silver, and suited, rather, for a wake

Laurence had been hoodwinked and cheated. He'd been living half a year in this gnarly hamlet, and even those whose fate depended entirely on him had kept secret these riches, which had never been equaled and never would be—that nasty habit of concealing treasures, thinking it only right and proper that they should vanish idly. But this time, it wasn't sorcery, not an apparition that disappears as soon as people see it. You could hold this woman like the horn of brandy; you could devour her like any other. Laurence stood up, grabbed the horn, drained it without stopping for breath, and, placing it on the table, told the forester:

"I want her for my wife"

Laurence was not requesting her father's consent. It's not required among highlanders. You can abduct a bride from her home, even against her wishes—in secret, if you're afraid her father and brothers might interfere and get the better of you, or openly, if her relatives are weak. If her parents are really abject, they're warned ahead of time, just as a courtesy

Since there's no priest in the mountains and no way to get to one, the complicated wedding ritual is replaced by an even more complicated ritual, but performed by a person chosen for the purpose, usually the oldest. The elders make the marrying couple jump across streams, flog one another with branches, crawl on all fours, and such like; the wedding goes on until the bride or groom falls down exhausted, which happens sometimes on the second or third day, if the ritual consists in moving cordwood or walking back and forth from one tree to another. Bandits are spared all this because they are not wed. Whether the unique nature of their business or their independent position is the reason, no one knows. A robber's wife has no right to children and no right to respect, no one greets her, women are forbidden to be in contact with her. It's not just that bandits don't object to this arrangement or fight against it (as to a fight, they might even pull it off, given their exceptional power), quite the contrary, they by all means condone depriving their wives of rights, and they're not barred from killing their wives even when the surrounding populace has paid a tithe to be left untouched. And since it's shameful to be a bandit's wife, an abducted woman, counter to all the rules, is allowed to divorce, although, in that case, no one and nothing safeguards her future life

The forester never imagined it was permissible to desire a dead woman, and wouldn't even have ascribed any meaning to such a thought. But now, once the murderous words had been pronounced, the former forester beheld that his deceased wife was alive, and in bloom. The possibility of losing her, the consciousness that they would drag her away, were completely intolerable. The host, half out of his chair, shaking, stammering, traced some signs in the air, clutching his throat. Laurence, intoxicated, was silent. All at once, her father darted into a corner, grabbed his rifle and fired without taking aim. He dropped it and fell on his face

The bullet lodged in a floorboard. Laurence didn't budge. Ivlita wasn't in the room. Frightened by her father's frenzy, she had run up to her room, locked herself in, covered up with furs, and was looking intently at the young man as though he had not remained below, but was standing before her, resolute, dressed to kill, triumphant; she searched for definitions worthy of him, but didn't find any, her thoughts were too few, she was worn out, enervated. She didn't think about her father

The shot chased off the image and replaced it with unbearable alarm. She needed to return. But in the room adjoining the dining room where Ivlita had left her father, Laurence, seeking her out, ran into her. The young woman recoiled. Laurence was not alone. Shadowy people were standing behind her bridegroom, among whom Ivlita recognized, although she had never seen them, Brother Mocius, the stonecutter Luke, and the postal convoy. Behind them all, the former forester was bent double. Ivlita started, shrieking: "You killed him, you killed him," pushed Laurence out of the way—and rushed into the dining room. But as soon as she saw her father spread out before her, she stopped. Her face assumed a calm expression, her head tilted back. Hastily unbraiding her hair and spreading it over her shoulders, Ivlita turned toward Laurence, who was swaying on the threshold, and asked, "You don't happen to know why my beloved father does not greet me?" And then she addressed the wennies, who had shown up on the outer threshold without daring to step across: "Friends, can you tell me why my beloved father does not come to meet me?" She walked around the table, wandered into other rooms, and returned, repeating: "My beloved father, why don't you come out to me?" And only after stepping around the prone body several times, she pretended to notice it for the first time. She cried out, fell on him, wailing: "Father, father, you're dead, but why did you leave without taking me along? I wouldn't have been a heavy burden for you, but when you abandoned me, you left me a sorrow not to be borne . . ."

After raising Ivlita, grasping her shoulders, and shouting into her ear: "I didn't shoot, your father did, he fell down in fright, he's not dead, don't give yourself so much grief"—Laurence, slowly coming to and gathering that, although still on his feet, he was unduly drunk from the prodigious draft of brandy, gazed with undiminished amazement at the young woman's face; the desire to possess her as soon as possible, compounded by his fury at being hoodwinked, returned tenfold, and there arose within the bridegroom, along with his readiness to turn beastly here and now, an unaccountable rancor toward his bride; he had to take something out on her, make her pay dearly, and all the more dearly for being so beautiful, for expressing so much of heaven. All the same, Laurence did not yet dare give himself free rein. He swept Ivlita up, wrapped her in a skin, determined to run home and get even with her there. But when he threw the door open to the frost and saw the wenny children before him, the thought sprang up that he didn't live alone and would be obliged to face the old wenny himself, withstand his attack; there was no telling how it all might end. Laurence slammed the door, set his burden on the table, baffled. Why leave? He could stay here in this excellent house. But the forester harried his sight and prevented him from initiating anything with an easy mind. Laurence didn't feel master here. The master of the house was lying there—deceased, perhaps, but formidable. Laurence had not anticipated this embarrassment, a weakness he had never suspected in himself. And suddenly he wanted so badly for the old man to live, for this to be really just a faint. Laurence rushed to the forester and turned him over

There was no determining whether the former forester was dead or alive. Laurence went out into the yard, hollered for the wennies, brought in snow, and began rubbing down the insensate body.

Since his efforts remained fruitless, the young man would periodically leave the old fellow's side, walk away, sit down, stare dully at the body lying on the floor, and once more set to chafing it. He found brandy in the house, dragged enormous furs into the dining room, from time to time he loosened them and directly pulled them tight

Several times it seemed his host had regained consciousness. It was only spasms of his dead arms. But then the former forester drew breath and opened his eyes. The old man fancied he was returning from an abyss he remembered nothing about, but returning transfigured, remade, no longer the former forester, but someone else, and the former forester was no more, and never would be again. What strange events had caused this, the old man couldn't comprehend, but the events were of distinct importance, irrevocable as the former forester's flight. The old man gazed absently at Laurence, who was holding him in his arms, at the snow strewn about the room, at the rifle lying nearby, at the table opposite, meaningless and mute objects. On the table, a curious heap of furs attracted his attention only because arms had slipped out from the furs and were hanging down on either side. It wasn't the first time the old man had seen those arms, but for a long time he couldn't recognize whose they were. He tossed and turned, moaned, gazed questioningly into Laurence's face. Gradually, the thought kindled in his consciousness that those were, as a matter of fact, Ivlita's arms, his daughter's

And then everything that had happened came back to him quickly and clearly. Laurence's advent, his insolent demand, the shot; and what horrible thing had taken place afterward, why was his wife laid out on the table, arms helplessly outstretched? The old man tensed, trying to break free of Laurence and get up. But the forester was dying. He no longer had any strength. His gaze, after shining momentarily with wrath and hatred, became clouded. "Is Ivlita dead?"—he moaned when he noticed Laurence's tears falling onto his own face and trickling down, mixing with his own. "No, she's sleeping," Laurence replied. And then the departing man's consciousness blazed up once more because of the young woman's presence. Hadn't Ivlita caused his misfortunes? Hadn't he buried himself alive on her account? Doomed to a vicious neighborhood? Hadn't he fired his gun and become overly agitated while protecting her? And she had brought their guest the silver horn, shared her love with the thief, right here, next to him . . . The whore, the tramp. "Take her," the old man imparted to Laurence. "Beat her, torment her, you'll never find such a noble body anywhere." But then, "Help me up, Laurence, lead me to Ivlita, let me look at her one last time, I spoke falsely, I want to bid my final farewell and on good terms . . ."

Gathering strength from some unknown source when Laurence lifted him under the arms, the old man stayed on his feet and took a few steps toward the table where Ivlita lay all wrapped up. He grasped the edge with his hands and rasped, "Show her to me, boy." Laurence threw back the skin. In a faint that had passed into sleep, his daughter presented her unbearable beauty to her father for the last time. The bodice she had torn in her raving revealed her breasts, the breasts of the forester's late wife. Her shoulders were fabulously naked, blindingly white. Tearing himself from the table, the father collapsed on his daughter and latched onto her throat with skeleton hands: "Whore, you wanted to betray me, you couldn't wait for me to die . . ." The woman's cry forced Laurence, swallowed up in his thoughts, to focus. Grabbing the old man's hands, he unclenched them with some effort, pulled him off and threw him against the wall. Ivlita, crazed, sat up, blood oozing along her throat. And the old man kept spluttering out, "Whore, whore, damned whore, you'll die like a dog, took a bandit's part, you'll hang with him, there'll be no rest for you, adulteress . . ." Clamping her hand over her mouth as though *she'd* been blaspheming, the half-naked Ivlita looked at her father without seeing anything. She didn't understand his words.

But the dying man's rattle was insulting, even without words, her throat was aching and hurt as though his fingers were still clenched on it. "Quiet, you maniac," Laurence roared at the thrashing old man. Seeing as he wasn't calming down, Laurence walked over and kicked him in the face. He scooped up Ivlita, sat her on his shoulder, went out, and set off with giant steps down the mountain

06

Spring in the mountains arrives with such a delay compared to low-lying areas that a highlander who descends assumes there's no escape for flatlanders, so to speak, from summer, humid and rank. This impression grows more intense if he journeys to the sea—if, in particular, he gets there not by road, but taking advantage of the river's current, which, in four hours, with dizzying speed, will deposit into the salt waves a raft or a large boat, heavily laden so as not to capsize in the rapids, and on which the pilots vigilantly keep watch in all directions for the right time to push off from the cliffs, otherwise, they'll break up—if highlanders descend this way to the sea, they simply land in hell

This discrepancy magnified the difference between the months spent in the hamlet and this businesslike and busy journey a hundred times, and Laurence, lying on the bottom of a bark rocking near the seashore while the wennies deployed the oars, since now they would have to row to reach the nearest port town, answered his comrades' questions reluctantly, suffered from the sun, and couldn't stop thinking about Ivlita. There, in the mountains, her presence conferred divine happiness; here, he was becoming convinced that Ivlita had tangled him in malign nets after taking away his freedom. Previously, his colloquies on the advantages of brigandage had largely been exercises in eloquence, but touring the villages that pledged fealty and robbing the post—those were exercises in daring, and now Laurence realized he was no longer at liberty to dispose of the business he'd begun, necessity ruled him, he had carelessly dabbled in playing with things whose powers he had no feeling for, and was now constrained to float aimlessly. It hadn't been long since his need for the treasures he sought would not even have been found in avarice, in a desire for change and luxury. When money fell into his hands, large sums of money, he didn't know what to do with it, gave almost all of it away, and the rest, buried in the ground, was lying idle, the way riches were pointlessly hiding in caves and on the lake bottom. Ivlita, once she took over his mind, had turned everything upside down. If she were a woman like any old peasant woman, there'd be no cause for anxiety. But her beauty remained beyond Laurence's grasp, she herself was supernatural, demanding excessive obeisance, gifts, offerings. He'd dug up his forgotten money, handed it over to her, watched her pour the coins from palm to palm, pick out a handful, and, spreading her fingers, lull herself to sleep with a golden shower. And those fingers, what rings did they not demand, what necklaces did her neck not await, what tiara her precious head? He could clean out all the sacristies, despoil all the wonderworking icons, and all of it, in Laurence's eyes, would hardly suffice to adorn Ivlita worthily. And it was no longer merely *possible* to rob, he *had* to

Spooked, the young man tried to calm down, reassuring himself that he was, no doubt, strong and would obtain everything. But self-assurance didn't help. His freedom had been forfeited, and life had withered along with it. As though his victims had infected him with the malady of nonexistence. As though the mountains where he was stuck for good had placed him in bonds, like a waterfall or a creeping glacier. The phantom most sweet had flown when, in order to prove its reality, Laurence had deserted and cast the monk down, and the poor fellow reckoned he had already suffered shipwreck

Once he'd resigned himself, Laurence was obliged to get back to business. Palavers and preparations began in anticipation of spring. But Laurence couldn't busy himself with some run-of-the-mill affair, making mischief near at hand. He needed a tenfold profit, something extraordinary. In the end, it wasn't worth robbing churches, either—a lot of complications and trouble with the locals. And when you got right down to it, could you really walk around the forest in vestments carrying gonfalons? And soiling yourself for the pleasure of drinking brandy from chalices also wasn't worth it. If the occasion presents itself . . .

And so you had to pluck up your courage and sail far away, to places where you don't feel safe, where there's no place to hide, places teeming with police, and attempt the impossible. And Laurence, grasping that his circumstances demanded extra focus, stubbornly struggled to drive off speculations on Ivlita and freedom

The deed itself was still far off, but there were already so many worries about how to unload weapons without being spotted by the shore watch. If not for Galaction's goggle eyes, grown to such size that you couldn't restrain your horror when you looked at them, the robber band would have been in serious trouble as to where and how to land

Galaction owned the town coffeehouse, situated opposite the harbor on the only street in town—along the embankment, stretching a considerable distance—and to all appearances he had no other occupation. He could invariably be seen strolling among the tables with a napkin thrown over his head to guard his bald spot from the sun's influence and checking to see whether any of his customers needed a cup of coffee and whether his guests were waiting for checkers, cards, dice, dominoes, or other games. The sight of the sea instills fear willy-nilly, you need to buck up your nerves now and then with black coffee, and since the town had only one dimension—length—no one drank anything but coffee, and since you wouldn't think of drinking coffee at home, the whole populace hung out at the coffeehouse, including children, peacocks, parrots, and cats. And since, finally, the port did a brisk trade, with cargo ships arriving and departing God knows when and agitation tormenting them all the time, the populace sat for whole days and nights in the coffeehouse and would eagerly have moved in for good if only they could have reached an agreement with the owner. This perfect arrangement of life in the port made finding people you needed easier in so far as it compelled everyone to live in sight of all

Sometimes, however, Galaction mysteriously disappeared somewhere and, when he got back, would tell his customers and friends (equivalent notions for him, by the way) either that he'd been ailing from constriction of the eyes and had gone to consult a renowned physician, or that he'd been ailing from distention of the eyes and had placed cupping glasses over them, or that he'd been suffering from his eyes growing fatter, lamenting that he never suffered their growing thinner; and so on, all in the same vein. With his eyes he squared accounts for all his liberties, and his witticisms were so flat, while his eyes were so horrifying, that by way of exception, everyone pretended to believe him

In fact, Galaction didn't go away to see physicians, but on the shadiest, most criminal business. If you needed to load or unload contraband cargo, keep a boat from leaving the port on time or make it meet with an accident while heading out to sea—there wasn't a fixer more resourceful or reliable in all these matters than Galaction. At Laurence's request he had even traveled out to the village with the sawmill, and in the tavern where the stonecutter Luke had been killed a bargain was struck between the seafarer and the robber band. Galaction, for a tenth share of the presumed take, was obliged not only to unload the weapons brought out of the mountains and shelter the bandits before and after the deed, but also to obtain all the intelligence necessary for carrying it out

The port town was already in sight when Galaction pointed to a small cove enclosed between two bluffs jutting out into the sea and suggested they steer toward it. When their boat reached the shore, entering a kind of grotto that hid it securely, their guide announced that they shouldn't unload right away, but wait for night

Laurence regarded with suspicion the pink mist, ravishingly transparent, that had colored everything. Flat fish are lying on their sides and you know neither their names nor use; sundry jellyfish; shells are weighing on something that's making them shift slowly and occasionally sticking its tentacles out; when the boat approaches, crabs plop from the rocks into the water, swell to frightening size and suddenly melt away; shades hurtle past under the water, but so headlong and blurred that you can't say who or what they are, in essence—and all this seemed hostile to Laurence, full of pitfalls and peril. Grabbing Galaction's arm, visibly upset, the young man demanded explanations from his conductor: what was that seaweed, what were those fish trying at any cost to be absorbed into the sea? But Galaction turned out to be a poor connoisseur of his native land and could say nothing more than that these fish were good for nothing, the seaweeds were useless and so didn't deserve names

The shore was strewn with bright jewels. Laurence scooped up a handful, scrutinizing them—were they valuable? But the pebbles dried and dulled

They lingered idly until dusk, glad that it wasn't hot in the grotto

When it got dark, they took the guns and scores of bandoliers from the boat and moved out toward the port. It was not yet midnight, and the whole populace remained within the coffeehouse. Therefore, passing behind the houses right up to the coffeehouse and descending into its cellar with the weapons presented no danger for the conspirators. Toward morning, Laurence and the wennies mixed with the crowd that frequented the coffeehouse.

And even though the highlanders' dress was picturesque, no one lifted their heads, let alone turned to look at the new arrivals

Laurence found these new circumstances extremely oppressive. He was flustered by being compelled to hide who he really was without really hiding, by having to pass for a merchant and spend the whole day sitting at a table doing nothing, sickened by the heat and the lack of brandy, and watching the townspeople scurry around under the figs and sycamores, bareheaded in all weather, but when it rained, barefoot under umbrellas, carrying their shoes to spare them. Time was slipping away, and there was no knowing when the moment for action would arrive and, most important, for returning to the mountains, to Ivlita. Now he no longer blamed her for anything, he wanted to see her, worried about her. At times, he had half a mind to give it all up and run away. But how could he return without accomplishing anything, empty-handed

But Galaction kept putting everything off, kept insisting it was still necessary to wait, the opportunity was too tantalizing and rare, it would be stupid to spoil it in haste, and so on. He alluded to information he'd received, read from some letters, made promises: soon everything would fall into place. In passing, he would come back to the terms he'd concluded with the robber band, review them, stipulate new ones, in a way you wouldn't notice, without threats, just by grimacing and gesturing. Laurence understood that Galaction was a finagler, thought scornfully of his tricks, and had resolved, if need be, to use force to get his own way. Whenever he complained to Galaction about the delays, about his intolerable environment, there was no end to his admonishing persuasion

"Wise up," said Galaction before bedtime, when he was heading home with Laurence, "this ain't the mountains. The authorities can't get at *you*, but you have your laws. *We're* within easy reach and so we live without laws. You rob, we burgle. But while *you* rob only occasionally and there's the possibility of using tithes to cut you down, since you're easy to find, we burgle continually, from our first tooth 'til our last, and you can't seal a deal, since you don't know whom to deal with. *You* attack from the front, but we steal on the sly, and always at retail. If you showed up at my place in your Sunday best for a reception (since you're a bandit, right?) and demanded tribute, the way you do up there, people would laugh in your face; here folks even laugh at my sickness. Down here, it's not just angels' wings they don't believe in—even *you* don't believe in them—here no one believes in anything, everything's mocked and everything's traded. Everyone thinks everyone else is a swindler and so they're always on their toes. *You* live by an established code, and if something does go wrong, you never betray one of your own, but the people here, while pretending to be rebels, will be the first to turn you in if they don't take a liking to you. And you'd never even dream up the nastiness they're capable of, their filth. Down here, you need special caution and different manners, you need to act skillfully, or you'll be dead before you know it"

And Laurence waited. The sea, poured out before him, didn't speak to him and only aggravated his boredom. Sometimes, wandering over the wooden docks, he tried taking a closer look at the work being done, how ships were loaded with the logs he had lashed into rafts on more than one occasion, fresh skins, dried fruits, how herring was brought in and nets were set. But he found this way of life alien and disgusting. He couldn't tolerate the local cuisine, primarily fish dishes, and grew sickly. Someone of his companions came down with a fever, a pretty malignant one. Watching people splash in the sea along the shore, Laurence thought how he could swim a raging river, but plunging into these waves would be just as disagreeable as living beside them. Nights were particularly cruel: it was stifling, but you couldn't open a window or the mosquitoes would eat you alive

One day, while walking along the embankment, he paused near a sailor mending his net, knocked him senseless with one blow, and heaved him into the water, without even thinking that there might be witnesses. Only when the sailor failed to resurface did Laurence take a look over his shoulder, but no one was there. In the morning, however, the body washed up on shore not far from the port and caused some talk. People were even saying that someone had supposedly seen the sailor attacked, and that they could easily identify the murderer. Galaction was particularly upset, started sweating, covered his bald spot with two napkins instead of one, paced worriedly among the tables, shouting that they needed to summon judges from the city. But, when Laurence told him that evening, "I did it out of longing for my wife, you're jerking me around," Galaction wasn't surprised and dryly called him a dumbass. "Your blood is fuming, seeking death," he added. "Why does it need to search?" Laurence snarled, "It seems like there's plenty, not just on the bottom of the sea, but even under the snow." "You got the bright idea of playing the fool," Galaction hissed, bugging out his eyes even more, "You want them to drag us all to jail tomorrow?" "Don't get smart, or I'll send you to the fish, too." Galaction wasn't frightened, but he didn't sleep at home that night, and when he came back before sunrise, he announced to his boarders, "Get moving, you can't stay here anymore; it's high time you got to work. Only, since there'll be extra expenses on account of your stupidity, Laurence . . ."—and he rattled off a string of new concessions

They loaded up the horses with boxes and marched for a long time along the shore road, then turned off into a thicket of cotoneaster, hid the boxes there, got their rifles, belted on their bandoliers, and continued their parade. The jackals that entertained the port nightly with their lament leapt now and then from the bushes and ran off, but there was no need to shoot them. After noon, when he heard a whistle, Galaction called a halt and a rest until evening

Not far away, a railway that cut across the savage land had been laid willy-nilly to join the regions that lay to the north and south, and along the sea so as to avoid the problems associated with passing over the mountains. Trains ceaselessly departed from certain debauched and flourishing cities for others just like them, slid into the woods and, cringing from the dreadful scenery, hurried to get beyond this district where the railway itself seemed, to the people who lived there, a silly, pointless gadget they never used, since they preferred their araba carts and their own feet

But no matter how natural it was in such a case to be wary of robberies, an unaccountable respect for the train secured it, since no one was daring enough to rob it. Therefore, Laurence's resolve to ascertain what rich people brought along and what the postal car contained was not only an innovation, but an exceptionally bold plan. The obligation to find out when the postal train would pass and the most convenient place to attack it had been laid on Galaction

Galaction could have sprung into action long ago, since his claim that the trains they wanted ran rarely was false. But he had decided to buy time for stipulating more things in his own favor. When Laurence suddenly did away with the sailor and sneeringly threatened him, Galaction, annoyed with the bandits and with himself, realizing that he had put too much heart into drawing things out, and certain that now, no matter what, they would outflank him, decided to act without delay

In the evening they went down to the railway bed and made it to the watchman's shack. Eliminating the watchman, his wife, and his small daughter was easy. Galaction was showing signs of agitation significantly beyond what was warranted. They let a train pass—it was the wrong one—took some crowbars they found at the watchman's and set off, some to twist rails, others to lug stones and arrange a bank across the tracks. Galaction took up lighting the fires necessary, as he explained it, for outwitting the engineer's vigilance

And yet the postal train, when it surfaced from beyond the bend, had no wish to topple over and stopped instantly before reaching the shack. That hadn't entered into Laurence's calculations or his accomplices', but there was no time for reflection. The highlanders took off running toward the steam engine, holding their fire for the moment. They were met with a barrage. One of the wennies sank slowly, sat for moment, and then fell over on his side. Laurence stopped, confused, and looked questioningly in Galaction's direction. But Galaction wasn't there. They had to respond shot for shot and move forward by crawling. There were evidently more defenders than attackers. Laurence ordered a halt to their senseless waste of powder, left one to keep shooting as a diversion, and led the rest on a flanking maneuver. Once they had determined that the return shots were coming from the engine and the cars just behind it, the highlanders decided to break into the train from the other end. But the doors were locked and the lights were out. It wasn't worth trying the windows and getting tied up in the passenger cars, that wasn't the main aim. Therefore, once they'd made a complete circuit, the gang charged the engine. The shooters hadn't counted on an attack from the rear and paid for their mistake with the engine. Laurence got through without losses and, after casting down several defenders while the rest retreated to the train cars, was on top. But more frequent fire came from the postal wagon and the following cars, and now in all directions. In short, they had captured the engine without gaining any advantage

Regardless of the heat of the action, Galaction's disappearance never left Laurence's head. Why was he running away? The bandit guessed there was some connection between his disappearance and the fact that the fires hadn't duped the engineer, and maybe even that the highlanders had encountered a barrage, but Laurence couldn't search out what it was, exactly. How long Galaction had been giving him the runaround! He'd been thinking about it, but never drew any conclusions. Meanwhile, they couldn't stay put on the engine and keep up their fruitless shootout with the rest of the cars. If the shooters hadn't yet made up their minds to take the offensive, they might work up their courage sooner or later. And if not, as long as they kept cool heads, they could easily hang on until morning or receive reinforcements even earlier. And retreating under those conditions in a strange land meant not escaping defeat and capture. They had to leave right away and admit the attack had failed

But once Laurence had rendered this wise decision, he flew into a rage like he'd never experienced in his life. To leave without achieving anything after months of planning and of humiliating, needless waiting in the port? When his goal lay just a few steps away? With one of his comrades killed? To return empty-handed and be the butt of everyone's jokes? And what about Ivlita? And the treasures for her, the point of the whole undertaking?

If Galaction were to turn up, if only, it would be rapture for Laurence to whack him. Thanks to this money-grubbing con artist, how many days had Laurence spent in the coffeehouse, footing a fabulously expensive bill for himself and his friends, and he'd been obliged to humble himself, hiding who he was! And why hadn't the train wrecked—had Galaction's fires warned the engineer instead of tricking him? The thought of betrayal was monstrous, but Galaction had boasted of being a seafarer, not a highlander, and Laurence had heard enough to know what sailors were like

Furious, Laurence delayed his withdrawal. When the night, half over, got fresher, he tried capturing the postal wagon. And he had already climbed up onto the roof, but it began to dawn on him that his hand was refusing to squeeze the trigger and hurt too much, shot through. There were more losses. Whistles that slipped between shots announced a new train's approach. More distant shots joined those close by. There could be no more delay. Laurence gathered his own, ascertained that no more had been killed, some were wounded, though not badly, and ordered a retreat. They carried the dead wenny

But the highlanders did not head for the mountains. They followed the same path they had taken the evening before with the owner of the coffeehouse. And the sun already stood high in the sky when they walked out to the shore and the town came into view

The coffeehouse was full, and Galaction was strolling among the tables with a satisfied air, narrating the night's current events: about how, not far from the port, a band of robbers who, it seemed, had met to make plans at these very tables, attempted to rob the postal train, but fell into an ambush, since they were expected, and were massacred. His effusions were interrupted by an extraordinary phenomenon

Four highlanders approached the coffeehouse, holding a stretcher cobbled from branches, on which lay a corpse covered in fiddlehead fern leaves. Behind the stretcher, with their hats off, several wennies were marching, carrying rifles and pistols, and Laurence, with bandaged hand, was bringing up the rear of the parade. Laurence passed to the front, coming closer to Galaction. Everyone turned toward the owner of the coffeehouse and saw that Galaction wanted to run, but could not, he was ready to fall down dead on the spot. "You motherfucker," Laurence screamed, "Say you didn't betray us." No answer came. "Cover his eyes," Laurence ordered. One of the wennies carried out his directive. "Take him to the dock." But when they grabbed Galaction by the arms, the condemned man, deprived of his only weapon—his eyes—tried to resist. He roared and howled, thrashed about, fell down, snatched at the earth, latched onto chairs. At last, they dragged him onto a gantry. Laurence demanded a rope. One of the customers hurriedly finished his coffee and ran off to bring one. They mastered Galaction and lashed him to the railing. "Gag him." The highlanders stepped back and shot, some sooner, some later

Then Laurence's accomplices came back, lifted the stretcher, and headed toward home. Several hundred people, crowding together by the coffeehouse, watched the bunch of toughs slowly recede along the shore until they turned out of sight

07

What a wind there was! It burst forth from under the earth, tossing up a prodigious weight of snow. Pines, whole forests of them, took off, with their roots. Along these expansive clearings the glaciers slid down unhindered onto the hamlet. But neither the crack of broken-up structures nor the screams of those crushed could pierce through the unheard-of blizzard

Ivlita, who had buried herself in the hay, lay for how long—hours, months, millennia, who knows—awaiting her hour. She'd never before suspected how unbelievably difficult dying was. Much more complicated than living. Had she alone been spared, had anyone else? Where was Laurence? From the moment Ivlita huddled into the corner, the reassuring voice had stopped wafting to her. Was it even now trying to shout death down?

Or do blasts only precede death, whereas *it* arrives silently? Most likely the latter. The roof no longer attempted to fly off, no one whipped the walls. Why so quiet, it would be better if the storm roared again, anything would be better, just not silence. What a trial—awaiting your final moments

But Ivlita did not die. Admittedly, she could not have assimilated this fact if the warm air that penetrated the chinks in the barn had not drenched her in resurrecting exhaustion. Ivlita calmed down, fell asleep, and when she awoke, could not tell for a long time where she was; not until the circumstances of the day when Laurence had abducted her appeared in her intelligence, her father's fury and curses and the love she shared with Laurence, interrupted by spring's onset and seemingly past its prime. What was wrong with her father? Who was looking after him? And where was Laurence?

Oh, if only her doom had freed her from hesitation and uncertainty! But Ivlita allowed with equanimity, and none of these left the slightest aftertaste, that Laurence might have thrown her over because he didn't need her, might be buried under the ice, or might simply have gone away on business. Did any of this matter to Ivlita? And she adamantly insisted: No, it made no difference to her

There, at home, filled with rapture, she had imagined love as something completely different. Could that imagined event really be brought to an end by a disturbance in the forces of nature? Could danger gain access to happiness? And, most important, was the phenomenon whose advent she had foreseen really not of the same order as the activity of mountains and waters, that is, infinite? And this satisfaction that had been taking form might have been engaging, but it was something else, a failed stand-in for her goal, a lie, which Ivlita had so stupidly credited

Caresses coursed with chills along her body. Spring had arrived, it was necessary to welcome it, to return to ordinary everyday life, in anticipation of true love. From this filthy shed where Ivlita had for too long been languishing, deceived, to rush back to the whimsical house. Would her father understand her? Forgive her? Of course. And although her neck had not forgotten his vise-like grip, Ivlita thought of the former forester with no trepidation

The growl of Jonah, one of the villagers, about whom Ivlita knew only that he had to urinate standing up, like it or not, after losing a leg during a bear hunt, while highlanders sit to do it, and that's the only way, brought her finally back to consciousness. "Dirty slut," he disgorged, "well, have you brought us good fortune with your unlawful sleeping around? Have you seduced Laurence to quench your abominable lust? Did you conquer him with your fucking beauty? Do you, coupled with death, think you won't get your comeuppance? Are you counting on your lover to defend you? But you even screwed him over and got him shot. And us, our homes? . . ." He drew closer, rearing up and waving his mitts. "Well, your case is clear, you're not even married, so you don't have the right to be a widow. For our common use, get it? That's how it works for any bandit's girl, and you've had it coming a long time. Well then, whore . . ."

There was nowhere to go. Ivlita wasn't frightened, she merely forced herself to enter into the meaning of Jonah's words. More abuse. But, really, he was right, she thought so herself. Those unpardonable blasphemies against rapture she was guilty of. That meant the storm had spared her to hand her over to Jonah. But did it make any difference?

And when Jonah started crawling in, Ivlita did nothing to defend herself. She looked at the beast with complete indifference, then turned her eyes away and sank into thought. Of course, she was guilty. Hadn't she been dreaming about Laurence from dawn until dusk and even in her sleep? Hadn't she been pumping the wennies for information about him on a daily basis? But had she really meant to work iniquity? Had she really earned endless humiliations and hardships? Certainly not, but how long would this drag on?

Jonah, however, once he'd leaned over her, lifted her skirts and seen her unbearable beauty, lost his nerve, shaded his eyes, and, shamefaced, limped back. Ivlita had plunged into expecting her new guest, but no one was there. Then she decided to go home. But before she stepped over the threshold, stones began flying at her. "Have no pity on her," Jonah was shouting to the highlanders, "This catastrophe's on her account, the witch. You can't even sleep with her, she'll cast a spell on you." One of the stones wounded her head.

Ivlita slammed the door and began piling everything she could find within reach against it. Stones knocked against the door and walls for a short time. The swearing and name-calling also died down with the knocking

Sinking, no longer able to hold back her bitterness, Ivlita shouted, thrashed around, tore out her hair. Only now did she realize how much she was bogged down in the human dregs, and humanity was the dung of the earth

And her thoughts returned once more to her father. He alone could be her consolation. Her father, in whose shadow she had led a crystalline life. If he were no more, everything would be stripped bare, turned to desert. Some people are drawn to people, others to things. Red admirals alight on flowers, and seeds fall and sprout. Ivlita had no one, and never would, except her father. Ivlita weeps

Her misfortunes were explained simply by her separation from him, not by the other reasons she'd discovered earlier. To return, therefore, and as soon as possible. Better to be beaten than to delay, death from parting was bitterer than any other

Ivlita scattered the furniture, flung the door open and ran out. The sky was so blue, and the sun so caressing, the plants so fresh and aromatic that the mournful aspect of the devastated hamlet was just an inconsequential trifle. From the heights, the lark that never lands on the trees sprinkled a trill of eternal return

Ivlita turned to head for her house, to run, to run . . . But the look of the lacy structure was so unnatural, even from afar, that Ivlita grew stiff as wood. The tower of the second floor topped, as before, the flat roof, but was hanging in midair. There was neither an upper nor a lower floor. The hummock was not a hummock, but a mountain of ice, and this ice had crumpled the outbuildings, now comical and pitiful, here sagging, there spread out completely flat. And the seemingly amusing spectacle was full of intolerable horror

The sensation of spring, the hamlet, and the highlanders standing a little way off disappeared, replaced by the sensation of running,
and Ivlita regained consciousness only at the place where her yard
had once been. But what had happened to the fence behind which
Ivlita grew up and lived her life, which would be no more; she had
known happiness she couldn't bring back. Fragments, ruins. Ivlita
clambered up onto the pile, kept closing her eyes and opening them
again, hoping to find anything that had been spared

She didn't think at first of her father. She couldn't entertain
even the thought of his presence here, amid the chaos. But a
strange object, half covered with snow, roused her curiosity. Ivlita
approached and studied it. Her buried father was dozing and taking
his repose in the snow

Ivlita had suffered too much to lose heart yet again. She just
turned away and shuffled off. Even without tears. To the wennies
who caught up to her, she said: "There lies my father. I don't know
when he died. In all likelihood, some time ago, and I missed it. Bury
him, please. I've already mourned him once and lost him by doing
so. It's not seemly for a murderer to remain with the victim"

As she passed by Jonah and his accomplices, who had not yet
dispersed, but were no longer making any move against her: "You
are right, at least in that portion of your accusation that concerns
my father's death. You may, therefore, judge me a parricide"

Jonah tried to mock her. "You think you don't have anything
to deal with," he drew out a laugh, "except sorting out your relationship with your father? That doesn't quite cut it. It looks like
everyone's facing enough work rebuilding the hamlet not to waste
time on you. True, like a hothead, I wanted to kill you just now. But
I wasn't thinking about getting revenge for your forester, but for
the insult. On second thought, however, I've decided to wash my
hands of you, since the avalanches rolling in are the best guarantee
there won't be any more deaths . . ." As for everyone's right to her,

not a word about it. Ivlita shrugged her shoulders and set off to the old wenny's

The old wenny was busy in his yard, near his house, the only structure spared by the storm, not counting the cretins' stable, and pretended not to notice Ivlita. He was actually listening carefully, kept track of her out of the corner of his eye, never ceasing to putter about. Ivlita was looking for protection with him, with an elder. Her father had perished, Laurence, too, most likely. Jonah and the others had just now wanted to beat her. But when she demanded a verdict, they abstained. Since she's not certain that if she stays in the hamlet and the wenny goes out to the pastures, they won't attack her again (while the women wouldn't dare intercede for a bandit's lover, even if they agreed to admit her to their society, which would be a singular courtesy on their part), Ivlita even begs the wenny to take her along to higher altitudes

Ivlita's request could not be fulfilled. Women, not just in view of their imagined weakness, do not frequent the pastures. Their presence there is just as undesirable as in the army, diminishing valor, readiness for self-sacrifice, and intuition. The beings lurking in the ravines and around the glaciers, now and then manifesting themselves to the shepherds, are sufficient proof that when spirits desire to harm a man, they need only incite him to love. And since, although highlanders much excel the earth's other inhabitants in purity and perfection, they are not entirely delivered from human flaws, for they, too, sleep with their wives, then, so as not to sink completely to the common level, it behooves them to spend a third of the year in chastity on the heights. And even if the presence of a single woman cannot lead all the shepherds to break the rules, it will introduce temptation, and then there will be no end to coupling with spirits and goats. And the wenny would not be able to prevent the shepherds from coveting Ivlita, all the more so because Ivlita was a bandit's widow, unwed, and must enter into common use

The stupor left Ivlita, and the words that she was, so to speak, generally available dribbled even from the wenny's lips to no purpose. A possession in common utterly like the moon and airy matter? However alluring this was, the cosmic enthusiasm in Ivlita had gone out, irrevocably. Now, she was not so naïve. Why should she be likened to eternal things, when her father had perished, her home was in ruins, and Laurence was gone? She alone was obliged to settle accounts for everyone, in order to prove that death is not death, but a miraculous transmutation. No, the others had died, and Ivlita along with them. No one had any right to her at all, since she was not of this world. The hamlet's laws deserved respect, but nature deserved more, and that these were not one and the same was clear, for the hamlet, notwithstanding the cretins' protection, had not been spared. Being an honorable widow is a law of nature; after an ill-starred love you want no other. A second love is unnatural

What did it matter that Laurence had been a bandit? And Ivlita grew ardent, quarreled, noted that she had passed from self-defense to defending her lover, and, consequently, justifying his murders. And the once-menacing moral world engulfed her anew in smoke, beyond which she couldn't distinguish a thing. Ivlita faltered. She was right only if Laurence was right, and if Laurence was right, then bear law was no worse than human law, and that meant Laurence and Ivlita were absolved of the murders, and the opposition between Ivlita and morality was no accident, but rather Ivlita, in her very existence and beauty, negated bedrock human precepts. And if that were so, could the wenny really judge her, when he considered highland statutes superior to lowland statutes only insofar as they were closer to animal statutes? No, Ivlita would not submit. Whether here or there, she would resist, weapon in hand

The wenny didn't just watch her, he devoured her. He was seeing this woman as was meet for the first time. No rules applied here, no, this wasn't a woman, but a sojourning feminine entity. And since the mountain ravines were swarming with her like, decidedly, adding one more wouldn't change a thing

And so when, several days later, the highlanders, after quickly fixing their dwellings, set off, all packed up, into the mountains, driving their goats and whistling shrilly, and proceeded up the canyon, making use of the remarkable bridges, Ivlita was bringing up the rear of the procession, armed with a rifle, although in this season none of the shepherds were carrying firearms, fearful of encountering the satyr, since the latter, having a goat's lower part, and an old man's above, attacks people only in the middle months of the year and when it sees a rifle, so it can sharpen its teeth on the barrel

What a journey! They were done with leaves and needles, ascended nearly to the sources of the stream that flows from the mercury lake in a narrow, but towering waterfall, so that the mercury, as it falls, has time to decay into water; they had to clamber up to the north along a damp clay outcropping. While the canyon hadn't yet been able to free itself from snow, higher up there was no longer any, all had melted away, well, just a little was left here and there. The sprouting grass was so juicy that the goats, after passing the winter on hay, refused to understand the journey's end had not yet been reached and they'd have to wait a while to relish it. Here were the last scattered junipers and thickets of rhododendron. The pastureland was beginning: long, narrow strips, bounded on the north by cliffs and glaciers that hid the summits themselves from view. It extended, dipping here and there, and then a stream, all in cascades, would cut across; or it rose, and to shift from one pasture to another, you'd have to surmount a wearisome col. That made movement so laborious that a day's travel equaled an hour's on the plain, and only after several nights of camping did the highlanders reach the hollow indicated beforehand by the wenny. Now they had only to emit a glottal sound and the goats would scatter over the grassy plots, risking descent right to the forest edge. In the evening, a labial sound compelled them to run back to the pen, jury-rigged out of branches. The next item of business after the pen was erecting huts, shelters for pails of milk and tubs of cheese. The highlanders themselves scorn huts and sleep wrapped in their cloaks, heedless of any cold or rain, under the open sky. When it really pours, they have to get up during the night, wring out their shirts, pants, and cloaks, and put them on again, perhaps several times

Their victuals: yogurt and cheese. Neither bread nor meat . . .

Ivlita, who had burst out of the hamlet for the first time, was too taken with her surroundings to suffer from all this. She was suddenly happy. Adversity, troubles, and the whole of intentional life had been left down below with the forest and the women. Here, you could laugh at hesitation and horrors. From now on, Ivlita would live like the shepherds: sleep all winter, and in spring take a stroll on a carpet of azaleas. The hard life is a fictitious life. Natural life is easy and cloudless

Once she'd grown accustomed to the pastureland, and the wenny, after elucidating everything, teaching her about the mountains and the mind, things you can't read in books, started repeating himself, Ivlita decided to find out what went on beyond the cliffs to the north. One day, she made an hours-long ascent along the glacial bed the wenny had christened the swallow's nest, until she reached a modest snowfield; from here she could see to the south not just the mountain where the wenny shot roe deer, but also the hazy outlines of the unfamiliar plain that lay beyond the mountain. Venturing next time to make an even higher ascent, Ivlita achieved a new field, more extensive and framed by crags, fettered in ice. A herd of turs drifted aimlessly over the snow, and Ivlita passed the day lying on a rock, observing the animals. But no matter how great her rapt admiration, when dusk began to fall and the herd started to leave, she raised her rifle and felled one of the beasts. What for? She didn't really know. Why such cruelty? Wasn't Ivlita imitating Laurence?

After all, she, too, was a murderer! But does a mirror reflecting something animate cease to be itself inanimate? Wasn't Ivlita's deed an exercise in futility, an attempt made with unsuitable means?

Unsuitable? A buck lay on the snow, its head bent back; blood was dripping from its muzzle. After lying there for a month or two, it would resemble the former forester

She couldn't fall asleep that night; it was too cold. There were the constellations slowly rolling across the heavens; they recede, fade, and only two greet the waning moon. The sky ruddies and soon flames up: the hour when barely perceptible fumes stalk over the mercury lake. No trace of fatigue. Ivlita perseveres and resolves to climb to the sky. She struggles with the ice sheets, now and then traverses tongues of snow that have become firm overnight, and cuts steps with her rifle butt. In the end, her rifle starts getting in the way. Ivlita leaves it in some crevasse and continues clambering up, clinging to every ledge. Sometimes it seems that if she stops for a moment, everything will collapse, so she crawls on until she reaches a shelf where she can imagine resting

The plain is already perfectly distinct. Bright rivers crisscross it, ending in an expanse that's just as bright. That must be the sea. Far, far away to the south, in the cloudless sky, are two cloudlets like crumbs. No, they're not cloudlets, they're snows, too, imprisoning the plain. That means there are still more mountains and Ivlita's not the only one struggling and prevailing

The heavenly orb was already falling when Ivlita reached the summit. She looked around. On the other side, the crest dropped off into an abyss, and in the abyss, fenced on all sides by ranges just like this one, lay paradise. She couldn't see the ground because of the shimmering of whitest wings, and managed only to make out that it was built over with white towers, where the wings flew in and out, and that it was crisscrossed by sky-blue streams. The streams merged into one, cascading into the abyss and then spouting back up in a fountain so majestic that its roar reached all the way to Ivlita. The wings exclaimed and exulted, except for one sitting by the fountain, preening. And Ivlita understood: it was a memorial for Brother Mocius

But the whirlwinds rose up, the mists rebelled and cloaked everything. In vain did Ivlita remain until twilight, hoping for the curtain to rise. And a second night passed without sleep because of the cold. In the morning, she had to hurry to the pastureland

With utmost difficulty, Ivlita descended to the upper field, crossed it, and was ready to mount the cliffs when a body of some kind that had slipped fell nearby. A tur? Ivlita hurried around a boulder. Before her lay a bloodied Jonah

"Ivlita, it's your fault I'm perishing," the highlander whispered when she bent over him. "I didn't dare when I had the chance, and I've been pining away ever since then. I've been stalking you relentlessly. I wanted to assault you, but, you see, it's hard without my leg"

"Jonah, don't die, darling, you mustn't. You must live. If you need me for the sake of living, take me, but don't die. Dying for love isn't worth it"

08

I f the city fellow with glasses hadn't shown up, the resumption of work at the sawmill would have brought on nothing new. They went back to cutting, planing, sawing, drinking away more at the tavern than they earned, and gossiping more than they worked. The hills and slopes were in bloom, even the cemetery was in bloom, and in place of snow, the almond tree now scattered its petals on the graves of the monk and the stonecutter

The little man arrived in a city carriage—God knows how he'd made it through on the local roads—and hired a room from one of the tavern keepers for an unspecified time after declaring to his host that he'd come to collect the butterflies called Apollos, so abundant in this locale, but, supposedly, not sufficiently studied, and after settling in, he actually did head off, armed with an enormous net, to ramble over the surrounding area. But in the evening, while he was dining in the tavern, he would listen attentively to what was being said around him, and when he caught Laurence's name uttered at one of the tables, approached those conversing and minted the most astounding news: "You're mistaken, comrades! Laurence hasn't been lost. He's just fighting his way slowly through ranks of police and their minions. But he'll be here, I assure you." And clasping his hands behind his back, the stranger turned around and exited

The next day, the drinking companions, on gathering together, had not yet managed to get to continuing their exchange of views as to yesterday's intervention by the butterfly lover when the tavern was rocked once more, and to a greater degree, by the advent of Laurence himself. No one had ever seen or expected to see him like this. He had grown up and into his manhood. His dark beard was not distinct from his face, dusty and sunburned. Of his splendid attire, only rags remained. His boots were torn, and only his rifle looked new. But there was such valor and magnificence in the whole setup that those in the tavern stood up and doffed their hats. Laurence, without replying, looked at them scornfully, passed through to the middle, and demanded food

The ensuing silence would probably have been broken by none present, despite the overwhelming urge each felt to address Laurence, but the new arrival, with his glasses and net, raced into the room, looked around, and when he noticed Laurence, rushed toward him with outstretched hand, jabbering: "Are you Laurence? I recognized you right away, though I've never laid eyes on you. Congrats. Glad to meet you. Basilisk. Just call me Basilisk. There *is* such an imaginary monster, but believe me, I resemble it in name only . . . You're golden, young man, and how! Don't get the idea it's just the government, we—I—we are also keeping tabs on you day after day as you push your way through, so elusive. And the folks here didn't have a clue, they thought you were a goner, the simpletons . . . We're all friends, right? Mine host, some wine! What kind would you like?"

Laurence had seen his fill of people during a month sitting in the port town and another month retreating. But he'd never met one like this. While the stranger's appearance was unimpressive, altogether small, round-shouldered, with a graying beard, and the net and glasses even made him comical, his eyes had such an iron cast that they immediately reminded Laurence of Galaction's, and he wasn't sure whose were more frightening. Just as then he had trusted solely on account of the eyes and paid handsomely, so now, also on account of the eyes, he couldn't just dismiss this little man, ridicule him, refuse to speak with him. The stranger gazed at him steadily, charmed him, and, without waiting for his reply, kept on speechifying

"You don't believe that not one detail of your remarkable retreat has slipped from my notice? And you're wrong not to. You ask how I know it all? That's my secret, for now. But I know not just that after executing the owner of the coffeehouse (a well-earned lesson for the traitor) you spent forty-eight hours shaking off gendarmes in the woods, laying out about twenty without losing anyone—the whole world knows about that—but also that afterward you were hidden in a cellar by a housewife who was boiling some nut jam when you showed up. Do you think she hid you because she was afraid of you? How wrong you are! What would it have cost her, when the police were literally digging everything up, to point out that you were, she might say, down below? And they would have nabbed you in no time . . . I'm the one who gave her the order to save you. There it is! And when her people carted you later to that cave where you managed to descend with the help of some ropes, who sent the ropes, if not us—in a word, me? And the warning that gendarmes were hurrying toward the village and that the only way out was by attending a church service, since the dimwits would never get the bright idea of bothering people at prayer, on whose orders, if not mine, was this thought suggested to you? And in that burg, who prompted you to head for the commandant's reception, not just to let the asses ransack the pub, but so you could meanwhile find out their further asinine plans—who gave you this assignment you so brilliantly carried out, if not me? Now you see I know a thing or two. And in step with your retreat, I arrived at such rapture not just because of your manliness, but also because of your active mind, that I hurried so we could meet and reason together. You are an Apollo, young man. We—I—can, along with you, accomplish such great deeds as no one ever dreamed of. Give me your hand in token of our alliance and friendship. I'll explain everything to you right away, and although you're very worn out from that long manhunt, we'll get to work tomorrow, since the matter brooks no delay. As it is, young man, you've taken too long pushing your way through"

This mysterious city fellow named Basilisk was speaking an astounding truth. Laurence assumed the adventures that followed his withdrawal from the port town had been a chain of accidental events, and explained the locals' help exclusively by his own influence. And now it turned out, someone unseen had been guiding Laurence and guarding him, someone unknown, but omnipotent, and it was *this* puny little man, a gabby butterfly collector. What was he after now, a reward for helping? Or maybe his spying was a game and Laurence had been allowed to get away so many times just to fall into a snare in his native village? Laurence grabbed his pistol. But Basilisk didn't let him think or act

"From how far can you hit a dog with a stone? One hundred paces? Excellent. How many of your comrades are fit for action? Quick, tell me, how many? . . . Fine, that's quite enough. I'll leave you for now and advise you to rest and catch up on your sleep. Come see me this evening, I'm staying upstairs right here in this building, and we'll come to terms. By the way, the police won't be any threat for another twenty-four hours. I arranged for them to be led off track and sent after a false trail. And in twenty-four hours we'll already be far from here. Isn't that right?" Basilisk turned on his heels and, waving his butterfly net, exited

For a long time after he was gone, Laurence couldn't get his thoughts in order. What did this unbelievable babbler want from him? Why did he want to use Laurence's strength and agility when, to hear him tell it, the upshot was, if Laurence had succeeded in anything at all, it was only thanks to Basilisk? And who would attest that this strange being didn't threaten him with the same thing Galaction had?

He, Laurence, had fled compulsory military service so as not to kill against his own free will. And what had come of it? Had he really wanted to kill Luke? Had he really wanted Galaction's death? Had he been free to choose his steps while falling back from the coast? Hadn't he been, right up to the present, goaded first by the stonecutter, then by the coffeehouse owner, and now by Basilisk? What worse servitude had he elected when he ducked military service?

By the sea he had blamed Ivlita, and for no reason, seeing in her an unwitting instigator. But now he was burning with desire to see her as soon as possible, and something, with only a few paces left to go, was driving him back. What was this power speaking through Basilisk's eyes? What was this new prodigy he had to contend with in order to win back his lost freedom? Ivlita didn't have anything to do with it. He, Laurence, was the one who had taken the wrong road, beginning with Brother Mocius

And unexpectedly, the tavern's customers, sitting around him, not daring to budge, seemed like family to Laurence; he wanted to embrace and kiss them all, call for an accordion, dance, bawl, and drink with joy that now, indeed, he had returned and seen his dear ones again, to recount his adventures deep into the night and vocalize together until dawn; to see, instead of snuffed-out faces, avid ones, catching every detail, to see a peasantry afraid *for* him, to sense that he was theirs, dear to them, that they were ready to defend him, lonely and weak, and make sure Galactions and Basilisks would not harm him

But Basilisk's disclosures killed any relish. The consciousness that he, Laurence, had been and was still a mere plaything rendered all his complaining hateful and all his criminal exploits wastrel. Why hadn't he been killed during the attack on the train or before that, during the attack on the post, or even earlier by gendarmes! You could taste and forget everything, as though none of it had ever been, emerge unharmed from irreducible agonies and consuming pleasures and sense death repeatedly. One thing did not pass without leaving a trace and, once settled, ate at his mind, bitterness alone, gnawing until it ruined him irreparably. And was ever there such bitterness

Bidding his landsmen farewell without even banqueting? And where was Ivlita, what happened to her, and how had he not yet asked about her? Laurence had only to pose the question and everyone reverently flocked together in haste. Ivlita? A number of people who'd been up there conveyed conflicting information. It was certain, in any case, that her father had been found dead in the ruins of his house, but had, apparently, died much earlier. Ivlita found him. They say she went mad. Everyone counted Laurence for lost, and bandits' widows, well, you know yourself. On account of her madness, mind you, it seems she was spared. Jonah, however . . .

The fellow who'd been speaking, before he could finish, flew into a corner from a terrific punch in the face. "Bull-fuck your mother!" roared Laurence, "I would have killed you, but I'm sick of getting dirty. You lie, tell me you're lying," but without waiting for a reply, he collapsed onto the table and started wailing like a professional mourner. The man he'd hit got up with some effort and, trying to wipe the blood from his eyes, muttered, "I don't know, that's what people say, don't take it out on me . . ." He was led away, supported under the arms, and the tavern emptied out. Even the owner stepped outside and left Laurence alone

It wasn't true, Laurence knew it was false—Ivlita wouldn't allow anyone, let alone Jonah, near her, even if she was a bandit's widow. But the shame she was slathered with just thanks to her situation glutted Laurence with brutal jealousy. Jonah, well, he'd sung his last aria.

On account of her madness, you say, they haven't slept together yet. But they forgot about him, Laurence? Lost, you say? What crap! And he grabbed his rifle and started shooting up the bottles on the bar, the glasses, all the glassware, riddled the ceiling, and ran out onto the square. Not a soul. Going on to waste more bullets, Laurence smashed all the windows he could see, shot up a flock of geese waddling near a puddle, wounded a pig that ran away squealing, and rampaged until he ran out of ammunition. He sank to the ground and lay there until dusk, just as lonely as before, in the dead-silent village. When it got dark, not a single light caught fire, neither in the sky nor in the windows. Laurence, after sitting up, stared for a long time into the darkness and listened intently, as though a sound or a ray of light would have been a support for him, when suddenly one of the upper rooms at the tavern was lit. The young man grabbed his rifle, but remembered he had no bullets left to shoot. In the light of the burning lamp, he recognized that morning's acquaintance. He could see Basilisk, hunched over with his hands behind his back, running around the room; he would come up to the window, glance out, and start running around again. Laurence watched the demon-possessed man, not merely without feeling any revulsion, but even drawn to him, ready to rely on him. He stood up, set off toward the tavern, groped his way in the dark for a while, until he made it to Basilisk's little room

When he heard footsteps, Basilisk forcefully threw the door wide open. He was frenzied and crackling with a speed exceeding that morning's: "You've gone nuts! Raising such a ruckus when the police are digging around the neighborhood. Even if they *hadn't* wanted to come calling, they'll probably drop in, and most likely before dawn, since your shots must have startled the whole surrounding area. I thought you were smart, Laurence, but get this, you're an ignoramus. I've just been to that baffling hamlet, wasted my whole afternoon making inquiries about your wife. She's out in the pastures with the old wenny, under no threat, and all the more since I arranged to let her know that you're alive and well. And you, instead of changing your clothes—take a look at yourself—got up to the devil knows what on account of some groundless gossip. Still, it's good you came here, or I wouldn't know where to look for you— these swine, your fellow villagers, are such cowards that no one wanted to go out looking. And if you hadn't shown up, rest assured, young man, this time you wouldn't have outrun the police, out here in the boondocks, they wouldn't hesitate to shoot you down to spare you from judicial red tape and unsound prisons

"Sit down and listen," Basilisk went tearing on, incessantly pac-ing. "I would have liked to explain everything at leisure, humanely, but now there's no time," and, after pulling his watch from his vest: "We have no more than an hour until our departure. It's a matter of looting, you see, but not the train, we'll take the train to do the looting. We need to relieve the administration of a much larger sum than you can imagine, and not a load of gold, even, since gold is too heavy to offer much value, but a load of paper money, incompara-bly lighter. The administration keeps its money in houses you have no notion of, but you'll soon get familiar with, called treasuries. So I'm inviting you to take part in looting the treasury. Get it? Now, here's the plan. The treasury lies *in* the city, consequently, you and your comrades are riding with me *to* the city. Further: I can't say exactly how much money we might get our hands on, but your cut will be one tenth. Although the share I'm offering you is modest, it's entirely fair when you take into account that, first of all, we—I—we are taking upon ourselves all preparations for the operation and are supplying you, so to speak, with the means of production; second, we will take all measures to guarantee against your capture and get you into the mountains. And third, and this is the most essential point, since the matter has to do with the progress of the party"

Basilisk stopped pacing and broke off his speech to see what impression it produced on Laurence

"Now, give me your undivided attention. The party is a society something like your association with the wennies, but more many-headed and in pursuit of somewhat different goals. You take money from those who have it or from the administration in order to enrich yourselves. We strive to take everything from the rich so there won't be any rich people and everyone will be equally poor. You liquidate bureaucrats, since they harass you; we want to liquidate the bureaucracy, since the system it upholds leads to the emergence of rich people, and so the bureaucracy eradicates us. You don't give a hoot what goes on in the world; you sit in your den and only go out after spoil. Our only concern is the world, where we want to establish equality and expedient coercion. You seek freedom, but necessity propels you, the party strives for what is necessary and is therefore free. Even if you don't understand this last point, I hope, all the same, it's clear we have a common enemy, and so our collaboration is entirely admissible"

Walking up to Laurence and taking advantage of the fact that Laurence was seated, the little man placed his hand on Laurence's shoulder and enthusiastically continued: "Laurence! A great exploit awaits, you alone are worthy of it. You will recover the loss that was Galaction's fault and will fall under the protection of the mighty party. The history of your retreat vividly demonstrates how valuable this patronage is

"Now, change your clothes. Here's your outfit: as you can see, I've given it some thought. As for the wennies, they escorted me to the hamlet and I relayed in your name that they should be ready and waiting behind the church

"Regarding your wife: believe me, you'll already be back before she has time to come down from the pastureland. You understand there's no sense returning empty-handed," Basilisk concluded, emphasizing each syllable, and rushed out of the room

At last! And Laurence, instead of changing, collapsed on the cot. What a flood of words, and he'd understood almost none of it. But Basilisk's eloquence had a refreshing effect. There was no refusing, he'd have to give it a try; anyway, it was more amusing messing around with this smooth talker than with hillbillies. And then there was the new ambit, with new and very promising possibilities

And Laurence felt himself brought to boiling at the thought of new crimes. He'd just managed to return, but after so many shoot-outs, he felt like fighting again, no longer retreating, but attacking, murdering, again and again. Once upon a time, he'd failed to get rich, now he would succeed

"What are you lolling around for?" Basilisk screeched, hurrying in, "The gendarmes are already in the village," and he rushed over to blow out the lamp. "They can't find their bearings yet only on account of the pitch darkness, and since no one's out and about"

But on this point Laurence needed no prompting. After scooping up Basilisk, he ran down the stairs and, without dropping his burden, raced to the church. Behind the church, the wennies actually proved to be assembled and ready, and the company made its way toward the forest, where they could wait out the night in safety. From there they could hear, first, firing, then shouts, and then, through the foliage, they began to make out purple: the police, frustrated that they didn't happen to catch their prey and that now they never would, since he had reached the mountains, decided to console themselves by resorting to pillage and arson. Basilisk forsook his garrulousness. The others were also silent. Laurence broke the silence:

"I cannot, Basilisk, stay here doing nothing while that's happening there. Our flight is shameful. It's paying me tribute, the village, *and* it's *my* village. I ought to defend it—my people are there. I'll be back, wait until morning"

"Don't you dare make a move." Basilisk became upset, recovering his seemingly dried-up eloquence, "The deed and the party await you, you're obliged. And where do you think you're going—you have no weapons, the enterprise might end lamentably, and then ours, too . . ."

But Basilisk's eyes were not visible in the night, and he had no power over Laurence. Laurence was already leaving, lost with the wennies in the darkness

Basilisk remained alone and, walking in circles around a tree, kept on talking to himself: "Fool, you think, 'They're my people, it's my village.' But I swear, when they thought you were dead and gone, they drank up ten times the quantity of brandy in their joy. You wanted to play at being noble, what a sentimental soul. And this taking a stand for them will end with them selling you out first chance they get. Naïve man, better not butt in. Such a splendid deed lies before you, but this, you can have it: dust, dreams, enthusiastic rapture . . ."

The shooting would die down, then pick up, and suddenly went quiet. The east was turning pink, and it was impossible to say whether the village was still burning or had already burned to the ground. But before the sun wheeled up, Laurence returned. He looked satisfied and exhilarated. "Well, finally," Basilisk shouted, "You, I should point out, are making us wait inordinately, going off after small potatoes, young man. Hurry up, let's get out of here . . ." They got going

On the way, Laurence told how, when he got back to the village, he had gathered the peasantry, rustled up some weapons; and the gendarmes hadn't finished rioting when they were lured, with their leader, into an ambush near the sawmill and massacred to the last man. "Not bad, right?" quipped Laurence, glancing into Basilisk's cold eyes. "And without your help . . .

"But don't think I did it just from pride," he tacked on. "While the administration fusses here, we'll have less worry taking care of your business"

09

The city where Basilisk and Laurence alighted was situated on the slopes of a mountain that first fell off steeply, then descended in terraces toward a pitiful river choked with sand. Over these terraces a net of magnificent quarters was cast so that if you looked at the city from the opposite bank, where its suburb was located and the railway station down whose very steps the gang had descended, the city seemed to lie in the palm of a hand. The city was exceedingly beautiful for its gardens, little houses, shops, but its chief attraction was the endless boulevard, simply called the Grand Boulevard and divided into two unequal parts. The first, long and broad, was accessible to all modes of transport—reckless automobiles, streetcars, buses, carriages, cyclists sped along, concerned only with squeezing by and disappearing in flight. The second part, ridiculously short and narrow, was closed to all hustle and bustle and, reserved for horse-drawn vehicles, not only bore a sign, "at the walk," but was paved so that any horse that deviated from the rules would immediately slip and fall. People who had skipped along the first part would reverently throng here, eyeing the way the flowers of virtue went driving, back and forth, in open calashes, from morning 'til morning, since driving for display was the chief civic virtue. And since the succeeding virtue was gluttony, the gawkers, in order to pretend that they were party, as they said, at least to this virtue, reared their heads up all day, picking their teeth, although they never ate anything

At the end of the boulevard was a square, all decked with boutiques, where the treasury building also hulked among the mansions

Basilisk, after pointing out to Laurence the valuables displayed in the windows, declaimed: "You won't find riches like these anywhere. And they say there's no woman in the world more beautiful than your wife. Look, if we pull off the job, you'll be able to come here and buy everything your heart desires." And when Laurence gave a mocking and impudent look in reply, he added: "Only no monkey business, especially now; be patient," and dragged the bandit away from the rings and earrings glittering behind glass

"Better have a look at that," the little man went on, striking a pose facing the traffic on the square and along the boulevard. "If you were conversant in the science of economics, if you kissed your belief in spiritual things goodbye once and for all, stopped being so naïve, the meaning of this marketplace, supposedly so sophisticated, when it's actually simple and instructive, would appear to you right away

"I will try, nevertheless, to explain a thing or two for you, and if, by chance, you don't grasp my words, don't interrupt, just hear me out to the very end, especially because a listener is, for me, the greatest of pleasures

"Well then. In the monetary system, of which this marketplace is the exponent, everything is defined by two actions: buying and selling. In so far as the desire to own, otherwise known as demand, equals the desire to provide, that is, supply, the monetary system exists in a state of stable equilibrium, and it's not for you or for us to cause it any harm at all. But gradually the thirst for selling, and therefore also for selling oneself, outstrips the hunger for acquiring—the system starts rotting and voilà, in the end a certain effort suffices to send it all to hell

"That everything here is for sale won't be news to you. But you should understand that every person here is possessed by a passion to be for sale. We won't even speak of woman, an outmoded phenomenon. But take young folks, they no longer seek out merchandise to sell, they offer themselves, usually to men, occasionally to women. Then the age arrives when you can't sell your front or backside even at a loss, and the bourgeois marries or acquires a friend so that he can trade his wife or friend. Those are the calashes where husbands offer their wives. See those two women, one older, one younger; the older satisfies her needs by trading her little friend. The time comes when you can't even trade your wife at a loss—you can move on to your children. That's the reason people here raise children. That said, those being sold get up to all kinds of tricks trying to turn the tables on their sellers and frequently pull it off

"You'll say: That means something's still being bought? Obviously! But only to be resold. And even if there's a limited number of utterly crazy people who don't sell anything and don't aspire to sell, they're branded as parasites and exterminated by any available means . . .

"Do you understand now why the boulevard is so honored while other parts of the city are deserted? Why the treasury has been sited precisely here?

"This system is corrupt unto abomination and we will destroy it. But behold, just when everything's ready to fall apart, by the ultimate contradiction, in place of a human being dying of thirst to be sold, a prodigal dying with the desire to squander arrives. You, Laurence, imagine you're a peacock from the highland thieves' nests, and that's all, but you're the monetary system's fledgling—you, dying with the desire to spend as lavishly as you can. Therefore, you're money's greatest foe and our fellow traveler. And I hurried after you into the mountains, convinced—what you will accomplish no one else can do"

Was the highlander listening to him? Rapt by the scent of perfume that had filtered from the shops onto the street and mixed with the scent of feminine sweat, Laurence narrowed his eyes, sank into sweet languor, and the deeper he sank, the more authentically Ivlita grew before him. And no matter how alluring was the luster of carriages, this scent he had never before experienced took the upper hand, and Laurence didn't just shut his eyes, he covered his face with his hands

"We're leaving, Laurence," Basilisk unexpectedly announced. "You've seen enough. It's time to get down to business"

Dusk was already manuring the earth, but the boulevard, once it was lit, did not permit keeping tabs on the sky as it dimmed above the houses and trees. The young man maintained his silence. Basilisk's blabbing wasn't conducive to conversation. Desires swelled and pressed on his heart. Once again, Basilisk was right. Laurence didn't know *what* he'd do if all this belonged to him. But he really did want it all, and what he'd do next didn't matter any more. A short time ago, he'd been inclined to blame Ivlita for his need to rob. But now, the desire for seizing and snatching ruled in its own right, unrestrained and inexplicable. It was just a few hours since they'd arrived, but it already felt, to Laurence, like the rigmarole here was the same as at the seashore. And he hurried Basilisk along

They hadn't crossed more than a few streets when the fancy houses gave way to shacks and the avenues to incredible back alleys and dead ends. Now and again, they had to swerve around a stiff cat or dog or a pair of brawling, drunken women. In the light of the streetlamps, the bandit surveyed the locals with revulsion. Emaciated, hunchbacked, reeking of urine, pustular, with putrefied faces, the inhabitants sat in their doorways, scurried from gate to gate, or defecated by the walls. Surprised that Basilisk wasn't talking, Laurence demanded clarification. But the little man no longer chattered, just answered quietly and concisely: "This is death.

It's for sale here at every step, presenting itself in the form of bottles of rotgut, card games, skirts, and rats, urging people to steal, poison themselves, commit crimes. Granted, I can see all this is artifice, the horror purposely maintained for the sake of the very same selling, but it makes me a little uneasy that the masters of the situation are so relaxed about trading in death

"Just think, Laurence, to be death's votary, to kill whenever you feel like it—your most cherished dream—this is an excellent thing. But here they make people kill not just in war or when they're putting down a rebellion. No, husbands are obliged to shoot their wives so the papers have something to write about, carriages run people over so there's something happening, poor people are obliged to be criminals and provide a chance to exercise false justice. And all just because death is an item for sale like everything else. And even though I know the cause of it all is, yet again, that very same monetary system (may it be cursed countless times), I can't help wincing when I think how monstrous today's overproduction of death is"

Basilisk stopped, cleared his throat, and continued sarcastically:

"Laurence, from your tale of how you massacred the police in the village, I grasped that you were insulted by my revelations about the party's help. You don't want to be guided. It's beneath your dignity. But, alas, don't be misled, don't imagine you're free. No, even your splendid death-dealing capacity is a fruit of the overall arrangement of things. You killed Brother Mocius because the plains perverted you, and the plains are perverted by the boulevards. And the clump of deaths keeps growing because death is what you sell, 'cause you, without noticing it, are not death's votary, you're a merchant of death. Might the party purchase of you several deaths for a suitable remuneration?"

The hotel they entered, fetid to a rare degree, was sunk in near-total darkness. When they had finally surmounted the stairway, on which two could not pass, the little man left Laurence standing in a corner and went into a room lit by a single candle where several bearded men were gathered around a table; their faces, already indistinguishable, were obscured by glasses and hats. Basilisk took a seat without greeting them and rapped out: "Everything's cleared up. The deed will take place day after tomorrow and, consequently, tomorrow will have to be spent in idleness. Since the police suspect something's up, I've taken measures so some of the comrades will let themselves be arrested tomorrow in possession of the tools of the crime, which will finally untie our hands. Martinian will do the throwing, no one besides him will be on the spot. The meeting is adjourned." He stood up, went out into the corridor, took Laurence by the arm and purposefully led him outside. Those who remained conversed for a long time and finally parted ways. One of the attendees first took one route, then turned around and walked back to a house where the chief of police was waiting for him

The following twenty-four hours passed for Laurence in a tiresome ramble around the city with Basilisk, all the more annoying because both had to be transformed, to glue on beards, squeeze into tight clothing and collars and carry a cane Laurence didn't know how to handle. Then Basilisk talked a lot more than he needed to and the prim highlander decided, whenever he got the chance, to show the little man that he was not always right

Basilisk made Laurence carry out such tasks that now and then the latter was ready to lash out. But Galaction's exhortations had not been vain and there was no need to argue. First the companions stopped by some kind of rooms where women, for the most part, were sitting and drinking tea, then they loitered around some stores, buying all kinds of rubbish and asking to have it delivered to houses that didn't exist, or rode from one end of the city to the other. From time to time, Basilisk noticed a familiar face, quickly turned away and pulled the young man after him. After a dinner at which Basilisk didn't allow Laurence to eat anything (explaining that Laurence didn't know how to handle a knife and fork) and ordered the waiters to give him only a shot glass of some kind of medicine, assuring them that his companion had already eaten, the comrades wound up in a new eatery, where people were dancing among the tables, but in a somehow peculiar way, and the music was vertiginous. Nothing resonated with Laurence, he had seen too much, it tired him and was monotonous to the point of nausea. In the evening they went somewhere beyond the city limits, to a garden where the music was real, his own kind, everyone was carousing, singing and drinking, naked women rolled their bellies and shook their breasts, and Laurence was ready to drink and go off to make use of one or two, but Basilisk again prevented him. What slavery! Then again, presumably *this* is expedient coercion

In the garden, some flower girl whom Basilisk called Anna revealed that the arrests hadn't taken place and the police knew the attempt was set for tomorrow. Basilisk gave a self-satisfied smirk and bought the most wilted bouquet; then they went back to the city. The house they now entered, extraordinarily magnificent, decorated throughout with gilt, marble, and paintings, was the most respectable house of assignation in the city. In a huge hall, with a fountain and plants, dozens of naked women were sitting. Laurence flushed, ready to pounce, but Basilisk detained him and chose one of the women, informing the madam they would share one. They quarreled for a long time. When they were led off to a room with a bed for six, the woman did not lie down, but recited a whole speech, whose meaning wasn't entirely clear, but which concluded with some indications about the following day. Laurence was no longer surprised, just confused. He wanted to sleep, he was tired of the whole thing. If Basilisk tormented him any longer, Laurence wouldn't be good for anything. They left, drove to the train station, bought tickets, took their seats on a train, but immediately got out and went to the nearest hotel. There, in one of the rooms, the comrade who had been the night before with the chief of police was waiting for Basilisk. The little man greeted him with a smile. Laurence, as soon as he saw a cot, crashed without waiting for an invitation or undressing

When Basilisk woke him, it was still night. Yesterday's comrade was lying next to him. "Don't wake him, he's dead," Basilisk snapped. "I suffocated him during the night. I'll tell you why later." They crawled out the window onto the neighboring roof, then dropped from there down into the yard and went out into the street. After a short trip down some alleys they knocked at a closed beer hall, where they were offered a room for the night. But Laurence could no longer sleep in the company of Basilisk, who took the liberty of killing his friends in their beds. More than once, the bandit felt like leaping on his companion, who also lay sleepless in his own corner. Day seeped into the room at a revoltingly slow pace. Finally, every object could be distinguished, and so Basilisk's unblinking eyes were also visible

What if the episode with Galaction was repeating? And Laurence determined not to do anything hotheaded so things wouldn't fall apart a second time. His stomach churned most of all because of the changes in Basilisk, because he had lost the magician's outwardly carefree attitude, he talked less and was smirking, letting the silence soak up his malice and pique. Now, genuine hatred flashed in the little man's eyes, and Laurence could not detect the reason for it

The hours of waiting were disrupted by a knock at the door. Someone entered the room. "Here's Martinian," Basilisk spoke through his teeth. Laurence turned around and couldn't keep from exclaiming

How old was this person who came in? No older than himself. The same height, same oval face, tender, the beard untouched by a blade. But his mien, the set of his head? Laurence saw it was his own mien, his own qualities, but not as they were now. Now, without a doubt, he had molted, become fleshless, become effeminate. This fellow was headed for certain death without hesitation or doubts, while he, Laurence, was scheming, cautious, and only faintheartedly postponing his finale. And suddenly the bandit had made up his mind to search out the exact year, month, and day he ceased being Martinian. But, God knows from where, a previously unfamiliar resolution surged over him: it wasn't worth finding out; and then exhaustion, unexpected and insuperable. And Laurence obediently gave in, no longer thinking, just watching, enraptured, and keeping an eye on the way Martinian walked catlike around the room, made broad gestures, spoke in a whisper, and his speech dripped, accentuating the silence. Only when Basilisk began shaking Laurence and shouting: "It's time to wake up, what's wrong with you, what are you doing, sleeping?" did Laurence shake off the enchantment. He got up, went out, without speaking, to the street, where he found a waiting calash. He got in and set off across the entire boulevard toward the spot

What was this mysterious attack of sentimentality? Now, Laurence was already recalling his childhood—he saw his parents' house, his first playmates, their pranks, antics, games. But he, Laurence, wasn't taking part in them, it was he, Martinian, Laurence before . . . Before what, exactly? But "it's not worth it" resurfaced, and then a thousand dear details flashed by—the stocky oaks he climbed, looking for squirrels; the ruins of the fortress where he hunted smooth snakes; the well with water not fit for drinking, but full of frogs; and in the copse, the horned owl's indispensable cry: "Snooze, snooze." The bumblebees' nest under the balcony and the nightingales in the jasmine. Nest wrecker. Laurence, by rights, deserved the nickname. How often had it been left to him to shinny up tall poplars in order to take newly hatched jackdaw chicks from their nests

The calash stopped. Without feeling the ground, as though floating on air, Laurence found himself at a glass door, opened it, and
made his way in to a hairdresser

The police knew perfectly well that a robbery was in the works,
and the party also knew that the police knew. But, since the police
didn't know about the latter fact, and the only comrade who could
have warned them went on sleeping under pillows at the hotel near
the train station, everything proceeded as planned. On the square
at noon, a shipment of bank notes was to arrive from the train station for delivery to the treasury. The delivery appointment had been
neither canceled nor delayed, for the police had determined to let
the attackers finish off the guards and then to capture the criminals
on the spot, which allowed them to resort to summary execution
(impossible in cases of preemptive arrest), and such a pleasure was
worth sacrificing a few hides

Since he'd wound up at the hairdresser's, Laurence turned to one
of the salesgirls and requested two packages of soap. He received
them, turned around, but did not walk away, remaining near the
door. He saw that the police had stopped traffic and a procession
had appeared: a dray was crawling along incredibly slowly, as though
on purpose, surrounded by soldiers and bearing a long box—not a
box, but Brother Mocius's coffin. And when the dray drew up even
with the hairdresser's, an explosion suddenly burst and shattered
the hairdresser's windows. In the unimaginable turmoil that arose,
he could make out that the wagon had overturned, someone was
running toward it, frequent shots rang out and people were falling,
that the crowd first tore at Martinian, then bent him to the ground
and trampled on him. Laurence saw how the pavement under the
feet of the guardians of public order turned scarlet, and then blood
flowed in fine streams in all directions. But he went on loitering, just
as rapt, thinking neither of his accomplices nor of their murders. He
wanted only to encounter Basilisk, shove him onto his back, and

trample him so the little man's blood would flow in streams just the way Laurence's blood was flowing

The dray was finally righted, the dead horse was taken out of harness, the sacred coffin was hoisted up. Now people—some military, some not—were already dragging the catafalque across the square to the treasury

Still haunting the shattered door, Laurence swung his arms out and threw a package of soap. It described a magnificent arc in the air and landed on the coffin. And Laurence heard nothing more, but saw the catafalque flung, together with the people attached to it, into the sky. Then the explosion reached him, so powerful, he was amazed the mansions withstood it. The guards were swept clean away, without a trace. The wennies, who jumped out from somewhere, dipped their hands into the smashed coffin. In a moment, they were already running away. Some belated shots rang out in pursuit

And suddenly Laurence beheld the Basilisk on a corner not far away, rearing, coiled, and licking its lips with its forked tongue

Laurence beat his wings once more and threw the second bomb

10

Now the day of the great hunt was approaching. A break from day-to-day life and a contest in daring, just enough carnage to knock the stuffing from the beasts for a whole year

Hunting small game is a run-of-the-mill task for a highlander. Taking his rifle, he wanders around in solitude from October on into June, dragging home whatever comes his way, but the snow and tracklessness don't much favor him. In the middle of the year, when it's customary to shoot rifles only at people, there is no small-game hunting, in general. Only once, after the second full moon, does the populace gather en masse, not excluding the women, to participate in the great hunt. The children sit at home for forty-eight hours, locked up with nothing to eat, and the same lot falls to the goats, driven into their pens

In order to participate in the great hunt, you must possess a quality native to every highlander—the ability to run effortlessly uphill and swiftly make your way through impassable thicket. You need to wield just one very singular weapon—a highland quarterstaff made of ash. You have to know what and when to shout

A flatlander has not the slightest idea how to shout in the mountains. When he's conversing, a highlander is already deafening. But if he shouts with all the force of his lungs and throat, his cry will carry an extremely long way through the canyons, amplified by its reverberating echo. And since a highlander's hearing is exceedingly acute, it's possible, with a favorable wind, to carry on a conversation between the pastureland and the cornfields

Therefore, on the great hunt, it's no trouble for the most distant hunter, using others to transmit his message, to notify the entire region covered by the hunt about whatever he needs to. Cries, normally throaty and only rarely accompanied by a whistle, which the wind mimics too closely, are, however, of quite different characters and convey, first of all, the nature of the beast a hunter has found. A supplemental cry tells whether the beast itself has been seen or could only be heard moving, whether a hunter happened on just tracks or a hole or a den. Some more cries, and everyone knows, based as often as not on nothing more than tracks, what kind of beast, its age, its notable features . . . And then it's already being communicated whether the beast is ambling off or charging directly into battle. There are also briefings as to the hunter's identity and location. And while the hunt is going after one animal, they flush out others, pursue them, lose them, and find them; when people attack or keep an animal at bay, they perish—for every detail and every human or animal ruse there is a particular tone, such that an observer initiated into the tongue and endowed with an ear can, without seeing anything and attending only to the exchange of shouts, compose a most detailed report on the hunt's progress and append what each participant accomplished

In addition, the beasts, from rabbits to snow leopards, are sorted by degree of importance, and while pursuing a low-level beast, if a higher-level beast is flushed out or its tracks are discovered, it's customary to give up the first for the sake of hunting the second

The quarry is dragged to one of the stations and divided by the chairman of the great hunt, who has lifetime tenure. The old wenny had been carrying out these duties for many years

And although Ivlita's absence—God knows where she'd headed off—worried the old man, he could, in view of the approaching full moon, neither send anyone to look for her nor delay the hunt. The highlanders had already spent a whole week hauling firewood from the forest, arranging it along the edges of the glaciers so that, when the wood flared up, it would form a chain of fires along the passes, unbroken as far as possible, stretching down into the valley, crossing over to the opposite slope, and describing a ring from which, until the fires went out, no beast could break free. Wherever water or cliffs broke the chain willy-nilly, ferocious dogs were positioned on the heights, never leaving the places they were left, and on the canyon floor, in the woods, where a forest fire would be unavoidable, women were armed with mallets and battledores for scaring off the beast

Darkness eventually closed in, they set off to light the bonfires, and it was not yet midnight when the range of mountains standing over the unpronounceable hamlet burst into flame. Until morning, the women beat tin plates. Now the sky has turned garnet red, and the men launch a centripetal attack, whooping and ululating. They're already broadcasting the news that they've flushed out a fox over there; here, they've encountered turs. The fox was foolish enough to swiftly hide in its den and was dug out alive, while the tur is unsuitable prey for the great hunt. After that, there was no news for a long time, as though the beasts, quitting the canyon in multitudes before the hunt, had escaped this time en masse. A shout from the pastureland guard reported that after the hunters' descent a pair of stray wolves had crept out of the forest, tried to get away over the ice, but was captured by the dogs. This news didn't cheer anyone

But now the highlanders had passed through the band of firs and let it be known from all points that they were entering the deciduous forest. Significant, exciting information began to come in.

At first a bear, a young one, tried to run away, but was compelled to turn around and earned a pike in the belly, it died, but mauled the hunter, and he was howling for help. Another hunter who discovered a she-bear with cubs had, evidently, even worse luck, since no messages from him, except for the news that, as he said, a female bear was attacking, had come in

There were lots of bears that day, battles ensued particularly often, once the hunters began to join up in pairs and trios. They had to rejoice that fewer vines would be spoiled that year. But there were almost no deer, only they chanced upon Crucifix once again, which outweighed all other events in importance

Crucifix was the nickname the highlanders had given an old buck (peerless for the size of his antlers) they'd been chasing for many long years, and without success. There were hunts when Crucifix never showed himself, since he'd left for neighboring forests, but after a year or two he would invariably return to tease the hunters. This time, he appeared to one of them out of thin air: the highlander was crossing a meadow in the fog, the mists parted, and the elusive creature stood at something like thirty paces from him. His quarter-staff struck the deer in the side, scratched him, a few drops of water and blood

The real hunt begins only with a deer. You have to run for hours, never stopping, and with enough speed not to lose sight of it for good; to be able to recognize when the beast is about to play a trick by doubling back and letting the hunter pass on ahead; to know where to appoint a rendezvous with fresh reinforcements so that, when you're completely out of breath, you can hand off the pursuit. In contrast to combat with bears or snow leopards, and to some extent, wolves, this really is a hunt in common, in which success depends on competent leadership and the strictest agreement

When he received word that Crucifix had been detected and was moving north-northeast, toward the upper reaches of the canyon, the chairman at once ordered an end to any other chase in favor of hunting Crucifix. Those occupying outlets from the forest to the east and those attacking from the north were ordered to stop, while the western units had to run, to the point of passing out, at the tail of the beast that had gone uphill, and the southern units were to hurry from the flank to back them up. The deer proceeded without tricks, but very slowly, stopping every minute and letting them catch up, as though some misgivings prevented him from trusting the headwaters of the little river. But was it misgivings? He didn't turn, and his behavior was so strange that the old man had to question whether the dispatches were accurate. One of the trackers reported that Crucifix must be exhausted, although the loss of blood was minimal. Exhausted, already?

But the wenny's perplexity gave way to alarm when the shouts conveyed that the deer had allowed a hunter to come so close he could not have missed and would have struck Crucifix in the head with the point of his stick had he not seen the deer carrying the tree of death between his antlers. The tree of death? Didn't that mean every one of the beast's pursuers was in peril of perdition? But would anyone really forgo the hunt?

The stream that flows through the hamlet takes its source not from the glaciers, like others, but from a mercury lake, overflowing in the finest cascade, and forming below the waterfall also something like a lake, but swampy, overgrown with grass, surrounded by bogs and birch copses. Into just this swamp the hunters drove Crucifix, who wasn't changing his path, but was traveling more and more slowly

At last, the deer ran out to the forest marge near the waterfall and halted. Toward him, cutting between him and the waterfall, ran the eastern unit of hunters. When they saw the elusive creature, they halted, not daring to move another step

The deer's antlers were tall, taller than he was, in the form of a cross, and no one could comprehend how he could bear such a crooked cross. A bony skeleton tree stretched out on the cross entwined and entangled it with branches covered in rosebuds

And suddenly the deer emitted a call, and a vague rumble was heard in reply, not exactly a thundering, nor a trampling. And no matter how dangerous the sight of death, the implication of the trampling, rapidly dawning on the hunters, was even more dangerous: wisents were moving in

The wisent has become nearly extinct in the mountains, like the snow leopard. Sometimes their herds, reaching a dozen head, still wander in remote northern canyons, and it even happens that herds, after joining together, abandon one canyon for its neighbor in search of better food or fleeing some kind of trouble. They say, however, that in years of great misfortune, the wisents migrate from the northern slope to the southern, increasing the magnitude of the calamity by their incursions. Admittedly, no one remembers the last time this happened

While it's possible to vanquish a single wisent, what can you do against an avalanche, even with a rifle, not to mention a quarterstaff? Take to your heels? It's permissible to be cowardly in life, but not on the great hunt, there's no retreating on the great hunt

When they heard the trampling, the western bunch of hunters also halted. And then they rushed out onto the swale, past the deer, toward their comrades. Everyone waited. You could hear the herd breaking through the forest, getting closer. Each knew: he would be driven back into the swamp or trampled. And the deer?

The animal let out another cry, truly mocking, and disappeared as though it had melted away. And with Crucifix's exit, the trampling died down instantly, and it became clear to the highlanders that there were no wisents, that it was a trick of the spirits that protected the deer

How much fury and disappointment was in the hunters' cries! But the wenny, on learning the outcome of the pursuit, did not grow angry, rather, he became even more unsettled. And although he could not forbid the unlucky hunters to fan out over the canyon, killing the pestering bears, and managed to conduct to a successful end a chase after some wild boars spooked from the lower reaches of the canyon, paying for it with an equal number of people, although a lynx turned up as a special bonus among their trophies—the incident with the trampling did not cease worrying him. A deer's mischief? No, a prophecy of shared perdition! But what kind, from where?

Moonrise put an end to the hunt. Taking advantage of the wonderful night, the highlanders, without flagging, dragged their quarry from all points to the wenny's station. And when noon arrived, a heap of beastly carcasses was already rising around the chairman's hut, and a row of human corpses they would have to bury, wrapped, avenged, in the hides of their beastly murderers or of an animal of the same species. If the murderer was absent, and its species likewise missing, the hunter was buried temporarily, until the day of vengeance . . .

Ivlita heard the exchange of shouts and discerned what was happening. But she, starved, exhausted, did not abandon the glacier on which the dying Jonah lay

At first, she wanted to descend and summon help. Jonah stopped her. He was dying, anyway, since he could neither begin anew his secret pursuit nor give it up. Let Ivlita stay with the dying man, not abandoning him needlessly

Once he'd voiced his request, Jonah spoke no more; she didn't know whether he couldn't or wouldn't. And so he reposed on his side, just as he had fallen, and gazed unblinkingly at Ivlita. She turned her face away, seated next to him, now tracing patterns in the snow with her finger, now staring into the valley, from which, along with fumes, first dusk was ascending, and then night. Were there stars in the sky that night? When day began to break, Ivlita called them to mind, but could no longer find anything . . .

The hunters' bonfires reddened the sky so that dawn lost all meaning. The drumbeat rising up from the canyon made waiting for death down below and up above solemnly triumphal to the point of absurdity. But were they hunting below? And here? Were not the fox they were finishing off there and Ivlita one and the same? And Ivlita suddenly realized that the haze creeping over the country was deadly. To stand up, to run, no matter where, if only to keep safe, live a little longer. And, strangest of all, where had her fear of death come from, why did things suddenly matter?

Ivlita jumped up. But the dying man's hand had latched onto her clothing and literally ossified. She'd have to unclench it . . . But Ivlita was in no state to touch Jonah . . . She wanted to save herself, saw that it was impossible, and froze with a presentiment of impending death

Jonah had held out in silence all day. But when the summons for the completed hunt rebounded along the glacier and the cliffs, he couldn't, in the end, restrain himself. His first words were barely audible, then grew louder, and, to the degree that night grew deeper, the dying man's voicing had already turned into a cry. How badly he wanted his friends below to hear him, too. Not despairing for a moment, he struggled furiously to overcome conditions unfavorable to sound, received no answer, and cried out unceasingly

Is it a human being roaring, or a tempest? What kind of person could rage like that? This legless fellow? Closing her eyes and covering her ears, Ivlita wanted to go deaf, but could not. However indifferent she had been to the wind, her skin was ready now to burst under its gusts (or the gusts of words), and she could not imagine bearing the trial any longer. If not for the hand

It didn't matter what he was shouting about. But his voice was so insolent, so insulting, that Ivlita recalled her father

And indignation took hold of her. Without opening her eyes, she stepped over to the place where the voice exploded from below, and when her foot felt something hard, she began stomping

The voice broke off, but did not fall silent, continuing to thicken. Ivlita stomped, but could not force it to shut up. She weakened and collapsed

And the roar unexpectedly quieted and an unimaginable silence ensued. Ivlita took her palms from her ears and heard only the water murmuring, flowing down from the snow-covered outcroppings. Nothing more. Not a cry or a howl. The water is murmuring. Ivlita listened, and listened more intently. Had it been murmuring for long? It had always been murmuring, always would, the gentlest song of death. Must be, Jonah's dead

Ivlita opened her eyes, but could not arrest her raised eyelids, and they went on parting more broadly, as though a moment were not sufficient to take horror at the spectacle of blood next to her in the nimbus of the new day. And Jonah's crystalline voice, montane, not human, streamed over the blood: "Ivlita, why did Laurence nurse you back from death, compel you to live? You would already be with me." "Jonah, are you speaking or dead?" But Ivlita learned nothing by bending over the corpse. Had the words been spoken by him, or had they only been heard by her? ...

Laurence? What did he have to do with her? And suddenly Ivlita felt her mind spinning, she was sick to her stomach; one after another, unfamiliar sensations she could not square with anything seized her, she felt light pouring from her and such warmth that the glacier was no longer made of ice, but was warm, already so hot you can't stand on it, it burns your feet so badly. And inside her, not just anywhere, but in a perfectly defined spot, unique in the whole universe, such a thing was happening that so distinguished the spot from all the same old stones, the same old ice, the source of a movement that began arbitrarily and on its own, the source of a sublime phenomenon, not subject to death, the rise of a new life

In reply to the tempest's (or human being's) curses, to the call of her mind (and the mind of the dying man), Ivlita answered with rebellion, a last effort to break beyond inviolable bounds. She triumphed

Ivlita broke into a run. But the dead man did not want to let her clothing out of his hand. Not strong enough to struggle against him, Ivlita was constrained to drag his corpse behind her. On the steep slopes, the corpse slid down more quickly, knocked her off her feet, drew her behind it, pulled her down into the snow, and she would get up after lying in the dead man's embrace, covered in blood. This flight went on all morning, until Ivlita neared the wenny's station. The slaughtered beasts showed black from afar, a magnificent hill

But the deceased had not managed to deliver his own quarry, too, when the soul-lacerating trampling reached them once more, ascending to the pastures. And then distant, frequent shots sounded, and voices full of mortal alarm. And Ivlita saw the shepherds toss aside the beasts they were already skinning, and without even thinking of the bleating goats in their pens, jump up and begin the descent to the fir forest in great haste. She shouted at them to wait for her, but no one turned around. She tore away. The dead man came loose

But Ivlita was chasing the runners naked

11

T he soldiers played the march with stress and passion, and the march, bursting through the wall into the garden, kept Laurence from concentrating. And meanwhile he had to revive in memory developments following the second bomb right up to these comradely revels—it was necessary to know them, if only for the sake of prudence, but Laurence couldn't recall anything for sure, and his already inebriated retinue didn't want to delve into any details. Who had picked him up, saved him from the police, deposited him at this drinking establishment? And what could explain his comrades' folly: carousing right next to a barracks and while the city was on alert and they were digging into every nook?

The table, laden with tasty dishes and with bottles, in particular, and spread in the shade of a magnificent cedar, shuddered every second from laughter, shrieks, blows, and other motions. What was Laurence to do with these people? They rejoiced at their success, and so did he. But he was hurrying home, to Ivlita. And then, these were outsiders he shouldn't trust; he just knew Basilisk. But Basilisk was absent, and his place setting, which hadn't been cleared away, gave the young man no peace

"Laurence, you're a treasure," someone across the table shouted. "The second bomb was a marvel. If not for you, it would all have been dust and ashes. Let me hug you, my darling dove"

Laurence felt hot and hemmed in and heavy because of the belt filled with gold hidden under his clothing, because of the banknotes sewn up in small sacks draped over his chest and back, stuffed into his boots and hat. Like he'd put on fat and grown four times as stout

"And your brave fellows, now they're *some* devils . . . The youngest one made good on the ruckus, went back into the shop to grab a perfume bottle and pour the whole thing over his head. Now robbing the jeweler is more than I would allow, they'd probably get caught red-handed . . . Hey, some red and more peaches, please"

Jewels? Laurence had inadvertently forgotten; after all, he'd thought about them earlier. And Basilisk had assured him he'd get to buy a whole lot. It would be better than hauling gold around

"Can't I get into the city?" the highlander abruptly interjected. "I need a gift to take for my wife, some emeralds, or something like that"

"To the city? Well, now you've lost your mind, comrade Laurence," his neighbor shrieked. "They'll nab you right away. The police are furious after being played. Now every place is dangerous except here, since this is our favorite and so the most dangerous place, and everyone's sure we could be anywhere, naturally, but not here. Dimwits. And what do they want with us? The money's lost, it's already rolling across the border with one of our trusty men . . . By the way, don't be alarmed: the police are the only ones who don't know we're boozing, the jeweler himself will show up here in person"

The military march blared incessantly. As though the soldiers, drawing valor from it, thought they needed to load up properly for some future heated engagement. And the more the French horns, never retreating, persisted, the more uneasiness found its place in Laurence until he became all ears. What tune was this, familiar to everyone, judging by his neighbor's words, never performed in peacetime and whose purpose was bracing hearts in the hour of battle? And since this tune might be forgotten after a long deficiency of wars, they'd begun playing it during attacks, as they said, on the internal enemy, while massacring workers, destroying schools, annihilating villages and, as an exception, finally, while the soldiers were quartered in brothels. What was the occasion now?

They sent a lackey to scout it out. He disappeared for a long time, and during his absence all events were subjected to the alarm. Therefore, when a dealer in colored gems who was subsisting off parties reveling in the suburban gardens turned up with his bins and trays, where, despite their owner's poor appearance, genuine treasures were on display, Laurence, without any sales pitch, parted with his gold, overpaying for everything—regardless of the conscientious tavern keeper's intervention—by a factor of three. If not for this brazen music, what joy he would have felt toward these presents for Ivlita, about which he'd been dreaming for months. Hadn't he bound himself to the conspiracy for the sake of these gems? But this unsolicited warmongering gobbled everything up, and, under the scourge of their trumpets, it struck Laurence that his exploits were hollow and his efforts wide of the mark

Neither police, nor perfidy, nor bullets had dissuaded him. And now the music started playing and Laurence realized he was weak, negligible, misguided; there'd been no point in starting the long drawn-out business, money was useless, since while pursuing it he'd been losing the main thing, which he could never recover

Why had he obeyed Galaction, followed Basilisk, taken his business beyond the confines of the mountains, descended into an unfamiliar world whose hardships he hadn't taken into account? Raised forces against himself to a degree he couldn't define? And for the sake of meaningless enterprises he'd turned his back on Ivlita, who was, perhaps, in life-threatening danger and had, just maybe, forgotten him, maybe . . .

Oh, to smash the trumpets, strangle the performers. An inadmissible disgrace . . . What's this? Why are they playing it?

When the scout returned, he affirmed what Laurence didn't dare think, but could almost smell. A cavalry squadron was leaving for the mountains today on a punitive mission to a village where, a few days back, some gendarmes had been lured into an ambush and massacred. People said it was the work of the same Laurence who robbed the treasury that morning. The soldiers were happy, anticipating the love of mountain beauties . . .

Mountain beauties? And him? And the party? Laurence jumped up, leaned across the table, scrutinizing his accomplices. Would the party allow it? Among the dismal bearded faces, the wise men who knew the prices of things and were possessed by an end that justified the means, he was such an unexpected sight that if any of them had raised their eyes, they would have seen the triple cipher of faith, hope, and love above the highlander's shining head. But the gazes of his comrades bore into the earth. No answer followed. You refuse to help? . . . You're handing them over to rapists? And suddenly peals of laughter and empty rhetoric seized Laurence

Ravishing. Things couldn't go any better. What luck that the party at whose disposal he remained, ready to do them service, did not reciprocate. For if the city was threatening his native village, Laurence, and no one else, must and would be able to defend it

"Comrades, I cannot hide from you the fact that this very seat remains empty on my account, since it was I who killed comrade Basilisk. During the course of a month, Basilisk treacherously sent me, Laurence, to life on a daily basis and then demanded a bribe, since I was supposedly beholden to him for my life. But when he'd played to his heart's content, he sent me, Martinian, to death. And so I resolved to kill *him*, too, in order to prove that a highlander is free, and that laws apart from economics exist, and forces besides the party

"Now, when the overcoats are going to pay for their insolence with their heads, a revolt is flaring up and not one of our shots will be fired in vain, no one will dare say we were led or that we are beholden to anyone whomsoever for our victory over the plains. A punitive squadron? The love of mountain beauties? We'll marry off every soldier, hand him a cherry, our sister death. . . . Farewell"

Everyone straightened up. Laurence, circling the table, kissed each party member on the shoulder and, backing away with his finger on the trigger of the pistol hidden in his bosom, reached the garden gate. The wennies imitated his movements. After letting them pass, he turned and leapt headlong onto the road

But his caution was misplaced. None of the party members had any intention of shooting. Sobered, they looked at one another, not without bewilderment, and when Laurence had disappeared, one of those present, shrugging his shoulders, said: "Still and all, Basilisk was an oddball. What the devil was the point of hiring that blowhard? That the police, it was said, didn't know him and he could throw perfectly? Silliness, we would have gotten by even without such a luxury. And now he's paid for his whim, and how much money, so necessary for the party, had to be allotted for his scheme"

And no one sat back down. After settling up with the surprised host, the guests left the garden behind and, with hands in pockets, went back to the city to put themselves in prison, a safe haven in their current situation

And Laurence and the wennies were walking toward the train station behind the squadron in a crowd of gawkers and little boys, to the accompanying mockery of that same march. Of the highlander's recent self-reliant confidence nothing remained. "His speech was what exactly?" Laurence reasoned it out: Was it slander against himself, or in killing Brother Mocius for no good reason, Luke in self-defense, Galaction in vengeance, Basilisk from a thirst for blood, had he really been killing just to kill, proving that freedom exists? But that meant there was no confusion, and those who suspected a boundlessly ill will in Brother Mocius's murderer had been right, and Laurence was, in fact, an evil man. At the same time, Laurence knew he was no villain, and he was sure that if paradise existed, space would be found there even for him. Then what was he? A plaything of the elements? And this thought—not exactly a justification, not quite an intuition about the universe or insurance against any eventuality, arising not for the first time and making itself his constant companion—embarrassed him. And the words spoken by Basilisk, that he knew how to kill, came to mind as wheedling. His speech before his comrades was boasting and nothing more

The train station presented a thoroughly outlandish scene. The square in front of it was jammed with pedestrians and carriages waiting for the punitive squadron to appear. The carriages were wallowing in flowers, and the pedestrians, mostly women, held armloads—bouquets and wreaths. But evidently the ocean of flowers was insufficient, since along the adjacent streets stood wagons, from which hawkers were calling out prices for roses, tulips, carnations, all red. The cream of city society, who had abandoned the grand boulevard for the holiday, gleamed with beauty in their calashes. But no matter how much gawkers and customers peered at them there on the boulevard, their faces had never flushed as they did now, had not blazed with the excitement, the frenzy that seized their beings. If they had seen the squadron at work, they might have behaved otherwise. But the thought of future massacres, the blood that would flow, enraptured them all, cheered them, made some cling to others, draw deep breaths, find life magnificent, and themselves likewise

The squadron's appearance elicited a storm of welcome. All who were sitting jumped up, and all who were standing raised themselves up on tiptoes, and there was no silencing the "Hurrah!" in honor of the future conquerors. A barrage of flowers began. They threw them from the windows of the surrounding houses, from the roofs; the imps who had taken to the trees threw them from the branches, so that the soldiers, leading their horses by the bridle and weakly defending themselves with their free arms, were marching in flowers up to their knees. The band struck up once more the march of blood and the cries of "Hurrah!" gave way to an equally unified and rhythmic: "Don't spare the bullets!" Women caught the soldiers' hands and kissed them, and those who were further off wailed: "Don't spare them," and blew kisses with both hands. When the squadron entered the train station, the whole square was ready to follow them. Doors were torn from their hinges, fences were broken down, and yet few had the good fortune of making it to the platform. There stood the military train, its cars decked in flowers from their roofs to their wheels

But if the soldiers were objects of adoration for the bourgeois (men and women alike), the chief honors, nevertheless, fell to their leader. Stately, with a broad backside exaggerated by the cut of his breeches, his chest enhanced by an attractive breastplate, and a crop in his hand, Captain Arcady smiled indulgently at the frantic ladies, never removing his chamois-gloved hand from the visor of his cap. While the soldiers were showered with flowers, he had to accept offerings as well. And, standing on the step of the car assigned to him, the captain tirelessly bowed to take from the tenderest hands some fetish or jewel and handed them off to an orderly, efficiently sorting his master's acquisitions inside the car. Here were rings hastily removed from fingers, brooches only just unpinned from bosoms, watches, crucifixes, and more. But the most numerous items were made from women's hair. How many of the city's women had not slept during the previous night so that, after shearing off a lock, they could weave a watch fob or a bracelet or a cross to be worn on the body. Several had contrived even to craft from their hair bouquets or initials placed in frames, under glass. But there were also those who simply brought their sheared plaits, tied up in ribbons. One beauty sacrificed all her hair to weave a rope from which she adjured him to hang the chief rebel. They had to resort to the strictest measures and, by establishing some kind of line, reduce the crush. One hour passed after another, and there was still no end to the queue of admiring women craving to kiss the captain's hand

Even Arcady began to feel nervous and tired because of this measureless immodesty. He would long ago have given the order to depart if he hadn't been waiting for someone. Finally, a certain youth turned up, mincing, heavily powdered and pomaded, escorted by envious glances. "Arcady," he cried out while still at some distance, "May the Lord bless you, may He help you accomplish your feat of arms . . . ," and, after embracing the captain, the youth whispered: "My dear, I love you more today than ever before. To live, it is necessary to kill. You see, our senses are fresher now than they were on the very first day. My hero, my god"

Laurence, persistently following the soldiers, had pushed his way through to the train and followed what was happening, spellbound and shamed. He recalled lording it over the villages, the receptions in the village halls and thought, how trivial compared with Arcady's triumph. What was the officer posing as? Some ordinary dirty cad like all the rest. And just the same kind of effeminate coward as was customary. But see, it was enough for Arcady to be entrusted with some affair, easy and shameful, and he was elevated to the heavens. And after resolving that the captain would not escape his bullet, Laurence sorrowfully chided himself for being ruled by envy

How much the last months had perverted him. Not that long ago, he wouldn't have thought anything of drawing his pistol and laying the captain low. But now he rebuked himself, no, it wasn't the time, he had to spare himself, the main thing lay ahead, and so on. Earlier, Laurence could only act, or, presumably, reason.

But now, it gave him pleasure to spend time contemplating and in order to prolong that contemplation, he sought out every possible justification for his weakness

Therefore, without undertaking anything, he climbed into the train along with several curious people who didn't want to let the squadron out of their sight and departed, together with the wennies, for his native land. Without any agitation he watched the local authorities, the clergy, and, again, the women greet Arcady at every station. In the car, the soldiers' conversations turned on one and the same tedious question—whom they would get to sleep with in the village, and that the mountain girls, although they had splendid bodies, didn't know how to put out and just lay there like corpses. "Lifeless beauty," the narrator added with the air of a connoisseur

But, when toward morning the hoary ranges became visible from the window and a pitchy, fresh smell wafted into his face, Laurence woke from a double dream. He couldn't wait for the first whistle-stop, even if it wasn't the closest to his native village, to abandon the squadron and get to work; and, taking advantage of the fact that, in view of track repairs, the train had slowed, Laurence ordered the wennies to climb off and then followed them. The confusion of the supervisor and his workers was so great when a bandit jumped out of a military train and demanded that they hitch up their horses, they didn't even attempt to delay. Laurence jumped into the cart and, backed by the wennies' whooping, drove, standing up, the four frightened horses toward the nearest settlement, which they passed without stopping, crushing several puppies and startling a bird. When the surroundings changed from flat to hilly, after five hours of brutal shaking, the mountains drew forward and the brooks began babbling. Laurence discarded the overdriven horses in a village once he had entered his own domain. But the reception shown him there tallied so little with custom and expectation that, thrown for a loop, he couldn't decide for a long time what to set his hand to. He was greeted with signs of honor, but coldly, almost with hostility. Instead of promptness, he soon heard reproaches. "A punitive squadron? And how could it be otherwise? What the devil made you brew up an attack on the police? They would have had their fun and left. Kill and rob at your own expense, if you like, but inciting the population, or even just preparing an ambush, no, it's not your job. The sawyers are idiots for listening to you. And now, knowing how it will end, they can't even come up with anything. Go on, you'll see, you'll get a load of thanks"

It had seemed to the enraptured Laurence that he need only arrive, lift an eyebrow, and ... But for the second time there was no one, not even over a horn of brandy, with whom he could share the impressions he'd brought from the city and tell about expropriating valuables. . . . His arm was not lifted to toss a handful of gold to his frowning landsmen, trembling for their own hides

And he was suddenly indignant: "Keep your cool and bear it when the gendarmes show up to violate and dishonor? Fun? And how many children who don't look like their fathers *or* their mothers would have been born in the spring? It's better to die like dogs than suffer that. Are we highlanders or not? Have we ever been slaves? Have we ever paid taxes? Look, they decided to call us up for service, but did anyone show up to enlist? I'm a deserter myself. And now you're worse than females. You're not dead yet, but you've already turned to clay"

But Laurence didn't shoot, didn't beat anyone, didn't even pound his fists. He demanded mules for himself and the wennies. With affected gravity, he stood on the threshold, waiting for the mules to be brought up, hopped into the saddle without using stirrups, and, adding nothing more, trotted off

He showed up in the village with the sawmill ahead of the squadron, for Arcady's cavalry lost a good deal of time pillaging and burning the neighboring villages. His compatriots met Laurence in such a way that his worst fears turned out to be rose-colored. On the square in front of the village hall and the taverns, the populace stood with white flags, waiting for death. When Laurence appeared, whistles, threats, abuse were heard. The mules were surrounded by a crowd determined to end the matter in a lynching. The wennies clutched their weapons, ready to defend themselves, merely awaiting a sign from Laurence

But Laurence, as though neither seeing nor hearing what was happening around him, looked, with his head raised, at an outcropping beyond the cemetery that rose up toward the forest, and so intently that the arms of the villagers nearest him fell, and their heads turned in the direction of the outcropping; the nearest were followed by those beyond them, their cries died down and the entire square, petrified, contemplated a great miracle

A snow-white archangel, whose fiery hair (winding round its wings and uplifted arms and falling to its knees) eclipsed the sky, was descending from the forest toward the village. The archangel's trumpet blasts penetrated the silence, and the copse creaked and parted from the blasts, and a sloth of bears issued toward the cemetery. But, after conducting the archangel, the bears stopped at the fence, settled back on their paws, and begged alms. The archangel, whizzing over the graves of Brother Mocius and the stonecutter Luke, headed for the square

A still distant, but distinct, trampling met it in reply: Captain Arcady's cavalry was bearing down on the offending village . . .

Laurence, leaping from his mule, swooped toward the sobbing Ivlita to catch her before she collapsed from exhaustion. Not turning, with his most dear one clasped to his breast, he passed the cemetery and, on the shoulders of the bears taking to their heels, plunged into the woods

And right behind the reiver—the peasantry

12

In the forest, where the soldiers did not dare penetrate at first, Laurence and Ivlita lingered five whole days, although starting on the second day, Arcady, who had placed machine guns at higher elevations, zealously sprayed the leaf cover, and it was no longer safe to nestle under the branches. But when, enraged by his stay in the depopulated village, where only turkeys and sparrows had met him, Arcady ordered the forest to be burned, they had to retreat by the most uncouth paths into the icy realm and, surmounting it, descend and set up housekeeping in one of the caves that had evidently belonged at one time to the satyr, but was not even frequented by shepherds now. Scrutinizing the drawings of beasts and the hunters stalking them, so numerous on the cave walls, Ivlita saw in the human beings her champions, and in the raptorial animals the foes of her future child

Last week's agonizing developments vanished into thin air as soon as they arrived, and, everything else forgotten, immersed in her growing love, Ivlita passed her days digging in the sands that covered the cave floor and finding, with inquisitive interest, fragments of flint tools and bones. It was, nevertheless, too bad she did not have at hand any of her father's books, with deposits of information she needed about the purpose of the fragments and the species of the bones. But this did not get in the way of sorting through her findings and giving Laurence lectures on human history

Daylight did not penetrate the cave, but Ivlita made no mistake in discerning night's approach. At that hour, she lost her fervor for excavations and gravitated, lying down and placing her hands behind her head, toward observing the movements of her belly, illuminated by the campfire. Who was it, a son or a daughter?

But the thought of the infant's sex called to memory the story of Ivlita's life, and no matter how happy Ivlita was that her life had worked out like this, and not otherwise, she preferred not to delve into the past, moved on to thoughts of Laurence, called him to her, if he was there. Sometimes she asked herself: why is he opposed to life? Is he really death? No, this is his child, after all. And can death be fruitful? And there was no end to such considerations, which seemed like pouring water through a sieve. Well, nothing else mattered, as long as she made it to that sacred hour

But the more her nature was sated with motherhood, the more starkly her nature was split in two, since her love for Laurence was also growing. No, you couldn't apply a quantitative standard where the quality was continually changing. Actually, Ivlita recollected the days when she observed Laurence from her father's roof. Then, his presence, scouring from Ivlita the scurf and scale of the past, endowed her with elevated feelings, opened her eyes to nature, transformed her hearing, turned her whole self from a young woman into a fragment of nature. But later, of her riches on that day when Laurence carried her off nothing was left except a filthy pigsty, pain in her body, disappointment and grief. Hadn't this torpor, however, helped Ivlita survive the blizzard, her father's death, and Jonah's insults. And now, in going up to the caves, Ivlita accomplished a double ascent. Nature gained once more its tongue for her, and Ivlita again sang the cretins' songs for hours. But, just like that, she was no longer a spectator this time, no, she took part in the cycle, and days and nights, wind and weather, were not merely parading before her. No, like the sun, she was carrying out constructive work on a daily basis, like a river, she was running along her magnificent course in order to empty into a nativity. When, lying in the grass near the cave, she watched bees gathering nectar from the clover and gentian, beauties flaunting their loveliness, ants founding a universe, she realized: her bonds made her kin to everything around her and nothing in the world was alien or inimical

She became attentive to herself, more intent on the world. While stepping, Ivlita avoided disturbing the soil and stones and hindering their purpose. When a hawk scudded above her, she wished it might achieve its goal. In its first advent, nature was comprehensible, but meaningless. Now everything found its place and meaning

Therefore, Ivlita knew now that there was no disorder in the world and everything was confined in a perfect structure. And whatever happens, nothing ever escapes this perfect structure and cannot do so

Turmoil, anxiety, fears—everything passed on, melted without a trace, replaced by imperturbable calm. When shooting could be heard, fires blazed up, Laurence arrived agitated, alone or in the company of clamoring highlanders, everything was insignificant, or significant, to the extent that the noise of a waterfall, an owl's cry, or the groan of a tree entering its senescence is weighty. And Ivlita no longer fled her thoughts, she meditated calmly on her father, and on Jonah, and on Laurence's murders. And her love for Laurence was likewise a calm love

At times, Ivlita didn't know whether she was more devoted to Laurence or the infant. But in allotting to one the mind's mind, to the other the belly's mind, by turns, Ivlita found comfort thinking that nature is absolute equilibrium. And since custom forbids a highlander from touching a pregnant woman, Laurence never stepped out of the imaginary circle Ivlita had drawn

Once he had hidden her in the mountains, settled her in the cave, supplied her with clothing of sorts, Laurence was almost continually absent and afterward only put in an appearance to top off stores of firewood and provisions. Animal existence was so natural and fitting for Ivlita (don't beasts bring food this way?), that Ivlita saw in the misadventures of recent months, in the complexity of human practices, an intentional path toward enlightenment and simplicity. Therefore, she hadn't simply stopped condemning evil, she found in it the most profound manifestation of good order and human uplift. And Jonah, like Arcady, and Arcady equally with the stormy springtimes, were agents of a higher reason that had given her the gift of cave-dwelling happiness. That was why nothing that happened after they left the village engaged her, and Ivlita never asked Laurence where he had been, what he had done, and what was new in the villages. And since the cave was not a fortuitous haven, but the place most suited for the nativity, it could not even enter Ivlita's mind that she should abandon the cave and that its order could possibly be shaken by anyone

Only on one occasion, when, in Laurence's absence, a crowd of peasant women barged into the cave with shouts and abuse, did Ivlita waver. "Ivlita pregnant?" The women pressed her, "How can that be? Once you're not married, a bandit's wife, you don't have any right to children. Even if it's a little late, you need to take measures to bring about a miscarriage"

Ivlita was retreating into the depths of the cave, not comprehending a thing. To what supreme level of well-being were these frenzied country women driving her? What were they pushing on her? She gazed at the wall decorations in vain, thinking that the millennia-old humans and beasts would instruct her at the decisive moment. But art, as usual, was silent, and the world was turning out once again to be imperfect, since Ivlita could justify neither the peasant women's intrusion nor art's detachment. And indifference, like the indifference of painting, exactly like what she had felt during Jonah's attempted rape, took hold of Ivlita. For no misfortune could compare to the collapse of the magnificent structure she had erected in the course of the spring months. The wind whistled in the cave, drenching her with moisture. Ah, yes, it's autumn

But the first of the hands threatening Ivlita had only to become bolder, and nothing remained of her brief hesitation. Hadn't the branches whipped Ivlita's face just so when, after parting from Jonah, she was running, out of her mind, through the forest? Hadn't the plants bent over her just so, pricked her, spit on her, vilified her, and hadn't it been obvious that the plants were dead people and every thicket a cemetery? But when the attacking women tore Ivlita's dress off and blood ran in ribbons down her enormous belly, art finally revived and the bears, coming down off the walls, surrounded her, ran after her, just as on that resplendent day, the first of her motherhood

And rapture stooped to Ivlita, pierced her, whirled her up, and, reconciled, immaculate, she attained, after torturous labors, the summit whose height is infinite, and proclaimed with trumpet sound the last and ultimate victory over death

The peasant women stood still. They looked with astonishment at the being nailed to the wall. Now that their eyes had grown accustomed to the darkness, they perceived that this woman with her hair flowing from the clefts was a phenomenon not of the same order as themselves, but akin to the mysterious prodigies and giants that gazed on them from the walls. And, beginning to lose their nerve, they were already asking whether there wasn't some mistake or trick here, the intervention of special powers, since if it wasn't a woman, she wasn't pregnant, and the whole story was a demonic delusion, there was no child at all, and the belly that disfigured such perfect beauty—a deliberate, brazen provocation for their sound mind

And one of them was set to touch the belly and destroy the illusion. But she didn't have time, the infant leapt for joy. In the light of the dying fire, the kicks looked mighty, as though the unborn child were tearing out into the open to chastise the blasphemers. And suddenly Ivlita gave up the ghost, her head drooped, and her body, together with her parting groan, came crashing down from on high to land at the feet of the womenfolk. And then the last flame also sank down, and darkness, silvered with a breath of smoke, engulfed those present. And a fearful panic at once overcame the peasant women. They fled back, but there was no possibility of making out where the exit was, they banged against rocks, howled, knocked one another flat on their backs, maimed one another. Those who managed to break free streamed out and cascaded to the bottom of the canyon

When Laurence returned that evening, he was met with wailing that carried forth from the cave. Overwhelmed by the darkness, alarmed, he lit a torch and stumbled upon several wounded women who were in no shape to express themselves clearly, and in the very depths of the catacombs—upon an insensate Ivlita

He tried for a long time to bring her back to reality, outraged, not comprehending the cause of what had happened. And what exactly had happened? Were the authorities involved and had their refuge been discovered? Or something worse?

For months, Laurence had been bearing with life in the cave and his hard luck, and the relative peace in his soul was unperturbed as long as Ivlita, too, abode in peace. And so it had consistently seemed to Laurence, also, that this state of things would go on forever: the cave over the precipice, Ivlita pregnant, soldiers in the village, difficulties finding food and useless riches he'd brought from the city and still didn't know what to do with. But today the phantom of constancy had dissipated and it was revealed that such a state could not continue, neither the cave nor Arcady in the village would go on any longer, and it was time for the pregnancy to end. Laurence could not, however, set his hand to anything definite and find the necessary denouement without having it out with Ivlita and while he bandaged her wounds, he made haste, worried not only about her health, but also sensing something even bitterer in the future

He reviewed once more in thought the road from his encounter with Brother Mocius up to the present, forced to reevaluate his deeds, which had already long ago ceased to appear impeccable. On the contrary, he was convinced that somewhere some shortcoming had brought on the flood of misfortunes, but Laurence was for the first time prepared to admit that this shortcoming was not in himself, but in the world around him, in the rotten social order, in the filthy administrative structure, in human banality, and in Laurence himself only as a reflection, and so he bore no responsibility for what had happened

It had been easy before to heap blame on himself. Life, they say, is wonderful, I am the only unhappy failure. But now, when Laurence was left, as it were, alone with himself, he already understood that his guilt could not remain any longer somehow undefined, but must be precisely ascertained, he could no longer exist in darkness, feeling his way about, otherwise he would not avoid even worse consequences. And it became clear to him to the point of absurdity that he, Laurence, and his environment, which he so despised, were one and the same and his own guilt was a scale model of generalized guilt

Laurence looked at Ivlita, turned back on the peasant women, recollected the day he had met his wife and the forester's death, compared how he resuscitated the forester's daughter then and now, and all of it lacked only the words so that everything would be made fast, and the seemingly stable scene of their stay in the caves would give way to a new one, actual and lethal

The consciousness that all existence was meaningless, wayward, drove him crazy. And how distinct were Laurence's present considerations from his thoughts during the time of Galaction or the Basilisk affair. Then, there were obstacles opposing him, but Laurence could surmount them. Now, however, he took cognizance not only of not being on the attack or staying in place (the cave age), but also of not even zipping off, persecuted, since there was no place to go, everywhere was one and the same sky, one and the same earth, the same people and stones and—enough to put your jaw out of joint from yawning—one and the same death

One comfort remained—Ivlita. Ivlita was with him, she understood him, she would disappear, worn down, like him, by banality, the plains, the mountains, it made no difference, and would die, but would not surrender to these misshapen peasant women, or he to Arcady

A comforter? What was wrong with him? Where had his musing led him? In what was she his comforter? A monstrous absurdity. Ivlita, that was all. Ivlita loved Laurence. What more did he need? Riches? But did *she* really need them? Look, he'd brought them, and had she paid them any attention? How many times had he told himself: exploits, money, that's not the main thing; and he hadn't listened to himself. Fool. What was he running around for when happiness was here, simple normal mutual happiness

It was like a weight fell from Laurence. And, lighter now, he felt just as innocent and green as he had been the year before. If only Ivlita would come round soon, they'd get through everything safely, and it would be possible, after disavowing his murders, to live a tranquil life

But when Ivlita, regaining consciousness, lifted her eyes, hostile in the light of the pinewood chips, while trying to push Laurence away and straining to enunciate something bad, what exactly Laurence could not immediately catch, the young man sensed that his fragile happiness was on the verge of falling to pieces any minute

And he divined what had happened in the cave before he arrived. Not the external event, that was not important, but the internal event, whose expression Ivlita now was. And although Laurence did not completely hear what Ivlita was attempting to utter, he got the message: her words must contain a verdict that would not only destroy the happiness he had nearly attained, but, most likely, would make it altogether irrecoverable. If only the silence would go on for as long as possible and the denouement arrive as late as possible. For it was horribly evident that the denouement of their romance was inevitable, that Laurence lacked the power to forestall it; and, a purportedly valiant man, he took fright, decided to draw it out, understanding perfectly that he could not draw it out to infinity. He admirably acknowledged that the time allotted him was dwindling, and, all the same, he clamped Ivlita's mouth shut, not wanting to let fall from her lips the inexorable judgment

Ivlita quickly understood why Laurence was pressing on her face. In not allowing her to speak, what did he want to forestall? Could this madness really go on? Could they think of persisting further in their errors? Persisting, if only for a minute? As long as the affair dealt only with Laurence, he had been free to act as he saw fit. But this one, the third, not yet arrived, was he not already showing Laurence and Ivlita the way? Were they really free, even now? Didn't they belong to the one to whom the future belonged, the one destined to be a monument to their love?

And as her powers returned, Ivlita struggled more insistently to remove Laurence's seal from her lips. She recalled that she had, in just the same way, wanted to force Jonah to shut up because Jonah had been crying out what she wanted to say now, he had already foreseen then what she was only now assimilating, after a second trial. She could not put it off any longer, she had been cruelly mistaken when she refused to listen to Jonah; Laurence would never dare keep her from speaking, he was only doing it because he was no longer her husband and not her protector, but the murderer of the whole world and of her offspring

Poor Laurence. This time, perhaps, he saw more clearly than ever and in the way most devastating to himself. He guessed that if he allowed Ivlita to express herself, he would hear what he had just told himself, her resentment aimed against his freethinking, she would invite him to repent, to renounce murder, fighting, to have done, as they say, with soiling himself. But Laurence understood plainly the difference between freedom and coercion and, after fleeing into the mountains in order not to kill on command, could he now surrender on command? And this violence emanating from Ivlita would have removed any possibility of repenting; he could not under such conditions lay down his arms, and while he recognized that he needed, all the same, to repent, Laurence was prepared to do anything that would keep him from having to hear out her injunction and would preserve freedom as though inviolate

And after pressing down on Ivlita with all his weight, while continuing to clamp her mouth shut with his left hand, the young man grasped the pregnant woman by the throat with his right, determined to strangle her sooner than let her speak out. He felt something beginning to seethe under his palm and a rattle he had heard once before escaped through Ivlita's clenched teeth. Hadn't the former forester torn at this throat in the same way? Laurence was already the same mad and dying old man. His fingers suddenly refused to obey and, despite his efforts, Laurence could not continue to bring them, turned wooden, together

With a force he had never supposed in her, Ivlita sunk her teeth into the hand covering her mouth, broke the other one that had grown into her throat, pushed Laurence away, and jumped up, raining blows, writhing in pain and rage

Unfit for battle, stunned, wounded, he staggered back toward the exit from the cave and as the light increased, the spectacle of the beauty with the swollen, paint-smudged belly became more repulsive, a vision so unbearable that Laurence closed his eyes, turned, and made a break to run off into the unknown

13

C aptain Arcady's authority was unlimited. He could send off peasants in whole families for resettlement and forced labor, confiscate their property, subject them to torture: probing with an iron or scourging, and execute anyone at whim, even without a court-martial. These rights were granted Arcady by law. Government custom allowed the captain and his soldiers to make use of local women to satisfy their needs. However, in view of the captain's peculiar tastes, boys were assigned to him, about eleven years old, no older, and green-eyed, without fail, the weaker sex was entirely placed at his troops' disposal

It would be a mistake to call such actions arbitrary or excessive. No, Arcady's behavior (and any other would have acted in exactly the same way in his place) was subject to a strict design, which was, to repeat, not the captain's property, but, after being worked out through centuries of government tyranny, framed the rite by which all punitive squadrons were inalterably guided

This rite began with seven days of mayhem. The task set before the squadron was: massacring as much of the populace as possible, spoiling their goods, and fouling their living quarters. When, toward the end of the week, only pitiful ruins of the dwellings remained, and beyond the village—hastily dug open pits filled with the shot and strangled, the epoch of social confidence was established

The extraordinary, epidemic flight of sawyers somewhat complicated Arcady's task. In order to reward the soldiers, he was forced to send them chasing after women in the surrounding area, and was left to content himself with God knows what and trample plantings, cut down orchards, and burn forests just to keep busy. But the populace had hidden in the mountains, where no detachment would be so bold as to penetrate. Therefore, the sack of the village with the sawmill lost all its picturesque quality, and no matter how much the newspapers tried to puff up events and satiate society, it was obvious that Arcady had not been especially fortunate

The epoch of confidence began with belles lettres. In all the village halls and taverns, on columns and fences a touching appeal was pasted, and since the district was never distinguished for literacy, meetings were called everywhere, at which it was announced: the administration, in need of working hands to rebuild the village and the sawmill, was recruiting volunteers, and those who stepped forward would be given the refugees' land and property. And on the next day, pitiful, starving shades actually began to arrive in the mucked-up village, expressing their willingness to help the economic steward and requesting the apportionment of this or that piece of real estate. That the newcomers were, in fact, the owners of the requested land and that no outsider ever showed up, about this fact not only everyone in the district knew perfectly well, but also Captain Arcady. But this was a regulation comedy, and Arcady pretended to believe in the newcomers' sincerity, making out that they were emigrants from some overpopulated village

During the first week only a few unfortunates crawled into the village, one at a time. But when they received what they asked for and no one touched them, the populace started to return in droves; a rumor circulated around the district that the soldiers were no longer acting up, that they were even removed from the village and occupying a special barracks built near the church, which they were forbidden to leave at night, that the captain had executed two who dared shove an old woman who was on her way to get water, and mayhem was mayhem, but now it was all past and Arcady was the most honorable of rulers. And in the inaccessible gorges and gullies, in the virgin or godforsaken thickets, the refugees bestirred themselves, preparing to return and transform the deserted village into a lively mill village

In vain did Laurence attempt to rally the refugees and rouse them to fight. To no effect, he picked his way through one backwoods nook after another, talked, argued—nothing helped. They answered him either with reference to the story about the gendarmes or with silence. And before the young man could be convinced that you couldn't inspire anything in his fellow villagers, the return began and he was forced to think no longer about an uprising, but about how he could hold back or slow down the backsliding. At times, the thought flashed through Laurence's mind that his efforts on this point would also be fruitless and his isolation was just a question of time. But engrossed in current affairs, he didn't let this thought gain a foothold, not knowing what he would do if he didn't manage to hold the peasants back. And he was prepared to pass a winter in the woods, even more than one, if need be, hoping that Arcady's patience was not infinite. The young man also failed to notice that his grandeur was melting away from day to day, and if everyone had not yet discarded him once and for all, this could only be explained by that fact that the comedy of return was playing out according to the rules. It still seemed to Laurence that he was the same Laurence he had been on the morning he first visited his native village in his capacity as bandit, although the wennies were in hiding and no one paid him tribute anymore, while the money he'd received from the party had been spent not on his wife, but to support the refugees who remained in the mountains

When most of the sawyers had returned, there was a new appeal, proclaimed at meetings just as solemnly as the first and pasted up everywhere. A most significant sum of money was posted for Laurence's capture and return, dead or alive. But the captain, understanding quite well that this was the very goal of the invasion, took into account also that, unlike the literature on allotments, the new proclamation could have no immediate value, and that among the highlanders a traitor would never be found for money. Therefore, when the latest literature provoked a panic among the peasants, who feared cruelty on the part of Arcady in his desire to find out where Laurence was, they were swiftly reassured, and Arcady did not, in fact, interrogate anyone, since he was confident: an occasion would turn up when a traitor would reveal himself, without fail—but disinterestedly like the artist Luke or, most likely, even unconsciously

What happened in the village with the sawmill was repeated in the cretins' hamlet. When Arcady dispatched a platoon of soldiers a few days after the incursion, the hamlet was deserted, everything had been carried from the houses beforehand, and the soldiery was stuck smashing just walls

Not counting the cretins, who had not abandoned their stable and who, for some unknown reason, even the soldiers wouldn't touch, the only person not wishing to leave the hamlet (and no one could make him) was the old wenny. He descended from the pastures at the first shots heard from the vicinity of the sawmill, calmly contemplated the ruin of his fatherland, received a series of rifle-butt blows and a wound from a fascine knife, and now, ailing, was lying on some straw in the cabin where Laurence and Ivlita once lived. And the wenny's stamina, about which Laurence had often heard in recent weeks, seemed to the bandit not wisdom, but a challenge tossed his way, and one of the fundamental reasons for the villagers' return. Not once since the day when the wenny's children had been taken by Laurence for instruction had the old man expressed his views about the way things were going. And from the time when Laurence departed for the shipping traffic with Galaction, the young man hadn't even seen the wenny and now concluded that he wouldn't escape a severe rebuke when they met. And with every minute that Laurence put off their meeting, the thought that it was necessary, that the old man had turned out to be right in his dark prophecies and judgments, and that his advice might be, especially at the present time, extremely valuable, irritated him all the more, and, in acknowledging that the wenny was right, Laurence would add, every time: right, but not once and for all—and he hoped, day after day, that circumstances would turn and Laurence would no longer be vanquished. And gradually it dawned on the young man that words were to blame for everything, and that words, which had raised him to the dignity of bandit, were now standing guard over him and suffocating him, and he needed a new word to ward off failure, a spell that undoubtedly only the wenny knew and could teach. This made Laurence go on pondering all the more (in the secret hope that, lo and behold, he would stumble on the necessary word) and act all the less, convinced that he had been tardy with his thoughts: he should have thought before acting, or not have thought at all. Where, however, could he stick this inflamed brain that kept him from sleeping, wasting him more than any battle or march. To return, but in what way? And when the word "return" had finally been pronounced by Laurence, when it arose in his head at the sight of the insensate Ivlita, after he lit up the pitch-dark cave, Laurence did not see himself saved, but on the edge of an abyss

His next impressions were of an expansive cirque filled with eternal snow, air slightly humid but without losing its purity, the finest feathery clouds, a clump of them lying at the very bottom of the sky, and indistinct voices. It was so good that all Laurence desired now was not to move, to stay like this in this place forever. Life is a swoon, and when it passes, blessed death arrives—waking life, full of snow and clouds. Laurence looked at the clouds that put tortoiseshell to shame—barely melting, but dwindling all the same—and on the extremely slowly draining, but, for all that, depleted day. The azure became now brighter, now bluer until, finally, unfaithful to both, it preferred a straw-colored hue. Alas, if choice exists, that means death is not yet, and the swoon is not over. Oh, to regain consciousness

The young man made an effort. There was pain throughout his body. What had caused it? Had he plunged down a steep slope or simply fallen down after losing consciousness? And how did it happen? How could he have fallen from the cave onto glaciers that lay much higher up? And his head, supposedly dead and empty, from which everything had ostensibly been eroded, had in fact lost nothing. Memories crowded in, so clearly delineated that they required no effort, you didn't even need to call on them, they were just there, in the most austere implacable sequence

The young man opened his eyes wide and peered into the depths, hoping they would deliver him from the past. But the heavens were turning gray, scarcely warm, and night, less forbearing than day, was stepping up to the rack

Alpine night! The concluding blaze on the jags edged in icicles has not yet been extinguished when, without giving dusk even half an hour's existence, darkness crawls out from under the snow, rumbling and booming, and a penetrating cold freezes all creation. The crags, spangled with diamonds and blemished by damp, throw on an icy veil so as to see nothing. The mountains sit up, stretch their numbed extremities and rise higher and higher, no matter how high they already are, turning the slightest hollow into a precipice, a gully into a canyon, while the valleys recede into immeasurable distance. And when it has risen up, the mountain tears through the sky, reaches the countless stars and, once covered with them, drops off—to sleep. What does it care about the victim on the rack?

Only some avalanches, and then as quietly as possible, laugh and slide down to the mountain's feet

The objects that have surrounded a person during the course of a life lose their materiality, becoming phantom and diaphanous. All night, freed from reality, they float, pure concepts, and in vain does a person attempt, peering into the darkness, to catch what, essentially, is happening and what his life was

And only long after midnight, bled by the search for meaning where there isn't any, the reader of his own fate, doomed to mountain solitude, turns out to be for the first time not alone, but in his own company, and, rapted to a fearsome height, floats, girded with himself and the saving circle of death

But Laurence endured the night and, when dawn descended, illuminating the pink glaciers with its blood, he was forced to return to his wretched existence, from now on deprived of all meaning. The answer Ivlita had given him—from which, because it was coercive, he had fled the evening before—while it had undoubtedly been a way out, no longer seemed so to Laurence. Can death, when there is no other way out, be a solution? Did returning mean regaining? After the bitterness of defeat came the bitterness of disillusionment. There was nothing to regain. Was he afraid to die? Oh no, how gladly he would! How content he would have been lying broken on the floor of a canyon or shot through the head. And, truly, what was to consider: whether it was a way out or not, there was no other outcome. If it were otherwise, everything lost because of idle curiosity—joy, gooseberries, the glades, the lumber mill—would remain forever out of reach. Laurence wasn't thinking about Ivlita. She had immediately vanished from his existence, set like the sun, leaving him to hunt for a way where there was none

But Laurence, looking at the whitening glaciers, had only to recall the old wenny, and all pain passed from his body. And the young man jumped up as though nothing were the matter and with swift steps, assured as never before, began descending along the glacier, taking running leaps across the crevasses or carefully crawling over them, or even taking them on a sled. And then along the cliffs, following shelves and ledges, seeking out chimneys and suitable ridges, he moved with inhuman spontaneity. It had seemed everything was finished, once and for all. But now his nature did not want to yield to his frazzled head and was latching onto the slightest pretext for action. This world was suddenly fine and fair, funny, just, one Laurence would never abandon. The curling ice formations hanging over the precipice, and the stream digging in far below under the cliffs heed the young man's steps with such attention, as though afraid he might stumble. A kite shoots out of a fissure, frightening the lizards, whose presence you divine at a distance by the stones they knock down; the grass, mowed by the goats that went down at night to their watering place and would go down, naturally, today, too, is a glorious place for a hunter. A grass snake judiciously makes way

Yes, if some witness who had seen the young man a minute ago met him now, he wouldn't believe his eyes. Laurence's face was transfigured to such a degree, full of valor, without a care, unwrinkled, unreflecting. Humming, Laurence sought a place where he could cross the stream, part wading and part leaping from one boulder to another, and took off running on the opposite bank in order to warm himself and dry off. Laurence had strength enough and to spare, and if he had recalled just now being in despair, he would have been amazed. But Laurence no longer remembered anything. He proceeded with a weightless gait and if the road that lay before him had been much longer and much more difficult, it would have been overcome with the same animal litheness. For the first time since the evening when Luke had attempted to intervene in Laurence's life with art, Laurence was the same as he had been before that memorable evening. If only the path led into infinity

The forest stretched out on the opposite bank, and Laurence rustled among the branches and boughs, as though a massive beast were going through the woods; he spooked a few fallow deer and chased them, whistling. Even when it was getting dark and fireflies filled the air, causing a multitude of troubles, Laurence did not slow his pace. And, reflecting that this night, for sure, was exactly the same as the night of Brother Mocius, he felt only bolder and more assured. How much simpler everything is when you know what you want. And he flew into the sleeping unpronounceable hamlet precisely as he would have a year ago on his way to a merry hunt

Laurence paid no attention to the barking of dogs provoked by his appearance, not the bark that greets a human being's approach, but the kind that meets the appearance of a ravening and blood-thirsty beast, drawn out and dismal. The bark of a few was taken up by the rest, the wennies woke up, listening closely, and the soldiers, who were not entirely comfortable in this godforsaken den of thieves, jumped up, grabbing their weapons

Laurence found the cabin rebuilt and lit from inside, and after knocking down the door with a blow, he burst in. Near the entrance, on the floor, stood a lamp, and the wenny was lying next to it, his head turned so the shadow from his monstrous goiter fell across his face, howling like a dog. And no matter how eerie the barking of the village dogs, Laurence disdained the sheepdogs, but here he could not keep from shuddering and shrinking back. Was it a death plaint, an animal's savage exhaustion or a desperate call in view of a mortal enemy's approach? What hadn't Laurence heard during these last months: the crying of rape victims and the bawling of torture victims; nothing could compare with this fount of overwhelming horror. The young man grew cold, began reeling, trying to catch hold of the wall, and collapsed in a dead faint

When he came to, there was no more howling and the old wenny with his disfigured yap was bending over him. "I know you came for advice, my wayward son," he wheezed, "you who mocked it in due season. You wanted mountain treasures and found Ivlita, the greatest of all. And what of it, were you content? Still, you took off for the plains? You promised to make my sons rich and famous. And where are they? You spent time on the plains, collected some money; well, did it come in handy for you? And I won't even mention the fact that the whole country's mucked up because of you. And all because you're a pretender, one of the unwashed, you knew perfectly well you weren't a highlander, said so yourself, but you pushed in among the highlanders. Going nowhere fast, spitting in the wind. And you had the big idea of committing murder on top of it all. What advice can I give you now? Die like a dog and rot, you demon!"

"What garbage," Laurence cried out, bouncing back. "You've gone nuts because of your age and your wounds, obviously. At last, I see that *you* are the pretender, not I, and your wisdom is nonsense just like Brother Mocius's riches! I don't know what kind of blackout came over me. I thought: *you* can give me some advice, *your* words mean something. They're crap, that's all. Just like all you highlanders. Get this, you old blockhead," the young man went grinding on right into the wenny's ear, "murder's the only thing makes life worth living. We travel, get drunk, work, sleep with broads, all according to nature's laws, like we're walled in. There's only one way out—murder. Nature intended such and such person or beast to make his way through life, but I messed with the plan, took a knife or a pistol and turned everything upside down, violated the order of the world, broke free. I celebrated the mystery of turning wine into blood. Don't bother searching, murder is the only way to make freedom visible. Especially when it's not caused by hunger, or revenge, or at war, but murder for its own sake. You've been blowing smoke about you people not dying, but turning into trees. If you like, I'll cover the barren cliffs with vegetation and every desert with a garden in bloom. I'll strike you on the temple and branching death will sprout from your head this very day"

"Die like a dog, murderer," the old man rasped. And, forgetting his years and wounds, he jumped up and threw himself at Laurence. He knocked him down and both rolled on the floor. The lamp tipped over, kerosene streamed out and ignited

Villagers and soldiers, attracted by the fire and noise, came running. But they could not step over the threshold. Through the shimmering curtain of flame that engulfed the floor and the unhinged door, they observed two grappling people, now falling, now ascending with a snarl and a roar

But those gathered began whispering among themselves, and then a rapturous word rolled over them: Laurence. They could see: one of the brawlers stopped, distracted at being hailed

Laurence? One of the two? The soldiers raised their rifles and began shooting into the flames

But in the morning among the ashes and roof tiles of the burned-out cabin they found no corpses. Just one trunk of a strange tree resembling a skeleton and untouched by flames

14

In the city, they did not yet know anything of the latest events. Laurence, the treasury and all that, had been forgotten long ago in favor of other, more current, stories and the name of the unfortunate Arcady was covered over by the same oblivion. Therefore, if on this day some verifiable information had arrived about what happened in the cretins' hamlet or in the village with the sawmill, it would have appeared in small print, and only for lack of other material, on the last pages of the newspaper, where no one, it goes without saying, would even notice. And at present there was more than enough material, and the most urgent, official information, not subject to any rewriting or abbreviation, and so you could say with certainty that reports of Laurence's latest appearance would not have landed in the news section—no space for them would have been found even in the provincial chronicle. Today, the city was graced with a visit from the emperor

In consideration of the empire's breadth and variety, its juridical, so to speak, head was deprived, naturally, of the possibility of frequently displaying his outward ugliness to the populace, so devoted to him for his inner ugliness, and all the more of appearing in places distant from the capital, like the city with the grand boulevard. And since, besides, the emperor, dubbed The Prodigal Frigging Hand, hated his people for the characterization bestowed on him, despised them for their servility, and feared them, without knowing why, then, although appearing before the people was an obligatory condition of any reign, viewing The Prodigal Hand was permitted on extremely rare occasions. However, in accordance with considerations intelligible only to his entourage, it was incumbent on him, nevertheless, sometimes to travel, and the emperor was even now traveling, and since the city with the grand boulevard lay along his route, he could not avoid the grand boulevard and was obliged to give its citizens an occasion for demonstrating once again all their slavishness and the baseness of their race

In all classes of the population, therefore, a phenomenal fever held sway, whose degree depended on the degree of each class's participation in the events described. And it reached virtually its highest degree among the police. Since the task set before the state's police force was in this case particularly difficult and ticklish

First of all, they needed to preserve the person of the emperor, since it was customary in the country's history for emperors to end their lives in violent death. This problem would not have been so complicated if it had been possible to know precisely from whom they needed to protect the emperor. Although there was a simple answer in such cases: from the party, the inadequacy of this answer was too obvious: the party had been in existence for not all that many years, while emperors had been dying violent deaths since the dawn of time. But in view of the fact that the other assailants were too highly placed and that they were inaccessible or simply unknown to the police, the police stood by their answer and, naturally, strove to prove that they were right. And in view of the fact that the party, knowing that the emperor was only the sign over a shop where others were enriching themselves, had no plan for assassinating him, the police, in order to have something to intercept, had to arrange for an assassination attempt on their own. But because, finally, plotting attempts on the emperor himself was risky and his lackeys didn't have enough spirit, plots were set in motion against those close to the emperor, who actually trembled in fear for their own heads on such trips. That's why the struggle against the party was the second, concomitant concern for the police

But since the attempt had to be carried out, all the same, not by the police but by the party, it was necessary for the police, if not to run the party, then, in any case, to urge the party on to heroic exploits. The whole question came down to getting rid of surprises, which, however, remained, for no matter how many hands the police had in the party, not all the party's leaders were its people. The robbery of the treasury had succeeded only thanks to Basilisk's quick wits, and this time they had to be especially careful so as not to repeat the episode with the treasury

Several facts made the work of the police easier during such trips, in part the etiquette that divested a crowned personage of all freedom of action and predetermined for several months how that personage would pass each day and along what streets he would move while carrying out the ceremonies that made up his schedule. And since it had long been established that the linchpin of his visit would be a solemn prayer service in the city's cathedral in the presence of all ranks of civilians and soldiers, high and middling, the cathedral was chosen as the next theater

This time, the pantomime was sure to come off particularly ravishing and elegant, since the main role was assigned to a woman remarkable in all respects. Actually, Anna was a flower girl, whose adventurous love affairs were known well beyond the bounds of the city. She wasn't beautiful, perhaps good-looking, but in her strange figure—a small head with a broad smile, flat chest, excessively voluptuous thighs and sculpted little legs—was so much charm and banality that the males of the city were driven mad. Anna, however, who could easily have become rich and made a name for herself, derived no advantage from all her attractions, remaining trifling and poor. That's why the glory of an unmercenary settled on her, opening all doors into society, which despised disinterestedness, and the police, resolved to be, at long last, sharp-witted, suggested to Anna that her genuine path in life, in that case, was the party. But to keep Anna from becoming too zealous in working for the benefit of the party, they kept her in reserve for some solemn occasion. And now such an occasion was at hand, and it was decided to release Anna into circulation

Everything was extremely uncomplicated. In the cathedral, Anna had to carry out an attempt on the person of the chief of the state's police force (it stands to reason that this was a decision of the police chief himself, who worked out the details of the attempt), but not an entirely successfully one, then to be apprehended and immediately put to death. Thanks to the attempt, the chief of police was making his tenure more secure and receiving his next ribbon, and rewards and promotions were being prepared for his subordinates. Members of the party, once they had been accused of aiding and abetting, could be, in part, sent into exile, and in part, incarcerated: new sources for police prosperity. And everything was so clear and preordained, even the fever that had seized the police gained hold, essentially, only over the lower and less responsible ranks, while its leaders maintained the most magnificent calm in fulfilling their loyal duty. From the outside, the only thing that differentiated the peculiar life of the massive police barracks from its everyday aspect was that all ongoing work was suspended and the barracks was transformed into a theatrical wardrobe. Day and night, apparel for all kinds of citizens was being sewn, since it behooved the costumed police both to embody a crowd and to represent a delegation of craftsmen and merchants, bureaucrats and teachers, and every kind of delegation imaginable, up to and including governing circles. And although the emperor knew of this, and if he didn't, could easily have guessed, seeing in all corners of the country approximately the same forensic types, etiquette required him to pretend that, as he said, he was pleased with the reception, to believe in the genuineness of the people presented to him, often ten times in one day in one and the same city, changing their costumes and makeup, and to pose questions, hear out replies and read with pleasure the patents and charters submitted to him. True, the costumers' tastes and the love of state folklorists for old-fashioned things led to the people who met the emperor usually being dressed as no one had dressed for many centuries already. But this only made everything more picturesque, and for the unfeigned philistine who watched the shuffling of costumed police, the spectacle turned out to be not merely amusing, but even educational

The Prodigal Hand was dressed in the same kind of antediluvian costume in order not to break the unity of the decor when, emerging from the train station, he had to clamber up onto the horse that was presented to him and, surrounded by his entourage, brilliant to a rare degree, ride through the entire city to the cathedral. And since the number in disguise was, nevertheless, insufficient to bank the road from the station to the cathedral, The Prodigal Hand was forced to move along at a particularly slow pace, thereby giving the ecstatic populace the opportunity, once he had passed them, to race forward along side streets and, in this way, fill the boulevard, which, cordoned off by soldiers, was, in fact, deserted. In the cathedral, what there was of baseness in the city and whatever vapidity could be brought were united for the meeting. And Laurence, scrutinizing the monstrous mugs, heavy-lobed, hawk-nosed and cross-eyed, and the feeble bodies, bony hands, bugged-out and unctuous eyes, the whole devil's Sabbath, asked himself with a shudder what the leader of these fiends must be and why a church was such a suitable place for bats, guano, sin and degeneration

After managing to jump out the window following his fight with the wenny and to flee the unpronounceable hamlet, Laurence considered Arcady's murder the last thing left to do and showed up in the village with the sawmill in search of the captain. But there he found out about The Prodigal Frigging Hand's arrival in the city and, seeing in this unexpected trip his one chance for redeeming the past, since to sweeten the theatrical effect they often pardoned bandits who turned up with a confession, he asked the village scribe to draw up a petition, carefully hid the sheet and, without disturbing Arcady's dreary sleep, set off once more for the city, where, so recently, he had resolved never again to make an appearance. And now, after gaining access to the cathedral thanks to his picturesque bandit's costume, Laurence was standing not far from the entrance, holding his petition, determined to press the paper immediately into The Prodigal's hands, since the hope for a pardon was an unhoped-for way out with respect to the future father who had returned to his senses

When she saw him, Anna could not for a long time recollect whether this was the same person she had met in Basilisk's company in the suburban garden on the eve of the robbery. But when she was certain he was the same, only then did it occur to her: yes, of course, that's Laurence, and everything was suddenly extraordinarily illumined, and Anna no longer saw anyone in the cathedral besides Laurence. But Laurence's very presence was so unnatural that Anna could in no way come to terms with it, and meanwhile, she needed to act. And allowing that Anna knew Laurence's tie to the party had been broken, and saw that he was alone, she was convinced that Laurence had planned something incredible, more magnificent than his former audacity. And although the object of his new plan could only be the emperor, the emperor whose approach the hautboys were already announcing, Anna did not consider whether she ought to get in Laurence's way, for to get in his way would mean renouncing what she had planned. And acknowledging that, no matter what, she had been driven into a corner and that if she did not shoot and kill the chief of police, she would all the same be strangled somewhere, Anna in the end decided to let Laurence act first and see what would come of it

And at once her agitation disappeared and was replaced by a sense of utter fulfillment. What fun it would be if he killed The Prodigal Frigging Hand or caused some unbelievable calamity here. And with the rapture, which, she tried to assure herself on this point, she had experienced once before when she met Laurence with Basilisk, Anna gazed at her hero, standing near the entrance on a dais and poised over the cathedral. The sunshine, penetrating the rainbow-colored glass, scattered bunches of alpine flowers around Laurence and cast a shadow from him in such a way that Anna, overwhelmed by the difference between him and the officials, had a vision: the whole area of the building was shrouded by Laurence, and the degenerates crowding around dissolved in him, along with the streams of people filing into the cathedral, more and yet more, the powerful of this world, preceding the emperor

No matter how repulsive the beings who already filled the cathedral, the look of those entering turned out to be even more shocking. Boys opened the procession, two by two, dressed in crimson broadcloth, in overly tight trousers that emphasized their loathsome, rickety legs. Their bloodless faces reflected inchoate vices. But on the muzzles of those who followed after them, carrying crosiers and wearing caftans embroidered with gold, the vices had been inscribed with diligent application, and, looking at the cavities and humps, bunions and sores that ornamented the courtiers, Laurence was more and more amazed. But this amazement gave way to squeamishness when the old men who were already completely decayed, so you couldn't tell how they were still bearing up, made their appearance. But, no matter how great Laurence's revulsion, which had begun to be complicated with fear, everything turned out to be trivial in comparison with the sensations that took hold of him: he shuddered, stiffened, stood transfixed, when he saw the emperor

Bringing up the rear of the procession, hunched over, wiping his eternally sweating hands, shaking the red beard dappled with gray that sprouted from his waxen face, wandering with the nervous gaze of his dull, bloodshot eyes, faded, paunchy, decrepit, Brother Mocius, dressed in a jester's costume, moved along, heading for the emperor's throne and noiselessly treading the marble of the church

Laurence's hand, grasping the sheet of paper and already on the point of being lifted up, hung in the air. Filled with trepidation, the young man watched Brother Mocius reach the throne, kiss the cross, and take his seat under the baldachin decorated with double eagles. The bandit couldn't believe his ears when he heard: "For the emperor Mocius, let us pray." To hand this person his petition, this pitiful pretender who had already been put to death once, someone like that—would he have what it takes? Could *he* really disentangle the contradictions that had been tied together in the course of the story to form the noose in which Laurence would perish? Breathe life into a brain drained of blood? Could he give sound back to the grass, clarity to the snowy ridges, and stillness to a shaking hand, and dreams to a hollow, unrestorative sleep? Could he reconcile Laurence with everything that had happened, rendering it suitable for toothless tales told to grandsons and granddaughters?

But, when Laurence recalled the misadventures of the past year, he forced himself to believe that Brother Mocius could do all. Brother Mocius would forgive him—he was, after all, one of his own, a neighbor, he would understand that Laurence had gone astray, had been punished as he deserved and that it was time to return to the sawmill, to his earlier tedium, hardworking and poor

Still, hadn't Laurence gone mad? How could this murdered holy fool, buried up there in the cemetery, not only be living, but in possession of the empire, ruling over impure spirits? And that he was now alive, who had been slain, you could handle that, but how could it be that he was a holy ascetic, supposedly, but when you took a closer look, he was pulling strings (and the pudding), the great prince of darkness, and so on, and so forth. And weren't his spawn just poor imitations of their emperor? And what about Captain Arcady's outrages? The gendarmes' brutality? Bureaucratic arbitrariness? The instigator of all the crimes that entangled the mountains and the plains—was he not this lout? And to think what Laurence had endured on account of his saintliness, which was in fact sin

And now to prostrate himself, abase himself, bending the knee, submit to his mercy and acknowledge the depravity ruling this world? Or was it better to finish off the creep?

And, nevertheless, there, high, high above the righteous hamlet, among the ice floes and stars, Ivlita was waiting for Laurence, reconciled to his evil for the sake of her future child

What hadn't Laurence borne on account of this woman! And it was still too little—he had to go on to new humiliations, mortal, to grovel in the dust once more and, possibly, even after death. "Isn't Ivlita Brother Mocius's ally?" flashed through the young man's head

The service was coming to an end. Incense filled the cathedral, and the sun's rays could no longer seep through the dove-colored density. The Prodigal Hand's eternally tired face became even grayer, melted, and he doubled up. Anna exchanged one or two glances with the police officers standing next to her, but prolonged the action. For as time slipped away, her rapture in the young man deepened, and she no longer wanted him to carry out the assassination attempt, on the contrary, she planned to get in his way. He would, of course, be apprehended by the police, beaten, hanged, this one and only decent human being. She had to save him; and no matter how pleasant it would be to see The Prodigal Frigging Hand prostrate, Laurence's fate was more precious

The clergy were crowding around the emperor. The ritual had ended. The bowlegged youths formed up once more, the gilded smut-mouths, the undead elders. They moved toward the exit. Laurence raised his paper again and, descending the steps, pushed his way through the ranks that separated him from the procession. "Should I submit it or not? Humiliate myself or kill him?" he was still repeating. Anna didn't take her eyes off of him, and when she saw that ten paces, not more, separated the emperor from Laurence and that they would shortly collide, she pulled a pistol from her purse, aiming at the emperor. But the hand of someone who had been following Anna rather attentively flung her hand up forcefully

A shot rang out, and the bullet, flying over the emperor, struck an infant painted on the wall vlita descended to the people. After her reconciliation on high, she decided to seek the swamp of daily life. The frosty nights that had begun to blot out the sun, and solitude, little suited her condition and would be entirely unfit for her newborn. She had to live among people

In the hamlet, where Ivlita returned on the evening following the fire, she was met with studied indifference. They already knew here about how the peasant women had paid for their attack and so there was no talk of taking hostile action against the pregnant woman. They steered clear of her, staring with trepidation at her awkward belly, and that was all. Whatever superstitions ruled the highlanders, however, Ivlita was so rich, refusing her proposal that they sell one of their houses to her meant missing out on an extremely rare business transaction; and that very same evening, Ivlita became, in exchange for a bundle of money that had become damp in the cave, the owner of a structure on piles, recently thrown together not far from the cretins' stable and divided into several miniature rooms

Ivlita didn't find her old friends. Laurence's clash with the old wenny made her the wenny family's enemy forever. When Ivlita tried calling on the spoiled class, those of Laurence's associates among the toiling class who had survived would not allow the woman to cross the threshold of their yard, greeting her with gobs of clay and abuse. But Ivlita didn't attach any meaning to this. She had no time for sorting out trifles. The nativity was approaching

The eldest of the wenny daughters alone refused to submit to her brothers' humor and moved into Ivlita's henhouse, dragging along a mahogany cradle, a gift from the spoiled—its luxuriant carvings and finish recalled the moldings and shutters of the palace that had vanished. Just as if by a wave of the hand, everything in the new dwelling was arranged and appointed. In the morning, the wenny daughter would busy herself with chores, after noon she would sit down to cut swaddling cloths and sew little blankets, and at dusk she would take up her guitar and, settling on her bed at Ivlita's feet, sing always the same ravishing songs. The nights were foggy and quiet. They were done with architecture and repairs until spring, and so the sun would come up on a seemingly desolate hamlet: there was neither a hatchet chopping nor a cry. Even the soldiers made no appearance. And it was like that the whole day

That's why when, during one of their suppers, the door slowly opened and admitted Laurence into the dining room, his advent was scandalous and shocking. The wall lamp weakly lit the man who entered, but even what Ivlita could see was enough. After a few days' absence, Laurence had wasted away and grown old. Laurence removed his hat, guiltily balling up the felt, and a gray lock fell into the bandit's eyes, half hiding his pupils, smoldering with a strange and baleful light. Not a hint of his bravery, strength, magnificence remained. His clothing was not just soiled, but even slovenly, and the former dandy, who would never before have dared show himself to his wife in such a state, didn't even think it necessary to apologize for his oversight. He was bent and seemed to have shrunk. And the former hero expressed nothing but impotence and improbable exhaustion

Without greeting her, shifting from one leg to the other, not daring to look Ivlita in the eye, Laurence haltingly told how he had wanted to plead forgiveness, but in the church, just as he was getting ready to hand over his petition, someone opened fire on the emperor and in the confusion that arose as a result Laurence had been shoved aside. What's more, someone began calling out "Laurence," which forced him to save himself by running away

Ivlita was listening to his story without any enthusiasm, as though knowing beforehand what it contained. But when Laurence, with bitterness in his voice, added that the silliest thing in this whole farce was that the emperor was none other than Brother Mocius, Ivlita flared up, and without warning, Laurence seemed so intolerable and repulsive that she clenched her fists and gritted her teeth to keep from attacking him

"Where have there not been any victims of Laurence," she thought. They were here in the villages, reposing in humble cemeteries and forest damp, frolicking on river bottoms and sea shoals, dwelling in the mountains, in cities; and even corrupting on the throne, ruling over millions and millions in an enormous empire, a man put to death by Laurence. Death penetrated everywhere, sparing no one, with unimaginable speed, and the last clod lost in the raging flood and ready from moment to moment to disappear was Ivlita and her womb

The contradiction between Ivlita and Laurence was so great there could be no thought of their reconciliation. And how naïve had been her wish for him to lay down his arms and renounce the past. Could Laurence, death itself, really cease to be himself? And how right the peasant women had been, asserting that a bandit ought to remain childless. But would Laurence really not remain childless, just the same, after infecting his wife and offspring with death?

Childless, just the same? No, no, her child would live, it was playing and wanting out. Ivlita did not fear dying, but would defend her greatest treasure. She would penetrate wherever you like, even to the edge of the world—to the birds, the beasts, the fish, hide like a toad under a stone, dig like a shrew into the earth—just so long as Laurence would never find her, could do nothing, and the infant, saved, protected, would enter the world and grow. And Ivlita, snarling with her hate-filled, fearless gaze, reduced Laurence to ashes, reddened in her anger, and Laurence, about to raise his eyes to hers, first lost his nerve, and then was surprised at her manifest hostility, threw down his hat and started racing around the room, waving his arms

As though he were to blame, after submitting to everything, that someone shot at The Prodigal Frigging Hand. And what was it, in fact, Laurence had done to make Ivlita begin hating him now? After all, hadn't he been killing all along—either in self-defense, or punishing crafty types (they were asking for it) or for her sake? Could she blame him because love had gone to his head? And what kind of artful ploy was this, puffing up a few murders (every highlander trailed as many, if not more) into an extraordinary affair, in terms of evil

No, enough rationalizing. If Ivlita didn't want him to murder and rob, he wouldn't; he was ready to while away his days with her in poverty. For now, it goes without saying, he couldn't live here because of the soldiers, but once they took themselves back home when the snows arrived, he would move in here. Ivlita, however, should not go back into the mountains. It was already cold, and then there was the child. Therefore, Laurence would settle in the forest and visit Ivlita when night came on. And Laurence lay down to sleep, without even taking his shoes off

Ivlita didn't shut her eyes for a whole eternity, and when, at the first cock crow, Laurence departed from her dwelling, she, too, got up, dressed hurriedly, gave orders to the wenny daughter and, without waiting for daylight, dashed into the forest. Her belly sorely hindered her, but the damp ground prospered her, and when, on the far side of the thinning leaves, dawn and fog disrupted the stars to the point of breakdown, Ivlita was already far from the unpronounce-able hamlet

The fog outstripped the sunshine. At first, it slid in toward Ivlita over the trees, slowing her pace, then thickened, descended, and trunks and branches were left floating in disagreeable dregs. Had it been long since the fog was in the pastures, dry and lightly eva-nescent? And now, oily and unyielding, it didn't leave the road—it insistently hid from the refugee both where the west was and the spectacle of healing autumn, long expected and arrived at last, happy and absolving and too short to weary

But Ivlita was going uphill, not losing time. And day, growing stronger, whisked the fog down, until the environs of the canyon she'd left behind emerged, first vague, and then evident to a fault. How distinct in content was the much-praised scene from those Ivlita had grown used to and examined with tenderness from year to year

In the sky, patently made deeper and not shaped like a cup, but like a funnel, ready at any moment to initiate a blizzard, the clouds were the color the sky usually is, while the sky was perfectly white, without a single blood-red drop, despite the morning hours, and blood, which now turned out to be the most normal and repulsive human blood, spilled, lay in spots on the leaves (especially on the other side of the dale, to the east of the wennies' hamlet), soaked into the moss, saturated the soil, now fresh and perfectly crimson, or a dried up red brown, or pink like an infant's, and of every other condition—and Ivlita noticed for the first time since Jonah's mur-der that her legs were wounded and bloody up to her knees. The snowy bodies rising up to the north, bordering the pastures, were just as empurpled and maimed. But without paying any more atten-tion to the glaciers or to her illness, Ivlita hurried on, panting, if only to make it in time, and thought, trembling, that if she loitered, instead of a new body, death would fall to her

In the glades, not just the grass, even the bushes were completely chewed down. Tomorrow or the next day the shepherds would pass over these places with whistles and sighing, breaking the silence with their concluding hustle and bustle after preparing everything for their long overwintering and hibernation, and driving the goats before them. If only she could sit for a while and rest

Here is the plot with its boxwood hedge, hung all over with bits of clothing and headwear and tresses of feminine hair and little crosses in honor of the satyr and with requests for intercession. Ivlita immediately recognized the hedge. Hadn't her way passed through here when, descending from the pastures, she had run naked in the direction of the sawmill? If the bears had not prevented her back then from stopping, there would have been no misfortunes. And tearing a lock from her head, Ivlita hung it, in a hurry, on one of the little branches. Take notice, my guardian!

And there's the village on the far side. You could reach out and touch it. Last time, in her delirium, Ivlita hadn't seen anything properly. And now, she studied with interested curiosity the human congeries, much more abundant and richer than the hamlet she had left behind. Although the view from here was not so expansive as from the glaciers, the plain was closer, and so it was easy to make out that the village with the sawmill was not alone, and that further along and lower down there were others, numerous and just as spacious, scattered over the limitless plateau, a new world, in which Ivlita would live a new life

Ivlita had only to begin her descent, and she ran into some peasants she didn't know, but who immediately identified her. "Ivlita!" Where was she going, they would detain her, you know, it's dangerous in the village. Some had just managed to begin speaking when others showed up. "Stop, it's madness to go down, those aren't people, but worse than beasts." Behind the peasants that had run into her, new ones rolled in, trying to persuade her, begging her to turn back. But she, with a rapt and inscrutable mien, continued on her way. And it bothered her not a bit that as she was approaching the village, she was already surrounded by hundreds. To these hundreds were added the villagers who came running from all around, and when Ivlita reached the village hall, in which Captain Arcady was quartered, the square in front of the hall was choked with a seething crowd of thousands

Captain Arcady, during the time he'd been staying in the village, had become accustomed to the fact that none of its inhabitants even dared cross the square, let alone stop opposite the village hall, and the customers of the taverns that lay across from the village hall, if, for once, they felt brave enough to pay a call on the tavern keepers, would only do so by the back entrances. "What doomsday is this?" thought the captain, sitting in his shirt at the table and tasting, despite its already being noon, his morning coffee, cursing for the umpteenth time Laurence and this savage country that had sucked him in with no hope for success. Yes, Arcady no longer believed it was possible to capture Laurence, especially after the fire incident, in which he'd watched the chance for selfless, unconscious betrayal go up in smoke, and he'd been so relying on it. And he had decided to write this very day a report to the leadership requesting transfer to another place and an assignment that could be carried out more conveniently. "What kind of prodigy is this?" he asked himself once more, got up and, yawning, walked to the glass doors that led to the balcony. On the square, directly in front of Arcady, stood a woman, two heads taller than all the peasants—they were familiar to him and had long since become irksome, but were today unnaturally transformed—who, being, in Arcady's view, if you will, too heavy-set, was, all the same, so radiantly beautiful that the captain at once surmised this had to be Ivlita, the bandit Laurence's concubine. But no matter how much Arcady had heard about her, the vision surpassed all his expectations. And could they really understand anything about beauty in the sticks? "If this woman were in the city, she'd be famous the world over, but here in this hole . . ." Ivlita rose up, not moving from the spot, sustaining the captain's gaze taking her in piece by piece: head, shoulders, bust, thickened braids. But what was this? Pregnant? Such a beauty? It can't be, and Arcady ran out onto the balcony to make sure he wasn't mistaken

The captain's emergence was met with shouts and threats. "Don't dare touch her," the peasants growled, shaking their fists. How's this, these scum dare make threats? The sons of bitches should be shot, and the cunt with them. But Arcady had been taken unawares. He, spoiled by the peasants' servility and cowardice, bound by the epoch of confidence, and certain that they would never, as he said, dare, did not have on hand a sufficient number of soldiers to disperse the unusual congregation. And was it worth it? Was it creditable that they would fight furiously for such a one? It could end badly! And then, on account of this whore, the administration would not praise him for the war . . . In short, rejecting immediate action, he put on a smile and, leaning over the railing, asked what was the matter

In response, the marble sculpture came to life and, emerging from the respectfully parting crowd, approached the village hall. "So beautiful, truly, if she were not pregnant, I'd be ready to change my tastes for her sake," Arcady muttered. And with great haste and polite antics he ran down the stairs, ready for anything they might ask of him and inviting her to enter. But Ivlita only came near the captain, said something to him, swayed, and once more entered the crowd. Rooted to the spot with his mouth hanging open, Arcady, daring neither to turn back nor to cry out, gazed at the beauty, who, passing the similarly dazed peasants, slowly rounded the cemetery and was hidden beyond the cypresses

When, with the coming of night, Laurence returned to the beyonsensical hamlet, he found Ivlita not in mourning, but wearing a pink dress in the latest fashion, broad and pleated, so that her belly was not very noticeable—a Sunday outfit—with a high hairdo and weighed down with the jewels Laurence had brought from the city, beautiful as a fairy tale and cheerful. The table was meticulously set and decorated with paper flowers, laden with dish after dish (Laurence's eyes caught fire at the sight of this abundance after so many months in the cave), and in the middle of the table lay a bottomless silver horn, seemingly the very same one. Laurence was embarrassed and asked what had provoked all this

"Simply an idle caprice." Ivlita wants a befitting celebration of their reconciliation and return to the little village

Of course, Ivlita was right, Laurence agreed. It went without saying, this bourgeois existence sure was the real, well-ordered life, and everything else was vanity, folly, and fidgeting. To be happy, nothing more was required than a sated mind and deep sleep. "Well then, wonderful," Laurence concluded, becoming surprisingly mushy and kinder. "We'll start life on a new footing." And, sinking into an armchair, he asked for some wine

Ivlita took the silver horn from the table, filled it with fragrant brandy and brought it to him. Laurence hesitated. He was too worn out and overworked to stand up to such a quantity. But the memory of their first encounter lashed against his vanity. Laurence accepted the horn and emptied it, without stopping for breath

Laurence had never drunk such strong brandy. Right away, everything became unstable, started wheeling about, and his breathing broke off. How weak he was. His legs were taken from him, and he saw stars, shifting, changing, jets of hot water were spurting, and then, it seemed, cold, and after that everything receded from him to an uncertain depth, at the bottom of which Ivlita was bathing, winged and rapidly approaching. Laurence felt Ivlita near him, stroking his head, unbuttoning his collar, taking off his bandolier, securing the pistol from his bosom. What for?

Gathering his strength, Laurence opened his eyes and looked at her questioningly and warily. But it was too late

Lifting the silver horn, Ivlita leaned over and, calling out, "Enter," struck Laurence on the head with such force that the young man rolled out of the armchair without even a groan

And the room was already filled to bursting. Captain Arcady, smiling and self-satisfied, soldiers, police, a few villagers. Dropping the horn, Ivlita turned away and withdrew into a corner. Not even looking when they dragged Laurence, bloody and firmly bound, into the yard. She remained standing like that until everyone left, last of all Captain Arcady, who had been pacing for a long time around the deserted dining room, hoping that Ivlita would suddenly turn back, would say something, and deliberating whether to break the silence. Losing his patience, he dashed out into the yard and walked around for the entire night, despite the unbearable cold, refusing to spend the night with anyone

As day was dawning, Laurence began coming to his senses. The captain, fearing an attack of rage, ordered the ropes to be pulled more tightly. But his precautionary measures were superfluous. Laurence didn't move a muscle. His gaze slid across the representatives of authority and settled on the house from which he had been dragged. Laurence never tore his gaze from this house until he was bound to a stretcher and carried away. Laurence wept

Before his departure, Arcady drew from his pocket a bundle of money, was about to send a soldier with it, but then became emboldened and, entering Ivlita's house, cast the money down on the table

Ivlita was sitting opposite the window, hanging her sun-petted head and crooning something, rocking an empty cradle

16

The young man, in crossing his horizonless prison cell and after resting near the wall, had only to resolve on four more steps, and he felt: in the sole of one of his shoes there was some kind of surplus that caused him pain at every step. But, preoccupied with his anger and bitterness, he didn't even wonder why

The narrow loophole of the ancient fortress (turned into a prison) that served as a window for his cell was not sufficient to light up the stone receptacle, but that made the brightness outside all the more blinding and objects in the outside world stood out all the more. Reaching into a crack, Laurence contrived to lift himself up and have a look, and the snow-covered mountains, the mountains of his fatherland that erased the horizon to the north-northeast, were just as near and obtrusive as if Laurence were looking at them from his native village. But now their sight did not instill joy, nor did it leave him indifferent. They oppressed him, with no respite, and Laurence, ostensibly self-contained, walled off from the world, but in reality, one who had not escaped that same old familiar, boring world, one chained to the mountains, surmised that in prison his last hope for redemption had been lost. At last he understood how small and intolerably cramped was the castle prepared for him

And Laurence decided he would make no attempt to get out and therefore would never leave from this time forth. Court and executioner were of no account. Life had been traversed, and death was already present in light puffy clouds. Redemptive death would lead him away into a dungeon without sleep, sun, and air

The young man played mechanically with the shackles that weighed down his legs and it seemed to him that it wasn't the first time he had reckoned up the links. But when was that? And, stepping back from one day to another in which, once he had reviewed a life that had not touched him at all, had indifferently passed by Ivlita's infidelity, Basilisk's perfidy, the mercenary Galaction, and the traitor Luke, always searching for the origin of these chains, Laurence finally recalled them ornamenting the spine and entwining the neck of Brother Mocius that evening. When the monk was flying from the precipice, the iron was disentangled and left shining on the riverbank. Wasn't Laurence, crouched down, worrying the chains just so, demanding from them the story of the man who had worn them voluntarily

It wasn't worth digging out: memories were just memories, for Laurence was still alive, but his mind was already dead. The penitential chains provoked neither revulsion nor fear; after all, he, too, had donned them of his own free will. They clanked, and that was all

Laurence tried standing up and again felt pain in the sole of his foot. He decided to take off his shoe. The sole was hard, thick, hiding something. Laurence tore the shoe apart, split the sole, and noticed there was a saw sewn into it

What could this mean? And no matter how much his mind had deserted him, Laurence still guessed the saw had been sewn in on purpose, someone had slipped him the shoes while he was being admitted to the prison so he could save himself, some unknown admirers were trying to help him, and betrayed by all, he was, nevertheless, not alone. And new might surged from somewhere, new resolve and hope. And hadn't he, all his life, sawn just like this through trunks and boards in his native village, hadn't the fine steel always destroyed chestnuts and pines, as it did now government iron? The work was done. A break until tomorrow. To run as soon as possible to freedom

The prison walls ceased not just to be formidable, but even sound. It turned out the frame around the loophole had been carefully loosened by someone and it didn't take much effort to push the stones out. Soon, the opening was so wide he could stick not just his head through, but also his shoulders

Down below, beneath the fortress, ran the river that, making its way from the paradisiacal valley and the village with the sawmill, became muddier and stouter. But no matter how troubled its waters suffering shortness of breath, the bottom was visible, and on the bottom some drowned man lay prone, surrounded by fish

"Can it really be Brother Mocius, yet again?" Laurence flared up. "If so, the monk is positively starting to meddle too much. Well, it doesn't matter, I spared him in the cathedral, today I'll get rid of him once and for all." And Laurence, crimson with rage, applied himself and, pushing more stones out, flew headlong with them into the river

When he had disappeared beneath the water, the swimmer opened his eyes. Fish were hurtling past in schools and looked especially huge through the emerald water, changing color and position every second, meeting together, circling, chasing one another, tumbling, and vanishing. In an eddy of sand and silt, turning now into trees, now into beasts' muzzles, now to ice and fog, they hurtled by. Sometimes a crayfish claw would butt in, threatening the swimmer

Several times, drowned people who had not lost their human image slid above Laurence. But whether Brother Mocius was among them, there was no chance of saying. Fighting the current, and not wanting to rise to the surface, Laurence dove deeper and deeper, suffocating, groping around and frightening hosts of fish

And the desire to pursue the monk unexpectedly disappeared, the search lost all meaning, and Laurence realized that not just his mind, but all of him was dying, there was no need to search when in death was everything, nothing to avenge when death is life without offense. And he sensed that, deceased, he was floating upward, escorted by fish, to the surface of another world and the unbearable lightness of eternal appeasement. But the fish drew back, the wind burst into his lungs, and the still unfinished day broke over his eyes. A shot, it seems. That means they've noticed the flight. Need to escape. Good thing the wooded bank across from the castle is close and reaching it won't be any trouble

First thing is shaking the guards from the trail and changing this prison garb for something passable. But, once he crawled onto the bank, the young man noticed that dusk was near. Let them follow. But which way should he get going? What kind of welcome was waiting in the first village?

Laurence's deliberations were interrupted by the sudden appearance of an unfamiliar villager who stepped out of the bushes. Laurence was ready to pounce on the stranger, but then he, waving his arms, cried out: "Don't be afraid, I'm one of yours, I have everything ready for you to change clothes." The villager untied a package. There really was clothing in it. In a minute, Laurence was transformed. Taking his hand, the villager hurriedly led him into the thicket, and after they'd passed through, took off running along the edge of the forest

Laurence had not yet had time to ask who his savior was and what this story in the spirit of what Basilisk meant when they reached some structures standing not far from the bank that resembled an inn and stables

His conductor entered one of the houses with the bandit and, saying nothing to his landsmen who were in the room, invited Laurence to sit at a table, wonderfully set, and fortify himself

"Hurry up," said the stranger. "The horse is ready, but the gendarmes won't be on foot, either, and you'd best keep them at a respectable distance. What can you do?" he added, as if justifying himself. "Everyone has to work. We've organized a concern to arrange escapes from the fortress. Sometimes it works out, sometimes it doesn't. Yours came off quite well. But when you're home, don't be stingy settling accounts with our emissary. The police, naturally, suspect some enterprising dispensation, but for now, they don't have enough evidence, and we give them the fattest bribes we can, so they don't keep us from earning our milk money. Well, get flying. Here's a weapon, just in case. And as for the way . . ."

And the stranger furnished the necessary information in brief

When Laurence had left, his hosts gathered peacefully together and, watching some mutton turn on a spit, waited for the gendarmes until midnight. But there was no pursuit

Laurence, when, toward morning, he had covered half the way separating him from the mountains, ran into a crowd of peasants (whether they were participants in the enterprise or simply fans, he couldn't tell) who warned him it wasn't safe to show his face in the nearest settlement and showed him a detour. He got a fresh horse from them and continued his flight

Why, for the third time, was he fighting his way back to the village where he had been betrayed and abandoned by everyone? What magnet drew him, despite all the prisons and his own resolutions, into the mountains, not permitting him to die in a foreign land? And although the question answered itself, Laurence pored over it for a long time, assuring himself that he was mistaken—altogether, as he said, *not* for that reason. But to the extent that his native ground came closer, he resisted less, and was obliged at last to admit that, no matter how hard he tried to think about something else, he was being pulled toward Ivlita

He was dying, so be it, but she must die with him. And no matter how distasteful it was for Laurence to note that he was moved by desire for revenge on a woman, and although he considered himself guilty for entering into her confidence and silly for plunging into so many affairs on account of a moll—and not just himself, the surrounding world and way of life were also to blame—the desire to settle accounts, to kill her, got the upper hand over all other considerations. And why the hell, he added, bestow meaning on seaweed, on his memories of Brother Mocius, and exaggerate Ivlita's role? A whore, that's all there was to it; a whore like all the others. But she'd get what she deserved, and the past would be wiped out with her

And to reinforce the threat, Laurence reached for his pistol. But he had only to touch his gun and Ivlita rose up before him, soaring aloft over the road and stretching her arms out toward him, in her superhuman glory, in her beauty, for the sake of which you could accept any humiliation, suffer every kind of want. And the young man bowed his head and let his arms fall to his sides. Letting go of the bridle, not noticing that the horse was going along at a walk, he was ready to weep in self pity

Such lack of will? Was he a bandit, or not? Honor, dignity—did these words still mean anything, or had they been hollowed out for all time? And had the name of Laurence really lost its shock music? So fainthearted before a whore? Laurence jerked the gun up and shot. But Ivlita melted away

No matter, he would find her there, in the hamlet. And the bandit gave his horse free rein to gallop, annoyed at wasting a bullet. As he approached his native village, he drank in the surroundings and once more acquired powers that would have no end

The sun had already spurned the hills, but the colors of sunset, splayed across the humid sky, two-thirds in cloud cover, and whirling in the air with the dead leaves, made the landscape soothing to the point of irritation. The shepherds' whistles and the bleating of goats descending from the pastures and intersecting, here and there, the road, channeling toward the villages, and the scent of fermenting corn spoke of an end to long and pointless tumult. From the forest that clothed the slopes of the nearby mountains, implacable, spotted with evergreens scattered among legions of beeches, the fogs flowed in streams, and the wind, evenly and lovingly, used them to cover the trees that had begun shivering. To keep his horse from slowing its pace, he had to spur and whip it every minute, but it insisted on its own way, as though considering it unseemly to gallop in the midst of this autumnal calm

The village with the sawmill was as familiar and ordinary as if Arcady, who had left the evening before, had never been quartered there. Despite the late hour, the whine of saws reached him from the mill: overtime before the winter break. The cattle, reluctantly yielding the path to the rider, the sound of little bells, the cackling of hens. In front of the taverns and the village hall a multitude of people, hurrying to talk their fill before the snows. They're beating tambourines and dancing

Spattering mud, dismounting and jumping back into the saddle at a gallop, peppering the air with bullets, Laurence hurtled past the gaping mouths of his fellow villagers. He was already far away when the people began exclaiming in response and the musicians, who had pulled up short, began playing a welcome; he didn't see the tavern keepers dragging skins onto the street and filling every jug gratis, and he didn't take part in the drinking celebration, the first since their liberation from the soldiers, with which the peasants rewarded themselves in plenty for what they had lived through. But the accordion's notes slid along behind the rider for a long time, and now and then, scaring them off, a lone clarinetist overstrained his instrument

Today Laurence could have tasted the delights of the reception he had been dreaming of. But there wasn't time

The path to the hamlet was too steep and winding. The horse couldn't go any farther. This played in Laurence's favor. "The gendarmes won't be able to ride through, either," he thought, "and on foot, can they really catch a highlander?" And, abandoning the horse, he ran, despite the slippery needles and the boughs and the acclivity, through the woods with the swiftness of a deer and was soon on the breakpoint to the other slope

Night was ready to step in at any moment and, it seemed, was only waiting for a long and fanciful pink cloud in the sky to dim. It smelled of moss and mushrooms. There was no wind, and even the red squirrels didn't shake the oak branches. Traveling along the western slope was much more difficult, he ended up sliding down every ten steps. Beyond the forest, on the grassy escarpment, keeping a foothold was inconceivable. Laurence tripped and went flying downhill. Here he is down below. The glade was spangled with fireflies, and the lights of the unpronounceable hamlet melted among the numberless stars. Above, the constellations, swelling with damp, differed in no way from the insects and conducted the same silent chorus. Neither birds (become altogether extinct), nor jingling bells, nor a stream to trouble the bottomless silence. And all of a sudden a rumbling hum that made the abyss still more apparent reached Laurence, something the young man had heard many times before, but had remained deaf to until now. The cretins were singing

How much Laurence had been dreaming during these last days about a return to the good life, lost through carelessness, but it had never occurred to him that he would *have* to return, no matter what, and that the good life was death. But now the meaningless, lifeless, useless sounds had touched the bandit and it became clear (why, however, so late) that only behind these nonhuman sounds was hidden a happiness he had stubbornly sought away from home.

Why, horrified (who cares about the rules of singing, were they really worth happiness?), did Laurence then, on the morning after Luke's murder, abandon the cretins' salvific stable? To return to them. To remain near them forever

The young man became suddenly alert. Shots, it seems. Most likely, the chase. Yes, and the cretins have gone silent. It's late to be dreaming of happiness

And Laurence ran off to Ivlita's house. Before the guard ran him down, everything would be over. He was about to break the door wide open with a blow when it opened on its own, and a woman, in whom he immediately recognized the wenny's eldest daughter, sprang up from the threshold and grasped the bandit's shoulder: "Quiet," she whispered loudly, "She's not well, she's been in labor two days and can't be delivered"

Laurence pushed the beldam out of the way and burst into the house. But when he saw a bed in its depths and was engulfed in groans, he paused, not daring to move. Giving birth? Could he kill both? Let the mother perish, but his offspring?

"Get out, don't you see?" the wenny daughter pressed him, shoving him into the next room. Feeling for his pistol, Laurence paced from one corner to another, stopping now and then to listen

The silence wasn't broken from outside. Time was passing. "Where are my pursuers, why are they dillydallying?" Laurence asked. Are they wondering how to behave? Or are they surrounding the house so they can propose surrender? . . . A futile business. That would cost them dearly. Should, however, determine what the problem is. Laurence went up to the attic and pulled himself onto the roof. No one. Evidently, the guard had decided to put off an attack until morning in order to avoid pointless shootouts. Most likely

Night wheeled slowly and wearyingly. The distant howling of wolves and growling of bears, still performing their weddings somewhere, could be heard for a minute without even provoking a bark from the village dogs, and then dissipated forever. Nothing except Ivlita's groans. Not one window, not a heavenly body shining. But in that blind and speechless night, something swelled, rotated, accumulated, the air had already become heavier, weighing down on his breast like lead. Why don't they kill? Are they creeping up?

And when the tension approached its highest point and, grasping his pistol, Laurence was prepared to shoot and shoot wherever his gun pointed, snow suddenly came down. Large flakes rapidly piled up, not melting, and now the barbed mountains they emphasized emerged from the hideous night, the sides of the dale covered in forest and patched in places by cliffs, the miserable creek, the few sleeping chimneys scattered on the glade, and right close up, Laurence's hand, still extended, the ill-suited pistol already dropped

"Why isn't Ivlita groaning anymore?" Laurence recollected and decided to go down. But his body refused to obey. He got to the stairs, couldn't bear up, and tumbled down. Was he really dying, and Ivlita would remain alive? Convulsively scratching the floor, Laurence made it, crawling, to the bedroom. The door opened part way with a lament

Next to the bed, feebly colored by a candle, the beldam was puttering about. The door made the wenny daughter turn her head. But Laurence no longer thought to interrogate her. A most lightsome smoke was emanating from the corner, and in the smoke swayed two trees—they were blossoming, but without leaves, they filled the room, leaning lovingly toward the fallen man, rendering him into rapture, and the words "the infant is dead, too" resounded far, far away from Laurence, a needless echo

NOTES

THE GOLDEN EXCREMENT OF THE AVANT-GARDE

1. See Roman Jakobson's essay written in late Spring 1930 in the wake of Mayakovsky's suicide. "On a Generation That Squandered Its Poets," trans. Edward J. Brown, in *Language in Literature*, ed. Krystyna Pomorska and Stephen Rudy (Cambridge, Mass.: Harvard University Press, 1987), 273–300. Zdanevich, typically, doesn't figure at all in Jakobson's overview of Futurism.

2. Il'ia Zdanevich, "O futurizme [On Futurism]," *Futurizm i vsechestvo 1912–1914: Tom I: Vystupleniia, stat'i, manifesty* [*Futurism and Everythingism 1912–1914: Volume 1: Speeches, Articles, Manifestos*], ed. A. V. Krusanov (Moscow: Gileia, 2014), 69.

3. D. S. Mirsky, "Voskhichtchénié (Ravissement), par Iliazd," *La Nouvelle Revue Française* no. 219 (December 1931), 962–63.

4. On May 12, 1922, a few months after arriving in Paris, Zdanevich presented a birthday lecture and rechristened himself "Iliazda" (later, Iliazd). The name was initially feminine and combined both his first and surnames. It also recalled Homer's *Iliad* and the Zoroastrian god Ahura-Mazda and evoked the Russian words for "star" (zvezda) and "cunt" (pizda). It is also a simple assertion in French of his existence: Il y a Zda (his intimate friends called him "Zda"). Iliazd subjected the name to several further transformations to designate the hero of his next novel, *Philosophia*, first published in 2008. I refer to Iliazd (both author and historical personage) before May 1922 as Ilia Zdanevich. "Iliazda. Na den' rozhdenie [Iliazda. For His Birthday]," *Filosofiia futurista: Romany i zaumnye dramy* [*A Futurist's Philosophy: Novels and Beyonsense Dramas*], ed. S. Kudriavtsev (Moscow: Gileia, 2008), 683–703.

5. Dates before 1918 are given in Old Style (Julian calendar).

6. Sofiia Starkina, *Velimir Khlebnikov* (Moscow: Molodaia gvardiia, 2007), 71–72.

7. Trans. R. W. Flint, in *Documents of 20th Century Art: Futurist Manifestos*, ed. Umbro Apollonio, trans. Robert Brain, R. W. Flint, J. C. Higgitt, and Caroline Tisdall (New York: Viking, 1973), 19–24.

8. "Poklonenie bashmaku [Shoe Worship]" *Futurizm i vsechestvo* 1:170, 180. Note that in his exegesis of shoe worship, Zdanevich consistently reverses or parodies critical moments for Dostoevsky's characters. He venerates not the feet, but the shoe. Rather than bowing down to kiss the ground, he urges human beings to tear themselves from the Earth. His praise for shoes is also an implicit criticism of Tolstoyan simplicity and any other "barefoot" back-to-nature movement.

9. "Pis'mo no. 12, I. M. Zdanevich—V. K. Zdanevich, Peterburg 1 marta 1913," *Futurizm i vsechestvo 1912–1914: Tom 2: Stat'i i pis'ma [Futurism and Everything-ism 1912–1914: Volume 2: Articles and Letters]*, ed. A. V. Krusanov (Moscow: Gileia, 2014), 77.

10. "O futurizme," 81–83; "O Natalii Goncharovoi [On Natalia Goncharova]," *Futurizm i vsechestvo* 1:132–33; "Marinetti v Rossii [Marinetti in Russia]," *Futurizm i vsechestvo* 1:147–48; "Protiv Kul'bina [Against Kulbin]," *Futurizm i vsechestvo* 1:185–86; "Protiv Gilei [Against Hylaea]," *Futurizm i vsechestvo* 1:187–92; S. Khudakov [pseud. Il'ia Zdanevich], "Literatura. Khudozhestvennaia kritika. Disputy i doklady [Literature. Art Criticism. Disputations and Papers]," *Futurizm i vsechestvo* 2:44–51.

11. Here, for example, is the second of Kruchenykh's poems "in [his] own language ... whose words have no definite meaning," where he mixes beyonsense with standard Russian (my translation):

> freet fron owngt
> I'm in love I won't lie
> the black tongue
> *that* was even among savage tribes

12. See archival drafts of an everythingist manifesto included in E. N. Basner, A. V. Krusanov, G. A. Marushina, "Ot sostavitelei [From the Compilers]," *Futurizm i vsechestvo* 1:28–29.

13. "Ot sostavitelei," 31.

14. "Protiv Kul'bina," 185.

15. "Nataliia Goncharova i vsechestvo [Natalia Goncharova and Everythingism]," *Futurizm i vsechestvo* 1:130.

16. "O Natalii Goncharovoi," 132–33.

17. Régis Gayraud, "Voskhishchenie. Roman [*Rapture: A Novel*]," *Filosofiia futurista*, 724–25.

18. "MV: Mnogovaia poeziia: Manifest vsechestva [MV: Manifold Poetry: A Manifesto of Everythingism]," *Futurizm i vsechestvo* 1:182.

19. *Futurizm i vsechestvo* 1:297. See the multiple drafts reprinted in the notes to the manifesto.

20. *Futurizm i vsechestvo* 1:299.

21. See Petr Kazarnovskii's reading of Laurence the sawyer in "Roman kak svidetel'stvo ochevidtsa iskusstva iz tupika, ili 'perevernutyi' sposob kak konstruktivnyi podkhod Il'iazda [The Novel as a Testimonial of One Who Has

Seen Art Out of an Impasse, or the 'Inverted' Device as Iliazd's Constructive Method]," in *DADA po-russki* [*DADA Russian-Style*], ed. Korneliia Ichin (Belgrade: Filologicheskii fakul'tet Belgradskogo universiteta, 2013), 93.

22. In a fit of anti-German sentiment, St. Petersburg had been renamed Petrograd at the beginning of the First World War. Zdanevich, like other male members of the group founded in 1915, participated intermittently, on short visits from the front.

23. A. V. Krusanov. *Russkii avangard: 1907–1932 (Istoricheskii obzor) v 3-x tomakh: Tom 1: Boevoe desiatiletie* [*The Russian Avant-garde: 1907–1932 (An Historical Overview) in 3 volumes: Vol. 1: The Militant Decade*] (S.-Peterburg: Novoe literaturnoe obozrenie, 1996), 269–71.

24. Janko Lavrin, a Slovene by birth, had helped guide Khlebnikov's research into South Slavic languages. He emigrated after the February 1917 Revolution to England and had a long career as a Slavist at Nottingham University. His early books in English, *Dostoevsky and His Creation: A Psycho-Critical Study* (1920) and *Ibsen and His Creation: A Psycho-Critical Study* (1921) grew from articles in A. R. Orage's *The New Age*. His interpretations of these authors' major heroes emerge from conversations in Zdanevich's St. Petersburg milieu and provide, in my opinion, insight into Iliazd's "transcendental criminal" Laurence and his "wrestle with the void." Kazarnovskii conjectures that Iliazd transformed Lavrin's Albanian adventure yet again into the story of *Rapture*'s Laurence ("Roman kak svidetel'stvo," 91–92).

25. He had published a book, *Natalia Goncharova. Mikhail Larionov*, in 1913 under the pseudonym Eli Eganbury, where Eli corresponds to his first name (essentially, Elijah or Elias) and Eganbury is the way a French postal carrier might make sense of the name Zdanevich written on an envelope in Cyrillic script (in the dative case). Scholars generally agree that he was responsible in whole or in part for the essays under the names V. Parkin and S. Khudakov in Larionov's 1913 companion volume to the Ass's Tail and Target exhibits. Khudakov's essay on "Literature. Artistic Criticism. Disputes and Papers" even quotes examples from imaginary collections of beyonsense and Rayonist poetry ascribed to other apparent pseudonyms for Zdanevich, preferring them to Kruchenykh's work. These examples, technically, are Zdanevich's first published poems, although he never acknowledged them. Zdanevich's name had also appeared with Larionov's on manifestos such as "Why We Paint Our Faces" (December 1913).

26. Tat'iana Nikol'skaia, *"Fantasticheskii gorod": Russkaia kul'turnaia zhizn' v Tbilisi (1917–1921)* [*"Fantastic City": Russian Cultural Life in Tbilisi (1917–1921)*], (Moscow: Piataia strana, 2000), 24.

27. Nikol'skaia, 22.

28. Nikol'skaia, 23.

29. A. V. Krusanov, *Russkii avangard: 1907–1932 (Istoricheskii obzor) v 3-x tomakh: Tom 2, Kniga 1: Futuristicheskaia revoliutsiia* [*The Russian Avant-garde: 1907–1932 (An Historical Overview) in 3 volumes: Vol. 2, Book 1: The Futurist Revolution*] (Moscow: Novoe literaturnoe obozrenie, 2003), 10–20.

30. Nikol'skaia, 35.

31. Nikol'skaia, 62.

32. Nikol'skaia, 76. 41° referred first of all to Tbilisi's latitude, but accumulated many more connotations: A fever sufficient to induce babbling; one degree more alcohol than vodka; the day after Christ's return from forty days in the desert; Zarathustra's age when he goes down the mountain to the people. In a further mystification, soon after his first Paris lecture, "New Schools in Russian Poetry," Zdanevich told his French interviewer, Raymond Cogniat, "the majority of the great beacon cities lie on the 41st parallel: Madrid, Naples, Constantinople, Peking, New York." See Raymond Cogniat, "Laboratoriia poezii: Universitet 41° [A Laboratory for Poetry: 41° University]," trans. Leonid Livak, in Leonid Livak and Andrei Ustinov, *Literaturnyi avangard russkogo Parizha: Istoriia, khronika, antologiia, dokumenty (1920–1926)* [*The Literary Avant-garde of Russian Paris: History, Chronology, Anthology, Documents (1920–1926)*] (Moscow: OGI, 2014), 815.

33. Nikol'skaia, 59. "Straining" connotes exertions during defecation and labor pains.

34. Nikol'skaia, 29.

35. In Russian, *pokushenie s negodnymi sredstvami*.

36. Kruchenykh issued several books on the topic over a decade or so, the last of which was *500 New Witticisms and Puns in Pushkin* (1924). Note that in this context, Zdanevich's lecture, "Tyutchev, Singer of Shit" does not imply any denigrating criticism of Fyodor Tyutchev's poetry. Zdanevich, in fact, considered Tyutchev one of the poets in the Russian tradition most sensitive to problems of poetic expression using a language gauged for pragmatic use.

37. Nikol'skaia, 92.

38. Sergei Spassky encapsulated Zdanevich's stance this way: "Long live beyonsense, but organized, not accidental, like what Kruchenykh proposes" (quoted in Nikol'skaia, 34). Vladimir Nabokov provides another familiar example of similar practices, most overtly in *Ada*, and, if we are convinced by Eric Naiman's *Nabokov, Perversely* (Ithaca: Cornell University Press, 2010), more discreetly in *Lolita*.

39. Vladimir Markov, *Russian Futurism: A History* (Berkeley: University of California Press, 1968), 336. Markov later exempts Zdanevich from his qualification about the "aesthetic" value of the works produced in Tiflis. "Zdanevich is to be praised for the purity and excellence of his *zaum*, which was never used before or after him in a major work of such proportions and on so large a scale. ... He was a 'classicist' of *zaum*, which he constructed and balanced in an elaborate manner. It is genuinely persuasive. Zdanevich displays in it unbelievable verbal imagination, and he never repeats himself. In a sense, it is a creation of genius" (357–58).

40. Petr Kazarnovskii, "Zdanevich, Il'ia." *Entsiklopediia russkogo avangarda: Izobrazitel'noe iskusstvo, arkhitektura: Tom I: Biografii A-K* [*Encyclopedia of the*

Russian Avant-garde: Visual Art, Architecture: Vol. 1: Biographies A-K], ed. V. I. Rakitin and A. D. Sarab'ianov (Moscow: Global Expert and Service Team, 2013–2014), 354.

41. "Novye shkoly v russkoi poezii [New Schools in Russian Poetry]," trans. L. Livak, in *Literaturnyi avangard russkogo Parizha*, 799; Cogniat, 815.

42. André Germain, "Il'ia Zdanevich i russkii siurdadaizm [Ilia Zdanevich and Russian Sur-Dadaism]," trans. L. Livak, in *Literaturnyi avangard russkogo Parizha*, 825. Germain's November 28, 1922 talk on Iliazd happens to mention another Futurist loss: Khlebnikov's death by starvation earlier that year. Suspicion of artistic revolutionaries from the East was real. Tristan Tzara had been arrested in Zurich as a suspected Russian agent in September 1919, and after the 1920 season of Dada soirées, the French press was full of invective. Marius Hentea writes that reviewers saw " 'literary Bolshevism' bent on 'destroying . . . everything that the French intellectual patrimony represents.' Dada's ideas 'are not French . . . [Dada] is an Asiatic, not a European, theory.' 'Extremists, revolutionaries, Bolsheviks, Dadaists—same flour, same origin, same poison.' " Marius Hentea, *Tata Dada: The Real Life and Celestial Adventures of Tristan Tzara* (Cambridge, Mass.: MIT Press, 2014), 149–50.

43. "Novye shkoly," 805.

44. "Novye shkoly," 797.

45. "Novye shkoly," 806.

46. "Novye shkoly," 807, 809.

47. "Novye shkoly," 810.

48. Leonid Livak, " 'Geroicheskie vremena molodoi zarubezhnoi poezii': Literaturnyi avangard russkogo Parizha (1920–1926) ['The Heroic Age of Young Émigré Poetry': The Literary Avant-garde of Russian Paris]," in *Literaturnyi avangard russkogo Parizha*, 50–51. Charchoune was a writer and painter who had left Russia in 1912 to study in Paris and then spent the war years in Barcelona, where he met Arthur Cravan and other poets associated with Francis Picabia. He returned to Paris after the war and made the personal acquaintance of Picabia and Tzara. Parnakh, who later introduced jazz to the Soviet Union (and who figures as the "hero" of Osip Mandelshtam's "The Egyptian Stamp"), had been in Paris since 1915. He presumably entered the Dada ranks in December 1920, after attending an opening by Picabia where Jean Cocteau was presenting a jazz band. Romov, who had probably gone to Paris in 1905 or 1906, was a printer with l'Imprimerie Union, a firm employed by the Parisian avant-garde, including Apollinaire. Livak covers their Dada activities and their first attempts to organize young Russian émigré poets on pages 17–42.

49. Cogniat, 814–15.

50. Livak, 71. Zdanevich had announced his new name in May 1922. I will refer to him as Iliazd in what follows. (See note 4.)

51. Livak, 73.

52. Livak, 90–92; Hentea, 194–97. Iliazd's recollection of the evening in a February 1936 letter to Tzara is reprinted in Robert Motherwell's *The Dada Painters and Poets: An Anthology* (New York: Wittenborn, Schultz, 1951), 306.

53. Livak, 109.

54. Livak, 110.

55. Livak, 112.

56. Livak, 70, 117.

57. Livak, 113.

58. Boris Poplavsky, "Stikhotvoreniia 1920-kh godov [Poems of the 1920s]," in *Literaturnyi avangard russkogo Parizha*, 659, my translation.

59. Livak, 122. Charchoune, who had become disillusioned about the Bolsheviks while waiting in Berlin for a visa to return to the Soviet Union, had publicly attacked Iliazd and his associates over the same issue in 1925, when they were openly pro-Soviet: "And when you go to take a shit, do you ask permission from Narkompros [People's Commissariat of Enlightenment]? My spit pursues you from the right—fellow travelers!" (103).

60. Livak, 136.

61. I would conjecture, also, that Mayakovsky's subsequent canonization by Stalin led in part to Iliazd's adoption of the dictum that "a poet's best fate is to be forgotten." In that sense, Iliazd's "suicide" was more successful than Mayakovsky's.

62. Il'iazd, "Venok na mogilu druga [A Wreath on a Friend's Grave]," appendix to Régis Gayraud, "1923—De *Ledentu le Phare* aux *Parigots*: Il'ja Zdanevic et la transformation de la *zaum'*," *Zaumnyi futurism i dadaizm v russkoi kul'ture* [Beyonsense Futurism and Dadaism in Russian Culture], ed. Luigi Magarotto, Marzio Marzaduri, Daniela Rizzi (Bern: Peter Lang, 1991), 235.

63. Petr Kazarnovskii notes that Iliazd's tone is quite similar to André Breton's first "Surrealist Manifesto," which appeared a year later. See "'. . . Taino v dvizhenii . . .': Rets. na kn.: Zdanevich, I. M. [Il'iazd]. *Filosofiia futurista: Romany i zaumnye dramy*. M. 2008 [' . . . The Secret is in Motion . . .': A Review of I. M. Zdanevich, *A Futurist's Philosophy*]," (Novoe Literaturnoe Obozrenie no. 101, 2010), 322. Given the history of such farewells in Russian literature, from Turgenev's "Enough" and Dostoevsky's parody of Turgenev with Karmazinov's "Merci" in *The Demons*, one should probably not take the solemn tone too seriously.

64. Régis Gayraud, "Mnogolikii Il'iazd [Polymorphous Iliazd]." *Il'iazd: XX vek Il'i Zdanevicha* [Iliazd: *The Twentieth Century of Ilia Zdanevich*](Moscow: ROST media, 2015), 29.

65. Milovoje Jovanović, "*Voskhishchenie* Zdanevicha-Il'iazda i poetika '41°' [*Rapture* by Zdanevich-Iliazd and the Poetics of '41°']," in *Izbrannye trudy po poetike russkoi literatury* [*Selected Works on the Poetics of Russian Literature*] (Belgrade: Filologicheskii fakul'tet Bel'gradskogo universiteta, 2004), 267.

66. Gayraud, "Mnogolikii Il'iazd," 30.

67. In depicting the vicious practices prevalent in *Rapture*'s provincial capital, Iliazd gives Baudelaire's "trivial expressions" his usual treatment by making them concrete: "The mind of man is glutted with passion: he has, if I may use another familiar phrase, *enough to resell* . . . . He never imagines that he is selling himself wholesale." (Baudelaire, "The Poem of Hashish: Chapter 1: The Longing for the Infinite," Aleister Crowley's 1895 translation modified to make the italicized idiom literal).

68. "Iliazda. Na den' rozhdeniia," 703.

69. Hugh Kenner, *Dublin's Joyce* (New York: Columbia University Press, 1987), 366.

70. Reviewers at the Federation publishing house suspected in 1928 that the novel might be religious. It featured, among other things, "some mystical state of the spirit." Olga Leshkova, a member of Zdanevich's circle in 1915–1916, even passed along some gossip from Moscow in August 1930, letting Iliazd know that the monk Mocius's appearance on the first page of *Rapture* had guaranteed its rejection. Régis Gayraud, "Voskhishchenie," 738.

71. Alfred Jarry, *Exploits and Opinions of Dr. Faustroll, Pataphysician: A Neoscientific Novel*, trans. Simon Watson Taylor (Boston: Exact Change, 1996), 21.

72. Gayraud, "Voskhishchenie," 725.

73. Jovanović, 268–69.

74. Nikol'skaia, 78.

75. The classic treatment of "poshlost'" (or, as Nabokov has it, "posh lust") for English-speaking readers can be found in section 2 of "Our Mr. Chichikov" in Nabokov's *Nikolai Gogol* (New York: New Directions, 1961), 63–74.

76. "Raskraska litsa (Beseda na Gaurizankare)," *Futurizm i vsechestvo* 1:155.

77. Kazarnovskii, "Roman kak svidetel'stvo," 84.

78. Elizabeth K. Beaujour, "Introduction," *Voskhishchenie: Roman* (Berkeley: Berkeley Slavic Specialties, 1983), xv.

79. Gayraud, "Voskhishchenie," 741.

80. Vladimir Nabokov, *Ada, or Ardour: A Family Chronicle* (New York: Vintage International, 1990 [1969]), 158. Nabokov is also fond of the "pretender" and paternity/parricide themes, especially in *Bend Sinister, Pnin,* and *Pale Fire*.

81. Kazarnovskii, "Taino v dvizhenii," 327.

82. Nabokov uses "Crime and Pun" to refer to *Crime and Punishment* in his *Lectures on Russian Literature*. I apply it here to Nabokov's own novel following an unpublished paper by Valentina Izmirlieva. Recall *Lolita*'s concluding sentences: "I am thinking of aurochs and angels [!], the secret of durable pigments, prophetic sonnets, the refuge of art. And this is the only immortality you and I may share, my Lolita" (309). Russian *tur* signifies both the Caucasian mountain goat (*Capra caucasica*) present (with angels) in *Rapture* and the extinct aurochs (*Bos primigenius*) Nabokov invokes.

83. Jovanović, 286–87.

84. We should not forget that Russian Futurism contributed significantly to the milieu in which Roman Jakobson (himself a minor Futurist poet) began

thinking about structural linguistics and in which the group of young scholars later dubbed the Russian Formalists (including Viktor Shklovsky) founded OPOIAZ, the Society for the Study of Poetic Language, in Petrograd in 1916.

85. Gayraud, "Voskhishchenie," 715–16.
86. Gayraud, "Voskhishchenie," 716.
87. Gayraud, "Voskhishchenie," 716–17.
88. Livak, 118.
89. Gayraud, "Voskhishchenie," 738.
90. Gayraud, "Voskhishchenie," 740.
91. Livak, 137.
92. Quoted in Gayraud, "Voskhishchenie," 742.
93. See Dostoevsky's epigraph for *The Brothers Karamazov*: "Verily, verily, I say unto you, Except a corn of wheat fall into the ground and die, it abideth alone: but if it die, it bringeth forth much fruit" (John 12:24 AV).
94. "Raskraska litsa," *Futuriszm i vsechestvo* 1:159.
95. I rely for many details in the following account on "Khronika zhizni i tvorcheskoi deiatel'nosti Il'i Mikhailovicha Zdanevicha (Il'iazda) [Chronology of the Life and Works of Ilia Mikhailovich Zdanevich (Iliazd)]," compiled by Boris Fridman in *Il'iazd: XX vek Il'i Zdanevicha*, 68–89.
96. Boris Fridman, "Vmesto predisloviia [In Place of a Foreword]," *Il'iazd: XX vek Il'ia Zdanevicha*, 12.
97. For an English-language treatment of Iliazd's Futurist books, see Gerald Janecek's chapter "Typography: Zdanevich and Others," in *The Look of Russian Literature: Avant-Garde Visual Experiments, 1900–1930* (Princeton: Princeton University Press, 1984).
98. "Posmertnye trudy," ed. E. Bozhur, *Novyi zhurnal* 168–169 (1987): 83–123; 170 (1988): 49–76. Il'iazd (Il'ia Zdanevich), *Parizhach'i: Opis'* (Moscow: Gileia; Düsseldorf: Goluboi vsadnik, 1994).
99. Il'iazd (Il'ia Mikhailovich Zdanevich), *Pis'ma Morganu Filipsu Praisu* (Moscow: Gileia, 2005). "Filosofiia," in *Filosofiia futurista*, 185–473.
100. Il'iazd (Il'ia Zdanevich), *Poeticheskie knigi, 1940–1971*, ed. Sergei Kudriavtsev (Moscow: Gileia, 2014).
101. Livak, 824 (note 66).
102. Johanna Drucker, "Iliazd and the Book as a Form of Art," *The Journal of Decorative and Propaganda Arts* 7 (Winter 1988): 49.
103. Gayraud, *Il'iazd v portretakh i zarisovkakh [Iliazd in Portraits and Sketches]* (Moscow: Gileia; Paris: Iliazd-Club, 2015), 30–32.
104. Il'iazd, "Filosofiia," *Filosofiia futurista*, 281.
105. Gayraud, "Predislovie [Foreword]," *Filosofiia futurista*, 17. In a further mystification, Iliazd had provided his birth *and* death dates in the colophon for the 1923 edition of *lidantIU as a bEEkon*, setting his end in 1973, fifty years after this first elegy for his friend and his own youth. He missed by two years.